*Love can move mountains . . .*

Strong, athletic, and driven, Tristan Sinclair is determined to fulfill his late brother's wish to climb Pakistan's K2, the world's second-highest mountain. He never expects part of the challenge will be getting along with one of his fellow climbers—or that the greatest peril may lie beyond the summit . . .

A passionate, life-long climber, Pakistan-born Farah Nawaz is skeptical of the hotshot from North Carolina. But as she and Tristan help each other conquer obstacle after obstacle, they find they have more in common than they thought—including a simmering attraction. And when suspicious deaths put them in the sights of a ruthless killer, they'll have to cover their tracks long enough to find out why—and stay alive for a future together . . .

**Visit us at www.kensingtonbooks.com**

# Books by MK Schiller

Unwanted Girl
Where the Lotus Flowers Grow
Eight Days in the Sun

**Published by Kensington Publishing Corporation**

# Kiss the Sky

## MK Schiller

**LYRICAL PRESS**
Kensington Publishing Corp.
www.kensingtonbooks.com

Lyrical Press books are published by
Kensington Publishing Corp. 119 West 40th Street New York, NY 10018

All Kensington titles, imprints, and distributed lines are available at special quantity discounts for bulk purchases for sales promotion, premiums, fundraising, and educational or institutional use.

Special book excerpts or customized printings can also be created to fit specific needs. For details, write or phone the office of the Kensington Special Sales Manager:
Kensington Publishing Corp.
119 West 40th Street
New York, NY 10018
Attn. Special Sales Department. Phone: 1-800-221-2647.

Kensington and the K logo Reg. U.S. Pat. & TM Off.
LYRICAL PRESS Reg. U.S. Pat. & TM Off.
Lyrical Press and the L logo are trademarks of Kensington Publishing Corp.

First Electronic Edition: January 2018
eISBN-13: 978-1-5161-0069-9
eISBN-10: 1-5161-0069-7

First Print Edition: January 2018
ISBN-13: 978-1-5161-0071-2
ISBN-10: 1-5161-0071-9

Printed in the United States of America

*To Patrick for his support and always bringing home a pizza when I needed it most*

# Acknowledgments

Thank you to the wonderful folks at Kensington Publishing, who have supported my work, especially my fearless editor and friend, Corinne DeMaagd.

# Prologue

Drew Sinclair woke up, shivering and alone on a narrow hospital bed. He couldn't remember how he'd gotten there. Even turning his head required great effort. The old linoleum and dated equipment told him he was still in Askole, a small village in Northern Pakistan. The cold, dark room suffocated him. He took a deep breath that turned into a violent cough. His head pounded, and his mouth tasted of desert sand. He closed his eyes. The last thing he remembered was talking to Tristan.

He'd told his brother how he hadn't made it. How he would try again next season. They would try together. He was going to tell him what he saw on the Savage Mountain, but he'd decided to wait. He was so messed up he wondered if the conversation had even happened.

He'd had headaches for three days now. They turned his thoughts into long-winding tangles, about as sturdy as strands of wet spaghetti.

The doctor came in then.

"You're up, Mr. Sinclair. You should rest." An American doctor? Here?

"I need to speak with my uncle. He's the general counsel to the US Embassy."

The man ignored him. He prepared a long silver syringe.

Drew's eyes widened as he saw the dark substance inside. "Did you hear me?"

"For now, you must rest. You're a special case."

He reached his arm up to push the man away. That was when he realized his wrists were bound to the bed.

# Chapter 1

As young boys, the Sinclair brothers were fascinated with Spider-Man. So fascinated they spent entire summers challenging each other to climbing contests. It started with the old oak tree in their backyard and continued to the drain pipes of four-story office buildings. Eventually, their climbs graduated to mountain summits. Tristan, being older and fitter, usually beat Drew. When the brothers eventually opted for elevations even helicopters could not manage, their mom had made the boys stand in front of her, hand over heart, to take a solemn oath they would not die before she did. She could not bear to attend her own child's funeral.

Melinda Sinclair died of cancer eight months ago.

Drew died on K2 twelve months ago.

Tristan often thought it wasn't the cancer, but the broken promise and shattered heart that killed his mother. Now, he had his own promise to fulfill. A promise made via satellite phone to a dying man. But for all his hard work and preparations, he'd never imagined the most difficult part of summiting the elusive K2 was the fucking paperwork.

He checked his watch once more, confirming he still had a few hours before his appeal meeting with the permit office in downtown Islamabad. He might as well spend the time searching for souvenirs. If he managed to climb the mountain, he doubted he'd be in the mood when he arrived back. He planned to head to the States after this climb. They would not expect him; he hadn't been home for a long time. He missed the smell of smoky barbeque and the feel of a fishing rod in his hand. Most of all, he missed his grandmother and sister.

He'd strolled around the modern mall in the city center for hours before realizing he wasn't going to find the right gifts here. For all his trouble, he might as well have been shopping at the Promenade Retail Outlets in Richmond.

He decided to try his luck at the local marketplace. Aggressive salespeople swarmed him like flies on a sugar trail. His six-foot-two frame, sandy blond hair, and bright green eyes made him the ideal target, the kind who might pay four times the going rate of an item, especially since the local market, unlike the mall, had no price tags and bartering became an art form.

"Come into this store, sir," a man in a colorful silk shirt called out as Tristan passed.

"Here, sir! We have western items," an older bearded man next to him said, pushing the first man out of the way.

They yelled out the names of brands and products as if the lines had been rehearsed for just such an occasion. "Gillette shaving cream. Oreo cookies. Ralph Lauren cologne. Prada purses."

He searched for the exact opposite of the objects they advertised.

Okay, so this wasn't working.

He ducked into a small nondescript store. Blinking as his eyes adjusted to the dim light, he breathed in a lungful of sandalwood smoke. Every inch of space inside the shop was crammed with display shelves covered in jewelry, figurines, and clothing. An older woman looked up from behind a long wooden table. She tugged on her head scarf and uttered a few words, possibly giving him a lackluster sales pitch or maybe telling him to get the hell out.

"I'm sorry, I don't understand," Tristan said, bumping his head on the sloping ceiling. He'd learned some Hindi and Nepali over the years. Urdu was similar, but nothing she said rang any bells. She held her arms out toward the small expanse of the store. The gesture most likely meant, *please look around*. So he did.

He didn't expect to find anything, but the books stacked on a bowing shelf caught his interest. He flipped through a small hardcover of Urdu poems translated into English. It looked used, the pages frayed and yellowed. This was exactly the kind of gift his Grandma El would treasure. She collected books, from rare first printings she would handle with white archival gloves to old garage-sale mass-market paperbacks she'd relish in one sitting. This fit somewhere in between.

She'd always told him there was a privilege in holding a book, in turning pages, in reading inked words written by people who were very different from him, and yet not different at all. She'd let him explore the library in her home with the plush blue carpet that sank down when he walked on it and the tall mahogany bookcases lined with every kind of book. As a kid, he hadn't appreciated it. Hell, he'd hardly been able to sit still. The only thing that kept a shred of his interest was his grandfather's chessboard, an antique set done in rosewood from the House of Staunton. His Uncle Elliot taught him and Drew how to play chess on that board, often recounting tales of his adventures in the East while showing the boys moves and countermoves. Tristan's methodical approach to climbing required similar skills as chess. The pursuits were as different as night and day, but they had intertwined in his mind from those afternoons spent with Elliot and Drew in his grandfather's library.

Picking up the book for Grandma El, he made a mental note to call his uncle soon. He added a few colorful bangles and a scarf for his sister, Julie. He was careful to step sideways as the aisle grew smaller. Heavy fabric drapes closed the lone window in the shop, keeping the space dim enough to see the rise of swirling dust motes. Several fans hummed, one with yellow and pink ribbons tied to the grill, a visual reminder the air was circulating even though the oppressive August heat gave no reprieve. He breathed in, inhaling another helping of heady incense.

A soft tune swirled around him. A feminine voice hummed a song he recognized but could not place. The melody, soothing and beautiful, reminded him of the ancient oak tree in the backyard of his childhood home, summer barbeques, and cans of cold beer straight from the cooler. Regardless of the flood of memories, the title escaped him, and the possibility of placing the song was fading faster than a winter sunset.

He looked around for the owner of the voice, wanting to make a visual connection. He wove through the packed aisles until he saw her standing in front of a shelf lined with jeweled boxes. Her back was to him. Still, how had he missed her? She wore a plain blue cotton scarf over her shoulders, a loose-fitting, gray tunic over jeans, and scruffy tennis shoes that had seen better days. She could be mistaken for a boy if not for the melodic voice. Well that and the soft sway of her hips.

He shook his head. It had been too long since he'd been with a woman. Not only was he guilty of leering, which was wrong in itself, but he was leering in a country where leering wasn't just discouraged, it was prohibited.

He brought his items to the wooden counter so the saleswoman could add them up. He smiled at the old lady. She pulled her headscarf tighter and ducked her head down, carefully inventorying each item. That wasn't an uncommon reaction. Tristan wished she'd hurry up.

Scratch that. What he really wished for was the damn permit to climb the Savage Mountain.

Scratch again. No, what he really wanted was for Drew to be alive. Right now, he could only control one of those things.

He'd settle just to know the name of the damn song the girl hummed. That would be enough. Just one goddamn win.

He glanced at the painting of the familiar mountain range on the far wall as the saleswoman tallied his purchases on a piece of paper. The artist had used muted water colors on an old parchment scroll. The saleswoman held up several fingers to indicate the price for his items. Tristan took out the appropriate rupee notes from his wallet. She wrapped the bangles in old newspaper to protect them and placed everything in a plastic bag. The transaction was complete. That should have been it. Would have been it. Except for that damn tune ringing in his ears, causing his curiosity to rebel against his better judgment. He wanted to hear the rest of the song.

He pointed to the watercolor. "How much?" He managed one of the few Urdu phrases he knew.

The song stopped. The sales woman looked at the scroll and back at him. She rattled off several quick sentences he could not understand. He sighed in frustration. He should have hired a guide. Then again, most of the people he encountered in Islamabad spoke English.

"She says it's fifty-two thousand rupees," the woman who'd been humming said in impeccable English. She had an accent, but it sounded closer to East London than the Far East.

Definitely not a boy. She was young, maybe a few years younger than him. Twenty-five or so? Her plump pink lips curved into a saucy smile. Her ebony, shoulder-length hair defied the popular long, silky styles adopted by most women in the region. The curls went in every direction as if challenging convention simply by existing. A thick tendril fell against her forehead. Her hair skirted the line between unruly and messy.

For some odd reason, she reminded him of the Karakorum mountain range itself. He'd always been obsessed with Karakorum, of which K2 was a part. They had fascinated him even as a child. There was a stark unadorned beauty about them. He'd never thought the same term could apply to a person, but he found himself making the comparison. She wasn't beautiful in a classical sense. There was no make-up, no jewelry, and her clothes were masculine. But she was intriguing nonetheless.

Her eyes though. There was nothing ordinary about those eyes. They were almost startling in color. At first, he thought they were a very deep blue, but the closer he looked, he realized they were violet. He was no geneticist, but violet eyes had to be extremely rare in general, and especially in this region. Long, thick eyelashes framed them, the kind of eyelashes most women removed every night, but he had a feeling they were permanent on her.

She stared right at him, almost rebelliously, as if taunting him to look away. Definitely unusual in his experience, no matter what side of the world he was on. Most women did not lock eyes with him without there being an element of seduction. But that was not the vibe she gave. It was as if they were having a contest to see who would look away first. He loved a challenge, but her eyes were so piercing, she just might be able to read his explicit thoughts. This was one game he would lose. *Damn, Bright Eyes, you're making me squirm, and I don't squirm.*

"Thank you," Tristan said after he realized his silent stare had slipped into the territory of awkward. He shifted his gaze back to the painting.

"You are welcome."

He placed his wallet in his back pocket and gathered the plastic bags with his purchases.

"*Shukria,*" he said to the saleswomen before heading toward the exit.

"Are you not interested?" Bright Eyes asked.

He halted. Did she read minds?

Oh shit, she was talking about the painting.

Tristan almost laughed at his stupid assumption.

"Not today." The painting of the Karakorum mountain range tempted his interest, but just like her, it was impractical. As a career climber, he only packed the essentials. He didn't believe in mementos and souvenirs. At least not for himself. He didn't even have a permanent address to store a painting, let alone a blank wall to hang it on.

Besides, the cost exchanged out to just over five hundred American dollars, a hefty amount for a shop like this. He could well enough afford it, but Tristan preferred to save his money for mountaineering equipment and permits and the million other expenses associated with the life he'd chosen.

She drummed her fingers on the counter. "You're American."

Tristan cleared his throat. "Canadian."

"Where in Canada?"

Shit. He'd been instructed to say he was Canadian when asked by strangers…just in case. He'd had no trouble, but not everyone was friendly toward Americans. Until now, he hadn't encountered any strangers that asked him for specifics.

"Quebec."

"*Comment vous appelez-vous?*"

"*Oui.*" He uttered the only French word he knew.

She laughed, making it clear his response wasn't quite right. "Well, nice to meet you, Quebec." She pointed to the picture. "She says there is a story to the painting if you want to hear it."

He couldn't help but grin. "A story, eh?"

She nodded, her sassy smile inching up enough to reveal a deep dimple on her left cheek. Grandma El always told him to go for the girl with sass. Sass was just backbone spilling out. Everyone needed a strong backbone. Grandma would know. She had plenty of sass herself.

"I can translate for you. I'm also curious." She spoke slowly. He detected the slightest Urdu accent. Bright eyes, deep dimples, and a seductive mouth—a surefire recipe for heartburn and bad decisions.

He gestured to the painting. "You know what this is?"

The smile curved a little more, exposing an almost identical dimple on the right cheek. "You can't live in Pakistan and not know Karakorum."

"You live here? Your accent doesn't quite match."

She shrugged. "That's an interesting observation, Quebec."

"Touché."

"So you do know some French."

Damn, the girl had a mouth as sharp as a razor blade.

"I suppose I do. Where are you from?"

"I'm Pakistani, born here, but I've lived abroad for a few years."

"England?"

"Among other places." She tapped her finger against her lips. "I bet you're a climber, right?"

"How do you know I'm a climber and not a tourist? Or do I just have a sign on my back?"

"I can tell from your build." Was it his imagination, or did she give him a once over? Did her gaze pause around his abs?

"Climbers don't have a build. They can be short and stout or tall and athletic. I've seen old and young. Hell, I've climbed Everest with a crippled man. There is no type. You'd be surprised."

She quirked her brow. "You climbed Everest?"

"I owned a trekking and touring company in Nepal."

"Oh." Her mouth tilted downward as if this news disappointed her.

"I should get going," Tristan said. The conversation had become enticing quicksand and he was getting sucked in fast.

"It's more than your build."

Too late. "Oh, yeah?"

"Tourists are usually enjoying themselves. You're far too focused to be on holiday."

"That obvious?"

"Not just that. It's the way you looked at the painting. There was respect there. Perhaps even a reverence. I've seen that look in others."

"You sure it's not desperation?"

"Maybe." She set the book in her hand back on the shelf. "I would say... It's more of a hunger. Or better yet, a thirst. Yes, a thirst that can't be quenched."

"And most likely won't be."

"I would not give up before you even start. You have to possess a good attitude."

Was she actually giving him a pep talk? "This isn't a self-confidence issue. I'm having trouble obtaining a permit."

"I see."

He jerked his head toward the picture. "It is a nice watercolor," he said with the ease of a man trying to churn out words into dry, humid air in hopes of keeping the conversation going. Which was to say there was no ease in it at all.

She conferred with the saleswoman who removed the painting from the clips that held it on the wall. She placed it flat against the counter. The edges began to roll. Bright Eyes pinned one side of the frayed edge and Tristan held the other.

Bright Eyes pointed to one of the peaks. "Is this where you're going?"

"That's Nanga Prabhat. It's pretty damn impressive, but it isn't where I'm headed."

"Well, you're a little too far north for Everest. Unless you're lost?" She pointed to the highest peak.

"I'm not lost." He placed his finger over the tallest peak. "This is where I'm going."

She titled her head, her brow furled. "I don't understand."

"That's not Everest."

"I thought it was the highest mountain in the world."

"It is." He chuckled. "The drawing isn't to scale. For some reason, the artist made K2 higher. It's actually the other way around." The distinction is what drove thousands of people to Everest every year and only hundreds to K2.

"You're going for K2 then?"

He nodded. "Yes. K2 is second in height, but many say it's more dangerous due to its slope and unpredictability. I would agree."

The store clerk began to roll up the painting, muttering something, most likely about how they were wasting her time. Speaking of time, he checked his watch once more. Traffic was going to be a bitch at this hour, and the permits office was clear across town. Bright Eyes spoke in Urdu to the saleslady. They chatted for a moment, probably forgetting his existence.

He opened his mouth to bid them farewell. Instead he said, "I want to hear that story."

"Good choice." She translated his request to the store clerk. The store clerk had disapproval on her face. "She says it's time for her lunch."

"Tell her I'll buy the painting if she tells me the story."

"As you wish." Whatever she had said caused the store clerk to move with a newfound speed. The scroll was unraveled once more. The old woman's voice, throaty and spirited, spoke for several solid minutes. The clerk focused on Bright Eyes the whole time and paid Tristan no mind. He did his best not to stare at her too. Another game he would lose.

His translator seemed as mesmerized by the old lady's story as Tristan was with her. The heat in the place made his T-shirt stick to his back, but she seemed at ease in the cramped store. The girl sighed, not the sigh of frustration or boredom, but the sigh of sweet dreams that were reserved for only the very young or the very optimistic.

"Well, don't keep me in suspense."

"Sorry. I'll do my best to tell it correctly." She took a deep breath before she began. "There is an old woman who lives on the base of a great mountain where you are traveling. People say she has lived a hundred-thousand suns, a direct descendent from the Goddess of the Mountain herself."

"Goddess?" he asked.

"You don't know about the Goddess of K2?"

Folklore of the region said a goddess lived on every mountain, a fierce spirit whose goal was to protect the mountain from those who wished it harm. "I've heard of her."

"Perhaps you will meet her one day. Anyway, this woman, who is of her bloodline, spends her days making paints from the materials of the land." She ran her finger over the edge of the scroll. "She creates pieces like this. She never speaks to anyone except through her paintings. The story goes that she lost her love to the mountain. They climbed it together and always held hands when they descended. A snowstorm halted them on one of their climbs." She used her hands when she talked, some of her gestures sweeping as if she was schooled in the ancient art of storytelling. "When the night air grew cold, he covered her with a blanket, but it wasn't enough. So he gave her his furs. But the winds were merciless. Finally, he lay on top of her, seeing her through one of the coldest nights the mountain has ever experienced. It is said it wasn't his body that saved her, but rather his heart. She lived, but he did not survive. He gave her everything he had to give, but the goddess was jealous of their love. Legend has it, when the wind howls just right and the stars light up the sky, she feels her lost love's hands clasped tightly on hers and hears the faint melody of his heartbeat. That's when she paints. She won't stray from the mountain base because his spirit still lives there. She knows with every beat of her heart he will reclaim her someday."

Tristan let out a low whistle. "That is…epically sad."

"Yes, but beautiful too, no?"

"I suppose." He pointed to the highest peak. "Do you think that's why the artist made K2 the biggest one in the picture?"

"Perhaps. This is a one-of-a-kind piece."

He ran his finger over the Oriental symbols at the bottom right side of the scroll. The artist definitely hailed from the Chinese border of the mountain. "What is her name? This artist?"

She asked the question to the sales clerk who pointed to the same etchings. Bright Eyes closed her eyes, the lines of her mouth tightening. "Maiden Shina is what they call her. Maiden Shina."

Before he knew it, the salesclerk rolled up the scroll, secured it with twine, wrapped it with more newspaper, and placed it in a larger plastic bag. He fished out the rupee notes from his wallet and paid for his purchase.

With the scroll under his arm, he followed her out of the store. They both blinked, trying to adjust their eyes to the sharp contrast in atmosphere. The harsh sun and loud noises almost broke the trance…almost. She adjusted the scarf so it covered her head.

"I'm Tristan by the way. Tristan Sinclair. I didn't catch your name."

She bit her lower lip. "Farah Nawaz." She used the Eastern pronunciation of the name, which slowed it down a few beats…Faw-rah. Her name was Farah. It was pretty. It fit her.

"Farah," he repeated to make sure he got it correct. Was it his imagination or did she smell like Hershey's kisses?

"Tell me," she said, "when you're standing on top of the mountain, what will you pray for?"

"That's not a when. It's an if, and a huge if at that. There is no guarantee I'll summit."

"Let me rephrase. If you make it to the top, what will you pray for?"

That was the last question he'd expected. Of all the meticulous planning he'd done, prayers never made the list. "Wasn't planning to pray for anything."

"That's a shame."

"Why do you say that?"

"You'll be so close to God, how could he not hear you?"

"I'll take it under advisement."

What to do now? If he was back home, he might ask her out for coffee, but that wasn't exactly protocol here. Who was he kidding? It wasn't protocol for him either. He rarely dated. He sure as hell wasn't about to start now. He lived a nomadic life, and if he needed companionship, he found it in a woman who was amenable to one or two nights of satisfaction. He doubted Farah Nawaz was such a lady, and this place wasn't the appropriate venue.

Turns out, he didn't need to ponder too much about it.

"*Au revoir*, Quebec. Best of luck to you." With that, she pivoted and headed down the street, not looking back. Not even once.

Eh, shortest love story in the world.

# Chapter 2

The city was built in the late sixties, the buildings and streets very modern. It resembled other large cities right down to the traffic jams. The ten-kilometer taxi ride took over an hour. His little detour with the strange violet-eyed beauty had cost him valuable time. Thankfully, the cool breeze from the open window brought clarity.

The sun shone low and bright, making the taxi feel like a boiling tin can. Yes, that was the reason for his fascination with her. Dehydration combined with very strong incense had made the encounter more than it was.

That's all it was.

It turned out, he didn't need to rush after all. The man he needed to see, the Minister of Expeditions, had decided to take a long lunch. Tristan sat outside his office, shifting in the uncomfortable metal chair. The Minister of Expeditions… Might as well have been going to see the Wizard of Oz and begging for a heart. Of course, if anyone asked his family, they would say it was a brain he needed. At least no one doubted his courage.

Finally, he made it into the impressive Office of the Minister. The man didn't stand up from his ornate desk. In fact, he barely glanced at Tristan, concentrating on the papers before him.

He pointed a gold-plated pen toward the empty chair. "You may sit."

Tristan took the offered seat and waited for the man to finish looking over his papers. There were portraits of the minister with his family vacationing in mountain areas.

"Are you a climber?" Tristan asked, hoping to break through the glacial ice forming between them.

The man shook his head. "My family enjoys the scenery and the climate of the hillsides. Pakistan is a beautiful country."

"She is," Tristan agreed.

If the man felt any camaraderie with Tristan, he did not voice it. "My profession involves granting permission for these kinds of quests, but I've never understood a man's desire to ascend to heights that he isn't meant to go."

"Who says he's not meant to, sir?"

The minister tapped his pen against his desk. *Tap, tap, tap* went for several seconds before he grinned. "Gravity."

"With all due respect, if everyone felt that way, we would still be traveling by steam engine and the moon would be a mystery."

"Are you saying climbing a mountain like K2 will better mankind?"

"That's not what I'm saying."

"Good, because at the heart of it, this is a selfish and self-centered pursuit, is it not?"

"I disagree."

"Then please tell me. What makes humans pursue such dangerous acts?"

Tristan tightened his hands around the wooden armrest of the chair. "I cannot speak for all people. Everyone has their own reasons."

"I'm sure you have a theory."

"Why do men want to do what is considered impossible? That's like asking why we want to know the unknown. Either way, I'm sure the answer to those questions are best left to philosophers and poets. I am neither."

The Minister of Expeditions rubbed his goatee in a way that suggested he was deep in thought. "I've done this for a long time, young man. I've seen men from every corner of the world come into my office to request permission from this government to climb one of our mountains. In my experience, there are two kinds of men who pursue such reckless dreams— the type who want to be closer to God and the type who want *to be* God. Which one are you, Mr. Sinclair?"

Tristan doubted this debate was a common exchange in the permit's office. "I'm neither, sir. I climb because you can't beat the view. Because climbing challenges everything I have in here." He made a fist and patted his heart. "And everything I have up here." He gestured to his head. "There is a sense of accomplishment unlike anything else when I summit. I don't feel like a giant. Quite the contrary, I appreciate just how grand the world is and I am in awe of it all."

The minister shuffled some papers around his desk. "I see."

Clearly, the wrong answer.

He could have at least offered a multiple choice.

It took two hours of waiting for this moment, but only twenty minutes for Tristan to realize he'd be denied again. He thought of doing something he'd never done before and use his family connections, but that might have the opposite effect here, depending on the political motivations of this official.

The minister droned on about the number of permits already issued and Tristan's other high-altitude climbs which, in his opinion, were too recent to allow for issuance of this permit. Tristan kept his composure and nodded along. Arguing would not win his case.

Why did he keep getting rejected? The official repeated what the others had said. They didn't think it was prudent to award him a permit considering he'd climbed Everest so recently. That didn't make much sense to him. He'd seen other less-seasoned climbers who had climbed more than one big peak in the same year get their permit. After all, permits happened to be a great source of income for this country.

His gaze fell upon a small photo in a white frame, the words *Riyadh Golf Courses—our Pearl in the Desert* written across the bottom. Inside the frame was a picture of the minister, smiling in a checked shirt with his arm around the shoulder of another man.

How did he not see it?

The most obvious explanation was always overlooked.

"Did my uncle tell you to ask me those questions or did you come up with them on your own?"

The minister looked at the photo and back at Tristan. "I'm afraid I don't understand. The man in the photo is a US journalist." The tap of the pen was less steady now.

"A US journalist who did an in-depth article on my uncle three years ago. In the article, he spoke of playing a round of golf with several officials of the Pakistani government and embassy officials in Saudi Arabia. Not to mention when I asked about my uncle, you never assumed the journalist could be my uncle, which implies you know who he is."

The minister didn't lose his cool. "As entertaining as this is, I have another appointment." Even being caught didn't faze him. "Do you have anything relevant to add to your case?"

"No, sir, nothing else. Something tells me I'm arguing with the wrong man anyway."

He left the office sans permit, but at least he had a few answers.

Goddamn Uncle Elliot.

Elliot was his father's best friend. Elliot was very powerful in Pakistan. Elliot had been like a second father to Tristan. Elliot was a climber himself, but gravely disapproved of Tristan's pursuit of K2.

How could he not have seen it? Hell, his family was already involved.

He didn't want to cast suspicion where it didn't belong, but watching less experienced climbers get permits with complete ease left little doubt that someone was blocking him. There was only one person who had the motive and power to do such a thing.

He understood it came from a place of concern, but Elliot needed to back off and realize why Tristan wanted to pursue this. Needed to pursue this. Climbing K2 was not another victory on his extensive resume. It was much deeper than that. This wasn't just for him. It was for Drew. Nothing defined a man more than the promises he kept and those he broke. Tristan refused to break this vow, even if everyone he loved disagreed with him.

He pressed the button for the elevator. Elliot wouldn't have his personal phone on during work. He dialed his office number, gave his name, and waited patiently as the secretaries at the US Consulate shuffled him around until he finally got to Elliot. Tristan entered the elevator just as Elliot answered.

"Tristan, it's great to hear from you. I was wondering when you'd get around to calling me. You've been in town for weeks, and I have to say, I'm more than a little hurt you can't make time for your favorite uncle, especially when we're on the same side of the world."

"How'd you know I was here?"

"The bigger the city, the louder the echoes."

"Are you free for lunch tomorrow? Say around one at the Shalimar? That's where I'm staying. You probably already knew that though."

"Of course, I do. All the climbers stay there. Best carrot juice in town. I'll be there."

The elevator doors slid apart at the lobby. A small government-run gift shop sat opposite the elevator banks. Tristan blinked several times at the display in the window.

What the hell?

Just when he thought this day couldn't get any stranger. Despite being worn-down and pissed off, he let out a hearty laugh as he took in the large display of identical, yellowing scrolls. The kind that were made to look old, yet were massed produced. They featured the Karakorum Range.

*One of a kind, my ass.*

# Chapter 3

A soccer match played on the large-screen television. Several men cheered as a goal was made. There were many foreigners staying at the Shalimar. They ranged from businessmen to Marines, but it was easy to spot the mountain climbers. Adrenaline and energy followed them like an atmospheric cloud. It permeated the air around them with equal parts excitement and desperation. Tristan knew most of them. The climbing world wasn't huge. They didn't have conventions or anything, but they would see each other at venues or read about each other's climbs. Many of them wrote books and blogs, chronicling their adventures.

Most of the climbers had returned from K2 or its surrounding peaks, already telling their tales of success or failure. Only twenty-six people had summited this year, a fairly low turnout, even for the Savage Mountain. Normally, Tristan would be sitting with his fellow alpinists, soaking up the stories of great mountain lure and heeding the warnings for future expeditions. But at this late stage, there weren't many groups heading out.

Tristan spotted Elliot as he walked in and waved him over. Elliot wasn't Tristan's biological uncle, but he was his father's best friend since childhood and Tristan's godfather. In many ways, it was Elliot who'd kindled Tristan and Drew's passion for adventure by taking them rock climbing at Jack's Canyon, hiking though Sedona, and orienteering in the painted desert. All the Sinclair children had referred to him as uncle. Elliot Cromwell was a tall man with more salt than pepper in his thinning hair. There were noticeable crinkles around his gray eyes, no doubt the effects of his stressful job.

"Tristan," he greeted, clapping Tristan on the back before cringing slightly. Every time they saw each other in recent years, Elliot looked surprised, as if he expected Tristan to be the clean-shaven youth of ten years ago. Not a tall man who sported shoulder-length hair and a rough exterior.

"Son, you look like an extra on *Game of Thrones.*"

Tristan arched his brow. "Is that a movie?"

Elliot laughed and took a seat. "You know nothing, Tristan Sinclair. Never mind, it's not important."

They exchanged a few pleasantries about the merciless heatwave and Elliot's job as Counsel to the US Embassy in Pakistan. Elliot ordered a plate of samosas and a carrot juice. When the conversation shifted to his family, Tristan grew uncomfortable.

"I thought I'd see you more often, since we're both on this side of the world. As it turns out, I speak to Julie more than you."

Tristan literally bit his tongue. Ouch.

Instead of continuing down guilt trip ally at breakneck speed, Tristan took a detour and reached for the cloth bag by his feet. "Well, glad we could make time to see each other now." He took out the large box inside and set the wrapped packaged between them.

"What is this?" Elliot asked.

"It's for you. A gift."

Elliot regarded it skeptically. "Hope you didn't buy it around here. It's almost a point of pride to swindle a westerner in some of the shops."

No shit.

"Got it in Nepal. It's legit. I know the artist. Open it."

Elliot tore through the plain parchment paper. His eyes widened as he took in the chess set. He opened the wooden box and examined the intricately carved pieces inside. He held the white knight up to the light and let out a low whistle. "This is some real craftsmanship."

"I remember you have a collection."

"I do. Thank you, Tristan. I'll treasure it."

"You're welcome."

"Do you still play?"

Tristan shrugged. "Not for years."

"What do you say to a game now?"

"What? Here?"

"Why not? I don't know when I'll get the chance again." Elliot signaled to the waiter. Within seconds the table was cleared and wiped down. "You can't appreciate the beauty of a set like this until you've actually grasped the pieces." He began setting up the board. "I don't think I've played you since you were seventeen."

"Yeah, on the Staunton set."

"Who would have believed our next game would be on the other side of the world?"

"You're gonna crush me."

"I'm out of practice too. I'll even let you be white. A small but distinct advantage."

Tristan placed the last few pieces on his side. "Sure." He slid the pawn on the shiny marble board.

"Ah, the Ruy Lopez opening. Named after a Spanish priest, you know."

Truth was, Tristan didn't know Ruy Lopez from Jennifer Lopez. He'd never commanded or memorized the rote operations of the game. He had grasped the strategy of it though. And he was glad for the distraction. It gave him an opportunity to measure the words he'd use with Elliot.

"Did you hear Julie was accepted to Harvard medical?" Elliot asked, moving his piece.

Tristan sat up in his chair. "No, I didn't know. That's amazing." He felt a sharp pang of regret that he hadn't called his sister in so long. He would call her tonight and congratulate her. He'd tell her the story of Maiden Shina and how he got fleeced at the local market. She'd find that funny.

"Your father is over the moon."

He was happy his father had at least one child who didn't disappoint him.

"How's Grams? Any updates?"

Elliot paused, his piece in midair. "When I spoke to her last, she said you had just called her."

"I call her every week. She's getting worse so I wasn't sure if she'd remember our conversations. I take everything she says with a grain of salt." These days, it was a few pounds of salt. After all, the woman insisted Tristan was in Poughkeepsie, despite his numerous attempts at explaining his actual location in Pakistan. Finally, he figured it might be better for her to go with Poughkeepsie. Poughkeepsie didn't make the news as often.

"Alzheimer's is a terrible disease. Your father found her an excellent caregiver and nurse so she can stay in her home."

At one time, when he was too young to remember or give her the admiration she deserved, his grandmother had been on a list of the most powerful women in the country. She'd single-handedly drawn attention to causes people were happy to ignore, including education inequality in the public school system. She was one of the reasons he still thought of North Carolina as home. A few more moves, and Elliot captured Tristan's pawn.

"How are things? Any adventures lately?" Tristan asked as he moved his bishop.

Elliot drummed his fingers on the table. "Not bad. I did a little hiking around Kala Patthar last summer. Well, truth is, I mostly enjoyed the views. I've been paying for that little excursion ever since." He rubbed his back. "Adventures are meant for young men to accomplish and old men to criticize. Not the other way around."

"You're still in good shape." Tristan gestured to all the white pieces on Elliot's side. "Plus, you're kicking my ass in chess."

Elliot tapped his head. "What's in here is definitely more limber than the rest of this." As if to drive the point, he moved out his queen. "Check. I have you in four moves either way."

"Possibly." Tristan recognized shit-talking when he saw it. He hadn't played in a long time, but in his analysis, there were still moves to be made. The game was far from won. He wasn't about to hand it over.

"You can resign, you know. Doesn't make you any less of a man." The mocking challenge in Elliot's voice invigorated Tristan.

"It does to me. I'm not resigning." Tristan moved his king to safety. He steadied the board, trying to envision all the different possibilities while waiting for Elliot to take his turn. He closed his eyes and emptied his mind of everything. His failed quest. His niggling guilt over Granma El. His sorrow and remorse over Drew. Even his anger at Elliot over the permit situation. Instead, he imagined the pieces and their potential paths.

"I'm retiring in a few months, Tristan."

Tristan dropped the knight in his hand. "Really? I thought you loved it here."

"Careful," Eliot said, picking up the piece and examining it for chips. Once he was satisfied he placed in on the square Tristan would have moved to. "I do love my job, but I'm growing tired of it. I miss things."

"Like what?"

Elliot looked around as if watching for listening ears. He leaned into the table. "Bacon and bourbon, two things you won't find in a dry, Islamic country."

"I can imagine."

"Most of all I miss my friends and family." The man's voice had a sad lilt. He'd been in Pakistan for over ten years serving the embassy. He'd left after his divorce. "Take it from someone who knows. The time you miss with the people you love is the worst kind of waste."

Tristan recognized the warning in Elliot's statement was meant for him on a much deeper level. On the board, he seized an opportunity to take out Elliot's rook. "What will you do when you retire? Somehow, I can't picture you playing golf every afternoon."

"Never was much for golf. I always joked with your father that it's the reason he became the politician and not me."

"Uh huh," Tristan said, leveling the board by taking out the other black rook. He wondered if the golf game with the minister was the last round Elliot played.

"Your dad misses you by the way."

"I doubt it. After mom's funeral, he told me to leave and never come back. He blames me for Drew's death."

"That's ridiculous. Where did you get such a foolish idea?"

"I guess it would have been when he said, 'Andrew's death is your fault, Tristan.' The statement, even for a politician, was fairly clear."

"He feels badly for the way he spoke to you. He was grieving. People say malicious things when they're grieving."

"When I told him my plans, he said if the mountain didn't kill me, the Taliban would. He just hoped my face wouldn't be on the evening news." The optics would be bad for his upcoming senatorial race.

"Well, you are going to be in their territory." Elliot waved his hand. "He's concerned. He didn't mean it. He tells me he's tried to reach out to you, but you're distant."

"He wants a photo op for the campaign trail."

"He wants his son back. He said things in the heat of the moment."

Tristan had no response. In many ways, he agreed with his father. "I'm not angry with him. We both need space."

"How much space do you need? You've put entire oceans and continents between you for years. I'd say you managed space quite well."

"It's your move."

Elliot shook his head before moving his knight in a defensive position. "He's already lost one son. At least give him a chance to be back in your life. And while you're at it, call Julie more often too."

"Every time I speak with her, she does what you're doing."

"Which is?"

"Trying to talk me out of it."

"Out of what?"

"K2. Except in your case, you're doing more than just talking, aren't you?" They were even in pieces now. Tristan had a decent position on the board. In many ways, the conversation was a reflection of the actual game they played.

"What do you mean?"

"My appeal was denied. Your pal, the Minister of Expeditions, gave me an interesting lecture."

"Well, I know him, but…"

"Stop it, Elliot. Neither of us has time for games." Tristan chuckled and gestured to the board. "Well, except for the game we're playing."

"I must say, it's turning into an interesting match."

"Why are you doing this to me?"

With each sentence, they made moves and countermoves, neither man taking his eyes off the other.

Elliot didn't relent. "You're in no shape to climb the Savage Mountain."

"The Sacred Mountain," Tristan said, capturing the black bishop.

"The Killer Mountain," Elliot countered, moving his knight out.

"We can do this all day. I'm in the best shape of my life." That was true. Years of training and experience had more than proven that.

"I'm not referring to your physical shape."

Tristan slammed his fist on the table. The pieces bounced but didn't topple over. "I am fine."

"Maybe you're an expert on Everest, but K2 is a different story."

Tristan captured Elliot's other Bishop. "I made a promise to Drew."

"You can't be serious. Drew's brain was bleeding out when he asked you."

"That was just a repeat of the promise we made when we were kids. The vow I made didn't die with him."

"You know if anyone understands that, it's me, and even I can't defend you here. Jesus, Tristan, one in four people die on that mountain. Do you really want to risk it?"

"I'm aware of the stats. I've studied them. You're not answering my question. Why are you blocking me?"

"Your father asked me to watch out for you, and this is the only way I know how. You're like a second son to me. I'm your godfather. I won't allow this, not as long as I have the power to stop it. Not to mention I helped Drew get his permit. I might as well have signed his death warrant. I won't do that again."

Tristan assessed the board. Using a hostile strategy, he'd managed to win quite a few of Elliot's pieces, tipping the scales in his favor. "Here's the thing, you won't always have that power. You're retiring, Uncle Elliot. Maybe you'll have the same connections in the permit office a year from now, maybe two years, but three years? Four? I'll come back and apply every single year until I get the damn permit. But truth be told, I might not be as ready as I am right now. I'm willing to risk it. Question is, are you?" He was hedging his bets here because the truth was he had enough saved for one more attempt after this.

"Careful not to get backed into a corner, Tristan. You keep missing the obvious threats."

"Is that advice or a warning?"

"Both." Elliot pointed to the board. "Your game play isn't rusty. But it is sloppy."

Tristan gestured to the black pieces that were now off the board. "I'm up by four pieces."

"Spoken like the true reckless maverick you are. Position over possession, Tristan. That is the key to this game. It's strategy, not attack."

Both men were quiet for a time, each digesting the other's statements. Elliot, a fierce and stubborn adversary, would not likely back down.

"It's your move, Uncle Elliot," Tristan said, breaking the awkward silence. "You don't even realize it."

"What's that?"

"The game is over."

"I'm winning."

Elliot shook his head. "You're too cocky for your own good." He moved his pawn one space. "Checkmate."

It clicked into place like a key turning a lock. If it had occurred to him twenty minutes ago, he might have had a chance, but Elliot had held the upper hand the whole time.

Tristan laid down his king, conceding his defeat. He shook Elliot's hand. "You win *this game.*" Tristan emphasized the last two words.

"Nice try." Elliot clasped his hand and shook it firmly. "You know why I think chess is the greatest game ever invented?"

"Because you love the strategy."

"That's part of it, but a small part. The amazing thing about this game is that all the pieces are unequal and the board is metaphorically tilted. Some pieces clearly have more influence than others. Not unlike this life. But even the most powerful have their limitations and weaknesses. That makes anything possible, doesn't it? Hell, even a pawn can win a game."

"I guess."

Elliot shook his head and adjusted his tie. "I'm getting carried away. In any case, you played well."

"You said I was sloppy."

"You were, but not without a few moments of brilliance. I'll admit you surprised me. You actually challenged me a few times. You were a prodigy once. You could have been a grand master if you'd kept up."

"I doubt it."

"You always had this intense fire to succeed. It took me a while to finally recognize it wasn't about chess, but a passion you carried in your soul. A part of your nature. I fear that very obsession is going to get you killed, but I also think you'd cease to live if the passion died out. It's your Achilles' heel and your Icarus's wings rolled into one."

Tristan knew two things. Elliot was kind of freaking him out, and he could really use a stiff drink, or ten, to get through this conversation. "If I promise not to fly too close to the sun, will you help me get the permit?"

Elliot reached into the breast pocket of his suit and took out an envelope. He slapped it on top of Tristan's fallen king. Tristan opened it and unfolded the paper inside. He skipped over the lines written in Arabic and Urdu until he settled on the ones in English. "Is this what I think it is?"

"Your official permit for K2. You're welcome."

"Why now?"

"You won't give up. It's in your nature. If I can't change your mind, then I can at least make sure you proceed with caution."

Tristan clutched the piece of paper, his own personal golden ticket. "Thank you."

"Don't thank me yet. I have conditions."

"You're kidding, right?"

"Just three small stipulations. If you agree to them, the permit is all yours."

Of course, there would be terms. Elliot was a lawyer. Tristan may be an explorer, but Elliot was a born negotiator. It was in *his* nature. Tristan waved his hand in the air. "State your terms."

"First, you go with an established climbing group."

Tristan shook his head, his fingers twitching to grab the scrap of paper and dart out the door. "I'm going solo."

"You'll have a better chance with a group. There is safety in numbers."

"Depends on the other numbers." There was also a greater chance someone would fuck up. But Elliot, an experienced climber himself, already knew that.

"Of course, there are risks, but I think the pros outweigh the cons in this case. Just to be clear, I won't concede on this. I've already spoken to someone on your behalf. His name is Ahmed Rana and he's local. He has a solid reputation."

"I know him. You already spoke to him?" It was odd to think Elliot had laid plans in motion for him. Then again, his uncle would have used the group idea to appease his father. Elliot was trying to create an alliance between father and son. He'd use whatever strategy and tools he could to achieve that end. He could hear the argument now. "Yes, it's a dangerous climb, but at least he's going with a group." Elliot was an accomplished negotiator.

"I'm an executer. I don't have time to dally so, yes, I spoke with him. He's for you joining, but apparently there is a hold out in his group so you'll have to do some convincing."

"And if I don't convince?"

"It's a group or nothing." Elliot wasn't letting up.

"I doubt I'll be successful. They don't know me."

"You'd be an asset to any group. You were voted Alpinist of the Year two years ago. Your resume opens doors. Use it. They will accept you once you state your case." He made it sound like Tristan was asking to eat at the popular kids' table at lunch. Elliot crossed his arms and sat back in his chair, signaling the conclusion of their debate.

Tristan saw the ink dry before he could raise any more objections. Even with a permit, the government checkpoint could still decline him with one phone call from Elliot. "I'll do my best."

Elliot nodded toward the bar. Ahmed Rana's tall, lanky frame sat on a stool, watching the game. "There's the man you'll need to see. I trust you on this, son. I have no doubt you'll honor your word to me just as you feel you're honoring your word to Drew."

"What are the other conditions?"

Elliot carefully placed the wooden chess pieces back inside the velvet-lined case. His uncle's hand shook as he placed the last pieces in the box. Nerves? "I want you to go home after this. Your family needs you. You need them."

At least that was easy. "It's my plan anyway. I sold my business."

Why?"

"I'm taking some time off after this."

"Excellent. We're in agreement on that point." Elliot folded the latch down on the wooden box and stood. "Thank you for the gift. I will cherish it."

This time the men embraced. "Good-bye, son. Godspeed."

"Wait, Uncle Elliot," Tristan called as the man was halfway to the exit. He turned. "Yes?"

"Your third condition. You never told me what it was."

Elliot smiled, but there was little joy in it. "I thought it was obvious. Don't die."

# Chapter 4

Tristan had met Rana while leading an expedition across Annapurna. When he discovered the other climber was also making a run for K2, they'd gone out for coffee and exchanged a few stories.

"*Assalaam-o-alaikum*," Tristan greeted, taking the seat next to him. He held the permit up, waiving it like a victory flag. He hoped it wouldn't become a flag of surrender.

"*Wa'alaikum salaam*. Please, brother, speak English. Your pronunciation sucks." Rana eyed the paper in Tristan's hand. "I heard those fuckers finally gave you a permit."

Those fuckers, as it turned out, was his godfather, but no reason to dole out those details. "Yeah, I got it."

He snapped his fingers. The bartender put down two silver cups. "We have to celebrate."

Tristan stared at the transparent liquid inside. The strong scent made it clear it was not H20. No way. Vodka. Vodka in a city where liquor was banished. "How?"

"It's all about who you know, my friend." Rana knocked his cup against Tristan's. "Congrats man, hope you summit."

"You too." Both men swallowed back the strong liquor. Tristan hadn't drunk in so long he almost winced. But he managed to swallow it down. It would not serve his purpose to look weak in any way. Rana would pick up on it. Man, moonshine and prohibition went hand in hand no matter where you lived. He slammed down his cup.

"So, word around the Shalimar is that you're the only game this side of China."

"That's not true. The Russians are still here. There is a Korean group too."

Tristan wondered if the strong liquor had diluted Rana's brain cells. "We both know the Russians and Koreans won't let an American in. Hell, you can't even get a visa into their countries these days. I'll pay you more than your going rate. I know that will appeal to you."

"Why do you think that?"

"Simple. You need my money. Heard the freak storm around the bottleneck buried most of your equipment last year."

"Is that what you heard?"

"It is. Also heard you had to finance heavily to replace it."

"Your ears are sharp."

"Always had a keen sense of hearing."

"Perhaps your only keen sense." Rana knocked on the bar twice. Two more rounds appeared before them. "Talking about a man's debts is a great insult in this country."

Tristan wasn't deterred. Rana barked loudly, but the proposal would make sense to him. "So challenge me to a duel, but only after we summit K2."

"Look, man, I'd love to do a favor to a member of the US embassy. But like I told your uncle, a member of our group vetoed you."

"You can change their mind. Hell, we both know you could sell heating oil in hell if you wanted to."

"I doubt it," he said, but his smile was smug. He glanced at his watch. "It's rather a ridiculous request anyway. I mean, seriously, we leave for Gilgit at 0800 hours. You're trying to jump on a bus that's already halfway down the road."

"You don't need to vet me. You know who I am. Let me talk to the holdout."

"It's not just that. I didn't give your uncle all the details. This is going to be a difficult climb."

Well, there was the understatement of the year. "Has the weather turned?" Tristan had checked the broadcasts that morning as was his habit, and the conditions were perfect. But every climber knew what made K2 such a challenge was the unpredictability in both terrain and climate.

"No, no, it's still clear."

"Then what?"

"We're not going the Abrussi Spur. We'll be using the Southwest Pillar."

"The Magic Line?"

"The very one."

Fuck, was he serious? There were a few routes up K2. The Magic Line was probably the most dangerous approach of them all. It had only been attempted a handful of times. The success rate of a summit on K2 was rare on its own, but traveling the Magic Line sliced those slim chances into the smallest percentages. Some climbers even referred to it as Suicide Pass.

"Why?"

"It was a group decision."

"So they overruled you."

"Actually, we all agreed. The traditional route has always proven unsuccessful for me. I'm ready to try something new." Rana had summited some of the highest and most challenging peaks in the world, but being a native Pakistani, K2 was the jewel for him. He'd attempted it five times, resulting in a failed summit each instance, either due to weather shifts or injuries. Once he'd almost been buried by an avalanche. For Ahmed Rana, K2 might as well have been an elusive whale named Moby.

Tristan considered tearing up the permit for all the good it was doing him, but he didn't have the stamina or the funds for another delay. Climbing was a rich man's sport. Most climbers were either self-funded wealthy men or they had plenty of endorsements. Although he'd been offered generous contracts, Tristan had no desire to use a certain company's equipment or wear their logos to get sponsorships. He'd had a decent savings from the inheritance left by his grandfather. He'd been careful not to dip into it too heavily, living frugally and taking odd jobs in preparation for the next climb, until he'd finally settled in Nepal and opened his own trekking company. This business of climbing didn't offer insurance and health benefits. There was no retirement package. Tristan's father had warned he'd run through all his money and come home penniless. Those harsh words pushed him to be the exact opposite of his father's prophesy. But a trip like this cost over a hundred grand, and he had just enough left for one more attempt... maybe two. It was now or never.

"I still want to go."

"We're doing most of this alpine style with very few fixed ropes. We're not going to hire much in the way of help either. No Sherpas or high-altitude workers doing the heavy lifting for us."

"I don't have a problem with any of that. I'm not a stranger to hard work. Are you questioning my ability?"

"Sinclair, no one is doubting you. You're one of the best mountaineers in the world. Just want you to be aware of the facts."

"Get to the point."

"The point is simple, my friend. This isn't a tourist attraction like Everest." There was an accusation in Rana's tone.

"What the hell does that mean?"

"Just making certain you understand if you stumble on this ride, you fall straight down. We're not hiring any Sherpas to set our ice screws and tie our ropes. There will be no porters to carry fucking lawn chairs and barbeque grills and cases of champagne while we trail behind them. No well-worn yak trails to walk along. We'll be roughing it, carrying our loads on our own backs, and cooking our own food. This isn't about getting on the cover of *National Geographic*." He gave Tristan a once over. "Or in your case, *GQ*."

"It was a *Men's Health* magazine, and you can stop giving me shit about it. We all have bills to pay."

Rana tsked with the authenticity of an overbearing mother chiding her kid. "I can't believe you went shirtless with a rope around your shoulder. Fucking lame, man."

"What can I say? The photographer had a vision. Don't worry about me. I can carry my own load." Tristan gave Rana a once over. "And maybe some of yours too."

The man smiled before downing the rest of his shot. He wiped his mouth. "Are you ready for this? You have your rescue insurance?"

"Bought and paid for." And never used, thank God.

"Brilliant. If it was up to me alone, you'd be in."

"Then why the long, scary speech?"

"Just wanted you to be prepared or as prepared as you can get in ten hours."

"So I'm in?"

"Wish I could say yes, but now that I know you're good with our route, there is still the issue of our little holdout." Rana ran his finger along the rim of his glass. "It's not me you need to convince. I was sold when your uncle asked me. This has to be a group decision, and as you know, it's not unanimous, which poses a problem...for you." He gestured to a group of men at a nearby table. "That's my group. Their curriculum vitae reads like a map of the Karakorum."

"Small group." There were four men. Tristan recognized Joseph Lino from a magazine article. They were all speaking animatedly, no doubt discussing their climb. An older man held up his cup, and the others all tipped their glasses to it. Their excitement was contagious, and Tristan felt it all the way across the room.

"I trust each of them with my life. You would have been a good addition, Sinclair."

"So which one is the holdout? Let me at least plead my case to the guy."

"I don't think it will help."

"He's got to see I would be an asset."

"Well, if you insist, I have no objection."

Tristan studied the group again. Possibly it was the blond man, the only one who wasn't smiling. "So which one is he?"

Rana grinned, his teeth shining like a pouncing tiger. "Her." He prolonged the syllables so the simple word sounded much longer. "And she's not there. I believe she's out back completing another inventory of our gear."

"Her?"

"That's what I said." He clapped Tristan on the chest twice. "Good luck, man. You'll need it."

# Chapter 5

Of course, there were female climbers, but not many. Even fewer who attempted an eight-thousander like K2. It would make sense a female would be more cautious. She might have camaraderie with the other males in the group and felt uncomfortable with a stranger. After all, they would be camping together and relying on each other for survival.

Whatever the reason, he needed to present a logical case for himself.

He turned to Rana. "I'll be back."

"Famous last words."

Tristan cracked a smile. "We'll see."

"Inshallah, my friend," Rana said, lifting his cup.

Tristan left the restaurant and crossed the lobby, heading in the direction of the back of the hotel where service vehicles parked. He didn't have to look too hard for her. Men were loading items into a truck. She was inside the trailer, giving orders to the packers, a clipboard in her hand. The balmy night air was fragrant with flowers and something else.

Chocolate.

Dimples.

Bright eyes.

"Farah."

She tilted her head up. "Hello, Tristan."

"You're a climber?"

She jumped down from the bed of the truck in one swift move. "You sound surprised."

"I am."

The corners of her lips tipped in an almost smile. "Why? Don't you know? Climbers don't have a build. They can be short and stout or tall and athletic. They can even be female."

She had backhanded him with his own words. He couldn't help a grin. Hell, he was probably blushing. Yeah, this one had sass to spare. "Why didn't you say anything the other day?"

"You didn't ask."

"I see. So it had nothing to do with your little deception?"

The girl had the nerve to cringe. "My deception?"

He crossed his arms and leaned against the truck. "Are we going to keep up the charade? I admire your devotion."

"You must be angry with me."

He shrugged. "Angry with myself, actually. It should have been obvious from the get-go."

"You think so?"

"Yeah, it took a minute, but it got clearer the more I thought about it. Maiden Shina. Maiden Shina. Maiden Shina. Made. In. China. Clever."

She reached into her pocket. "I was planning to repay you." She took out an envelope and lifted the flap open.

He stared in disbelief at the beige notes picturing a mustached man surrounded by a large maple leaf. "Canadian money?"

"I thought it would make it more convenient for you, Quebec."

Despite himself, he laughed. "Woman, you've got some balls."

"I was making a point with the money."

"Which is?"

"We all have our reasons to lie, don't we? But this isn't a joke. This money really is for you, and it's the same amount you paid whether it's the American dollar or the Canadian dollar or the Pakistani rupee."

"I don't want your money."

"But… It's not my money. It's—"

Tristan held up his hand to stop her. "Just tell me why."

She looked unsure. "I'm not a thief."

"Did you do it for fun then? A way to pass the time?"

"Hardly. I don't expect you to understand."

"Try me."

She placed a strand of her hair behind her ear. She spoke to the men with an authority in her voice. They all stopped what they were doing and scattered. "The shopkeeper. I grew up with her daughter. We were childhood friends. Anyway, my friend is very sick, and the family needs money for medical expenses. I offered to pay for it. It's not much money for me, but it is a fortune to them. Her mother would not accept help from me, even if it means her daughter cannot have the treatment."

"Why not?"

"That is our culture. She has a lot of pride. Her husband would never allow me to pay. We just finished arguing about this when you came into the store. I noticed you looking at the painting. Maybe it was wrong, but I saw an opportunity to give her the money without hurting her pride. It would help everyone."

He quirked his brow. "Everyone?"

"Well, maybe not everyone. But you did get something out of it. The painting wasn't authentic, but the story is a true legend. I figured it was worth your time. Anyway, I was planning to leave the money in this envelope at the front desk for you. My intentions were good. I hope you understand."

He did understand. She had used him, but only as a mechanism. A means to a justifiable end. He couldn't fault her for it. "How did you know I was staying here?"

"I recognized you. I've seen you at the hotel, and I know who you are."

How the hell had he missed her?

"You know my climbing resume then."

"Yes, and I've seen your...photo shoots. I think the article was called 'Adonis the Alpinist' if I remember correctly."

That damn cover was gonna kill him. "I'm a mountaineer. That's it."

She held out the envelope to him again. "It's all there. You can count it."

"I don't want the money. Is your friend going to be all right?"

Farah nodded. "She had surgery today to remove her gallbladder. She's recuperating. Thank you for asking."

"I'm glad she's okay. But I am curious. Was the shopkeeper really telling me the story?"

She shook her head. "No. We were discussing the weather. The story was mine. It's one my amma used to tell me when I was a child."

Not exactly a warm and fuzzy bedtime story. "You're a very talented actress to keep up with two different conversations at once."

She frowned. "I don't believe that's a compliment."

He inhaled a lungful of air. It smelled of wild jasmine and chocolate. Why did she smell so good? "It's not."

"You shouldn't hold such a grudge. There's a long history of western climbers being careless in their shopping habits when they arrive here."

"Oh yeah?"

"There are cases dating all the way back to Eckenstein. He was—"

"I know who he was. He was in charge of one of the first expeditions on K2 back in nineteen hundred." Eckenstein's partner, the famous Aleister Crowley, an openly bisexual man who believed in the occult, received more attention in the history books. Of course, his likeness was prominent on the *Sgt. Pepper's Lonely Hearts Club Band* cover. Interesting she had brought up Eckenstein.

"A little earlier, actually. This was his first expedition, the one he didn't consider successful. Anyway, he spent hours negotiating the price of a jeweled dress, bartering until the shopkeeper finally accepted his terms."

"So, what happened? The guy took his money and ran?"

"Just the opposite. He made the purchase, but he no longer wanted it."

"What was the problem?"

"It turns out he wasn't negotiating for the dress after all, but rather the woman in the dress, although he had no idea. Quite a scandal."

Tristan laughed, a gut-busting laugh, something he hadn't done in a long time. "Well, guess it could have been worse for me."

"Exactly."

"Why don't you want me on your expedition, Farah?"

She tilted her head down. "It's too late for us to take on any joiners." With that, she climbed back into the trailer of the truck. She turned on a flashlight and jotted notes on her clipboard.

Tristan wasn't about to be dismissed so lightly. "It's not too late. Did you forget I owned my own tour company? I understand how expeditions work."

"I'm sure you do." Her tone had enough salt to season a dozen pretzels.

"I don't believe that's a compliment."

She kept adjusting boxes and opening them up to count the contents. "Look, I've seen what companies like yours have done to Everest. People treat it like an amusement park. One huge rubbish pile where everyone is clamoring to get to the top, not caring what they leave behind never decomposes."

He understood her argument. Everest wasn't the same mountain climbed by Edmund Hillary and Tenzing Norgay. Somewhere down the line, mountain climbing became a business. Summiting Everest developed into a rite of passage for anyone who'd ever handled an ice axe. Farah, being a purist, held Tristan responsible in part for ruining nature at its best. In truth, most climbing companies left a carbon footprint the size of Sasquatch.

"My company isn't like that."

"Whatever it's like, I don't want you polluting *my* mountain."

"K2 belongs to you now?"

"Yes. It belongs to me and everyone else. I decided a long time ago it's my job to protect it. I won't let people like you turn it commercial. Why are you here? Is there not enough money to be made on Everest?"

"Is that what you think I'm doing? Starting a new company on K2?"

She let out a long breath, the curl on her forehead lifting. "Aren't you?"

"No. I'm not scouting out a new business venture. I'm here for myself."

"I'm sure there are other expeditions for you to join."

"Not this late into summer. Look, I get it. When you're up there, you have to be able to trust every man on the team."

"I have to trust myself most of all, and my instincts tell me you're not good for me."

He arched his brow. "Good for you?"

She swallowed, her eyes widening as he repeated her words. "I mean, good for our expedition. I'm sorry, Tristan. I really am."

"It's because I don't pray, isn't it? C'mon, be honest. At least give me the courtesy of looking at me."

She turned her head, giving him a full-on stare with her intense eyes. He'd thought her eyes to be mysterious, but they revealed everything. Her fear, her uncertainty, her vulnerability, her pride, and most of all, her strength.

"I'm not some religious zealot. I just think of this as a spiritual endeavor, not another line to add to my biography. I've seen what you have done. It's impressive."

"But not to you."

"We're just very different in our goals. You're the man who skied off Denali and snowboarded Everest. But I'm the climber who's tried and failed four times. This will be my last attempt. I won't risk an exhibitionist slowing me down."

Even as she pounded his hopes into dust, he still admired her tenacity. The fact she was out here checking equipment spoke volumes, especially considering her teammates were inside indulging in a meal. No doubt she'd worked damn hard to get here, probably moved mountains in the process. Tristan had worked hard himself, but doors opened with less resistance for him. Her world was a million times harder. Hell, she couldn't even give her friend money for an operation. She stood and went back to her work. He watched her count out packs of freeze-dried food.

"You're wrong about me, Ms. Nawaz. I am not your problem. I'm your solution. I will make sure we both summit."

This caused her to stop and look up. Her mouth parted. "You can't promise that."

"I can, and I can back it up too. If we don't summit together, then I'll pay for your next trip."

She tilted her head, the disbelief clear on her face. "Are you serious?"

"I am."

"You understand that even though I'm a local, the cost is still the same for me. It's almost a hundred thousand." She sighed. "And that's US dollars."

"I'm aware. We can draw up a contract if you'd like. One that states I will fund your next expedition so long as you allow me to go on this one. Is it a deal?"

"Why do you want this so much?"

"I have my reasons. Why do you want it so much?"

"Because ever since I was a child I was told I couldn't do it. That made me want it even more."

"Who told you that?"

Her voice dropped to a whisper. "Everyone. The entire universe."

"Ever consider the universe is right?"

"Never."

"So you want to prove them wrong?"

"I want to prove me right. Do you understand the difference?"

"Yeah, sister. I've been where you are."

"It wasn't just that I shouldn't do it. It was that I couldn't. It was physically impossible no matter how hard I worked or how much I wanted it. My DNA wasn't made for great things." Her laugh bordered on sad and cynical. "As if having a vagina is a handicap."

"We're not so different, you and I."

She quirked her brow. Tristan held up his hand, wishing he could erase the last two seconds. "Not that I have a vagina. Definitely no vagina."

The melodic sound of her laughter bounced around the metal walls of the trailer. "Didn't think so. I don't have balls either."

"Glad we could clear that up. C'mon, Farah, let's prove the universe wrong together." He held out his hand. "Deal?"

She didn't respond for a few moments, her expression thoughtful. "Let's get some dinner. You should meet the other climbers."

He almost asked her to repeat herself. "So I'm in?"

She nodded and gripped his hand. She squeezed tight. "I hope you're ready for this, Everest. I'm counting on you."

# Chapter 6

It's been argued that the long, arduous journey to K2 through the rocky streets of Skardu was more dangerous than climbing the mountain itself. As the creaky old passenger van screeched and bounced along dirt roads and made hairpin turns around steep, rocky cliffs, Tristan was inclined to agree. The Karakorum Highway, commonly known as the KKH, or the old Silk Road to historians, was not for the faint of heart. Cut into the steep cliff of a mountain, it resembled a highway in some places, but in others, it was only small patches of rocky road no wider than a railroad track and just as smooth.

On one side of them stood a monolith of rock, and on the other a cliff dropped off straight into the Indus River. There were more than a few times a wheel or two didn't connect to the road. During those seconds, every passenger leaned to the left side to keep the weight distributed. God forbid, they encountered a vehicle traveling the opposite way. Whenever this happened, the drivers negotiated who would be allowed to pass because there was only room for one car at a time. They typically won as their driver, a loud, boisterous man, seemed hell bent not to let anything slow them down.

Occasionally, they would pass a government checkpoint where a military official would climb aboard the van and verify their credentials. It all seemed surreal, especially with the Rolling Stone's *Bridges to Babylon* album playing on the radio. Apparently, Rana favored western rock and roll.

Tristan distracted himself by focusing on Farah. She sat in the first set of seats on the bus, looking out the window, unfazed by the drive. She must be used to it. He couldn't understand how anyone could be used to this. Then again, she'd had four failed summits so she must have taken this ride before. If she summited, she'd be one of twenty elite women and the only Pakistani to hold that distinction.

He wondered if there was a deeper meaning to her words from the other night. *You're not good for me.* He shook the thoughts from his head and turned to the other members of the team. The blond man, Malcolm Ball, didn't seem all that welcoming, but he tolerated Tristan's addition. Then there were three more men in the group. A hulking, broad-shouldered, jovial Swede named Bjorn. A short, stocky Italian, Lino, who he recognized from the article. Meeting him last night, it was clear he took great pride in sharing the same name as the first man to actually summit K2 back in '54. Edelweiss was the seventh member of the team. He was the oldest and had the least experience. Tristan had watched him while they loaded cargo. Edelweiss's hefty muscles left little doubt about his strength, but on K2, stamina trumped brute force.

The number of oxygen canisters labeled with the man's name was a concern too. Tristan always made sure there were plenty of canisters for his clients, but he never used supplemental oxygen himself. The canisters were heavy and weighed him down too much. Although it helped at high altitudes where the air was incredibly thin, the canisters became a drug. He'd seen climbers become disoriented when their supplies ran out. Even when changing canisters, a climber could make a stupid mistake. Tristan relied on his body to give him warning signs and confirmations if he should continue a climb. Supplemental oxygen might rob a climber of those natural defenses. The mind could be more dangerous than the mountain.

Rana sat next to him. Tristan nodded occasionally as the man rattled on about the trip. A few rocks hit the top of the van. Tristan tightened his grip on the arm rest. Their driver uttered "*Inshallah.*" Rana went into a long narrative about the time a group of climbers were wiped off the road by a mudslide before they even set foot on base camp.

Um…not exactly the kind of story he needed to hear right now.

"What's wrong?" Rana asked.

Tristan tilted his chin toward the first row of seats. "What's her story?" He wanted to change the subject, but he was also genuinely curious. He kept his voice low, but there was no need. The wheezing of the engine over rocky terrain masked the question.

"She's succeeded on a few of the peaks on Karakorum. She did Eiger too."

Farah Nawaz surprised him at every turn. He didn't peg her for a Swiss Alps kind of girl. "Really?" Then again, there weren't that many female alpinists to begin with.

"She studied in Europe. Anyway, K2 has always been her goal. Like me, she's tried and failed. We both have scores to settle. She's pretty impressive."

"Very," Tristan said.

Rana elbowed him, wiggling his brows. "And she's pretty pretty."

"So I noticed."

He frowned. "Do me a favor and stop noticing."

Clearly, Rana had a crush on Farah. Tristan couldn't blame him. The more he got to know her, the more interested he became. She was intriguing. Yeah, that was all there was to it.

"Understood. I'm just surprised I haven't heard of her before."

"She keeps a low profile."

"Do you know her well?"

Rana looked at Farah and back at him. "Well enough to know she is not for you."

The warning was clear. Back off.

"Understood, brother. Just asking a question." Rana was right. He had to trust her, but he needed to remain detached. His interest in her was careless, and nothing spelled danger in brighter letters than carelessness.

He turned his attention to the other climbers. "Do you think everyone on the expedition is up for this challenge?"

"You're worried about Edelweiss. I get it. He's old. He may not have as many big ice summits as the rest of us, but he's got solid credentials. Malcolm's an asshole, but he knows his stuff and he vouched for the man. They hiked Kala Patthar last year. Besides, this trip is as personal for him as it is for you."

"You know about Drew?"

"I read about it. Let me offer my condolences. It had to be very difficult."

"Thank you." Tristan did not want to open up those wounds now. "How is it personal for Edelweiss?"

"He has history on the mountain too. His grandfather attempted a summit bid back in forty."

"I didn't know there was a summit bid in forty."

"Heard he received special permission. He went with a small group. They faced a severe storm. When the team cut their losses to head back, the man refused to descend. They had to choose between leaving him behind or all dying together." Those were the kinds of decisions men needed to make at eight thousand meters when the air was so thin breathing became a luxury.

"So Edelweiss wants to finish what his granddad started?"

"Quite a bit more, actually. Last year a group of climbers took the same route as us. They came upon his grandfather's remains. They took a picture. The man is surprisingly intact. Edelweiss wants to bury him."

It wasn't unusual to find remains on the mountains. It went without saying if you died on the mountain, you'd be buried there. All climbers accepted that possibility, but it was rare to hear of someone going in search of the dead.

"Don't tell me we're going to look for a body." They were explorers, not archeologists. Then again, if anyone understood the importance of a proper burial, it was Tristan.

"Relax, we know exactly where he is. The climbers recorded the longitude and latitude. Edelweiss understands if we run into trouble, we'll have to skip the funeral. But I did promise him we'd try."

"Is this why we're doing the Magic Line instead of Abruzzi?"

"It's part of it. Like I said, that was a group decision. I want to try it too. The normal paths have never been successful for me."

Tristan wanted to ask Rana more, but the van groaned to a screeching halt. Everyone got out. They'd arrived in the Hunza Valley. Tristan's muscles burned and ached. His six-foot-two frame had been cramped in a tiny space made for a much smaller form for the past six hours. But there was little time to stretch tired legs. The day after tomorrow, they would make it to the remote village of Askole. That was as far as they could drive. From there, it was at least another sixty-mile hike to the Baltoro Glacier. And that would take them to the foot of K2. Then they could start their climb.

It took only a few minutes before a group of porters surrounded them. They all wanted to be chosen for the journey. One trip hauling supplies would feed their families for a year. But they were only using porters to get to Concordia Base Camp. Tristan paid his porters in Everest over the standard wage, but even that felt like a crime. He'd always had a hard time with the idea they were only paid about two dollars a day to strap heavy luggage on their backs and haul it across the rough terrain. But this was the way of life here, and the cost of living was low. The men wore shoes with holes in them and threadbare sweaters, yet Tristan had no doubt they were all skilled climbers. Climbing was part of their genetic make-up, more of a craft than an occupation, passed down from father to son. The men even had a union to protect them. They sat hunched on the ground waiting for Rana's decision. He asked them questions about their experience and assessed each man's ability. Tristan stepped away, not wanting to impede on Rana's leadership role.

Standing at the exit of the hotel, he sucked in a sharp breath. The air tasted different here...cleaner and sweeter. It was as if he'd never inhaled properly until that moment.

"You ride?" Malcolm asked, clapping Tristan on the back. He wore his hair pinned on top of his head. A man-bun was one look Tristan was never going to understand.

"Ride?"

"Horses. There's a polo match tomorrow. We can play with the locals if you're interested. That is, if you know your way around a horse."

"I've never played polo, but I can ride a horse." He couldn't think of an odder invitation.

"We'll see. I'll make the arrangements," Malcolm said, heading inside. The other men followed him.

Having spent hours in a stuffy van, Tristan couldn't imagine being indoors. He decided to go for a walk. He stretched first, grateful the feeling had returned to his stiff legs and back. He took in the sights before him. All of those sketchy moments in the van might have been worth it just to stand in this spot. The isolated lush green valley was surrounded by five of the most pristine snow-capped mountains he'd ever seen.

Glacier mountain water trickled over rocky landscapes, creating waterfalls. Juniper shrubs, cypress, and lemon trees bordered them, scenting the air. His career had allowed him to see more than his fair share of beautiful scenery, but this was different. The landscape looked fresh and new, as if man hadn't gotten a hold of this place and polluted it with his grimy fingerprints. A part of him refused to blink, afraid it would kill the illusion.

If there was a heaven on earth, Tristan was certain he'd found it.

"Welcome to Shambhala," Farah said. "Or as we locals call it, Hunza Valley." She wore the traditional *salwar kameez* today, a long shirt over loose pajama-style pants. A matching scarf in dark green draped her head. In this light, he could see hues of gold and red standing out among her ebony strands of hair.

"I thought you went inside."

"Just to freshen up. I have some friends to visit in the village. May I walk with you?"

"The honor would be mine." He whistled as they walked down sloping streets. Because of their vantage point, they could take in sights on the hills above them. They passed stairways carved of stone, magnificent old forts that had to be a thousand years old, and colorful fields overflowing with purple blooms. Everyone smiled at them. Drew had told Tristan how friendly the people of Hunza were. He saw that now. Almost every person they passed waved in greeting. "Shambhala, eh? That's a Buddhist principal." She arched her brow. "You know it?"

"Nawaz, I lived in Nepal. I know my Buddhism. Shambhala is a mythical country though, a place of peace and beauty and safety that lies somewhere between the Gobi Desert and the Himalayas. That's a large expanse of land. People have died trying to find it for centuries. What makes you think Hunza Valley is Shambhala?"

She lifted her head to the sky, a soft smile on her lips. "My eyes, that's what."

Taking it all in, he had to agree with her. Maybe Shambhala wasn't just a fairy tale or a catchy Three Dog Night song.

She plucked a long stem from the path. He was no botanist, but the distinct scent left little doubt about the plant origin.

He quirked his brow. "Is that...marijuana?"

She nodded and gestured around them. Holy shit, it was everywhere. Stalks grew in neat cultivated fields, and in other places they shot up from the ground in wild clumps over five feet tall.

"It is a native plant. The Hunza don't smoke it though."

"Why cultivate it then?"

"The cows graze on it."

He whistled. "Must be some happy cows."

She shrugged. "Some say they are a bit lazy."

He let out a laugh so hardy it echoed through the valley and caused folks to look in their direction. "I bet."

"We do eat the seeds though. They are good for the health."

"You keep saying 'we.' I thought you were from Islamabad?"

"On my papa's side." She patted her heart. "I'm from Hunza too. My mother's people come from here." She opened her palm, revealing a handful of wheat-colored seeds. "Care to try?"

When he held out his hand, she dropped a few seeds onto his palm. They tasted like granola. "Not bad."

"There hasn't been a murder here since I've been alive. There are rarely any squabbles in fact. Most people live to be over a hundred years old."

"Really?"

"Well, at least we think so. They don't keep official records. But they credit it to drinking glacial water and a diet of apricots."

"And pot seeds."

"Yes, and that."

The breeze blew her scent toward him. God, she smelled so edible.

"Do you wear perfume?"

She laughed. "No."

"You smell like chocolate. Anyone ever tell you that?"

"It's coco butter. I buy it in the pure form and use it every day. It's beneficial for the skin."

One thing was for sure…. It may be good for her skin, but it was very, very bad for him. Not only did she turn him on, she smelled like the most delicious dessert. The universe was definitely testing his will.

"I see."

"I can give you some."

"That's okay." The last thing he needed was surround himself with that smell. "I like walking with you." The statement was so simple and honest. The words just came without thoughts of context or consequences.

"I like walking with you too. I was hoping to speak with you alone."

"On what?"

"I appreciate your offer, but you don't have to fund my next trip. There won't be a next trip. This morning I made a decision this would be my last time trying for K2 no matter what happens."

"Why?"

"I can't put my body through it again. It's been physically and mentally taxing."

He understood her reasons. There was a fine line between conquering dreams and understanding limitations. "Then why agree to let me come?"

"Your conviction was compelling. I don't have a lot of people on my side, so it's nice to meet someone who understands. Who wants it as much as I do, whatever the reason."

"I'm proud to be on your side, Farah."

She looked away, a faint crimson blush coloring her cheeks. "Why did you sell your business?"

An ache formed in his chest. "It was time for me to move on." He didn't exactly have regrets, but Everest had been a major part of his life for so long he wondered how he'd function in a new domain.

She chewed on her bottom lip. "Crossroads are hard, aren't they?"

"They suck."

She cracked a smile. "Tristan, so we're clear, I know this place, and everyone here is accepting and welcoming. When we get to Askole the day after tomorrow, that's not the case. It's a much smaller and more remote village. You and I won't be able to walk down the street together there."

That was a shame, but he'd learned long ago if you wanted to live in a culture that wasn't yours, you had to respect tradition. "I understand."

It wasn't just a warning about culture though. Today was special. Today belonged to them. He intended to enjoy it.

She waved and chatted with the locals along the way while chewing on marijuana seeds. They stopped at a roadside stand in the bazaar. Tristan purchased chicken tossed in an apricot curry and bottles of water for them. They sat in plastic chairs to eat. Some boys kicked a soccer ball. It headed in their direction. Tristan kicked it back. They kicked it at him again. He finally picked it up and threw it back. "Not fair. Three against one."

The boys laughed as they ran down the hill. "Is that a soccer field?" he asked, pointing to the large park they entered.

"You mean football."

"Yes, that's what I mean." Some things he'd never gotten used to. Referring to soccer as football was one of them.

"Sometimes football. Sometimes cricket. Some days, it's used for polo matches."

"Malcolm invited me to play tomorrow. I'm surprised they have polo here."

"This is the birthplace of polo."

"Is that a fact?"

She stopped at a stall and looked through a rack of scarves. The bazaar wasn't crowded, but there were many trinket and hiking shops along the route. "Yes. The gist of the game started here centuries ago. They used a goat's head for the ball."

"Well, thank goodness for modern intervention."

"You ride horses?"

"I grew up on a ranch in North Carolina. Horses I know. Polo, that's another story."

They reached an intersection, and she turned. The area became more sparse and rural, the noise and bright colors of the marketplace giving way to small huts. The city was a network of stone paths interconnected by smaller farming zones. All of it surrounded and protected by the giant mountains of the Hindu Kush, as if the gods themselves had built a fortress to protect this land.

An old woman walked across a swaying land bridge. Tristan stopped, surprised by her spry steps. There was a gap of several inches between each plank, but she didn't even look down.

Farah nudged him to keep moving. She understood what he was thinking. "That's probably part of her daily commute. She can do it with her eyes closed."

They walked until they came upon another village. Really, it was just an area with many small, identical mud huts. A tiny woman came out of one of the homes, an axe almost as big as her slung over her shoulder. She had freckles and hair the color of straw. The dress she wore was not a salwar kameez or the burka he'd seen the other indigenous women wear. It was a long black dress embroidered in rainbow threads around the cuffs and hem. On her neck, she wore several chains of varying lengths decorated with shells and colorful beads. The woman smiled widely in greeting and embraced Farah.

Farah nodded toward Tristan and spoke to the woman, making an introduction. To Tristan, the language didn't resemble Urdu. He held his hand out in greeting. The woman looked at it with confusion, holding her axe tighter. He shoved it back into his pocket. "I guess this is where I leave you." He bowed slightly. Apparently, when it came to Farah, he was doing all sorts of gestures outside his comfort zone. "Take care." He tried to hide his disappointment their day had ended already.

The woman said something that made Farah laugh. "She says I've brought a giant to her doorstep."

"Tell her I'm a friendly one."

"Tristan, this is Asmaar Auntie." Farah gestured to the hut. "She's inviting you in for tea."

"I couldn't impose." He looked around, both surprised and unsure about the invitation.

"She'll be insulted if you refuse."

"Well, the last thing I intend to do is insult anyone, especially not someone with an axe."

Farah translated for the other woman. To his surprise, she laughed loud as if it were the funniest thing she'd heard. Asmaar Auntie led them inside. Thankfully, she set down the axe in a corner. He took Farah's lead and sat on the floor on thin straw mats. The woman heated up water on a small portable stove. The quiet scene erupted as three young girls came running inside, all talking at once. They wore colorful dresses, their long gold hair woven into tight knots at the nape of their necks. All three girls had bright blue eyes.

They ran around Farah. One sat on her lap, bouncing up and down. He noticed then the girl's eyes weren't blue as he thought. They were the same shade as Farah's eyes—violet.

"Are you related?" he asked.

"In a way, but not a direct relation." Farah kissed the head of the little girl who sat in her lap. She introduced them to Tristan, but he couldn't keep their names straight. Farah opened her bag. She had a colorful notebook and pencil set for each of them. Their faces lit up at the small presents.

When she took out the small plastic dolls, they danced around the room until their mother quieted them.

"Let's practice," she said to one of the girls. She pointed to Tristan.

The girl giggled. "Hellllooo."

"Hello," Tristan said, returning her smile.

The girl started to speak, rattling off a sentence Tristan couldn't understand.

"English," Farah said.

The girl pointed to herself. The words came out much slower. "My name is Farida."

"That's a pretty name."

Farah glowed with pride. "Farida is going to school next year."

"That's wonderful," Tristan said. He listened as she told him about the school. Farah corrected her when she slipped into her native tongue.

"You're close with them," Tristan said to Farah after the girls turned her their attentions back to the presents.

"I tutor them. They are learning English. I have a few students in this area."

"You teach?"

"A little during the off-season. I want to do it more."

"This isn't a typical household, is it?"

"I'm sorry. Of course, you're confused. I should have explained. This family is Kalash. They are a group that lives in this region."

"I've never heard of the Kalash."

"I'm not surprised. There are less than three thousand left. There are a few theories how the Kalash became indigenous to this area, but the most popular is that we are the descendants of Alexander the Great."

"You're kidding."

"The story goes that when he conquered the area, several of his men fell madly in love with the local women and stayed behind to make families. We are the last of their tribe. That's why many Kalash have blond hair and light eyes. At least in theory."

"So you're Kalash too. That's why your eyes are violet?"

"On my mother's side."

Tristan nodded toward the axe in the corner. At first, he'd wondered if it was to ward off possible predators. He leaned in and lowered his voice to a conspiratorial whisper. "What's with the axe?

"Are you worried?"

He pinched his fingers together. "Well, it doesn't make me feel at ease."

She laughed. "Asmaar Auntie works in the fields. She uses it to cut down the wild vine branches. She farms potatoes. Most of the women here work."

"Is that common?"

"For us it is. Women are seamstresses or farmers. Some are even carpenters."

"And some are mountain climbers."

Farah smiled, a soft blush spreading across her cheeks. "I think I'm the only one who holds that distinction."

Asmaar Auntie poured them tea into two tiny chipped cups. Her hands were calloused and scarred. Tristan asked Farah for the proper words to thank her. Then he attempted to repeat them several times until Farah finally translated.

"She supports her children with the potatoes she farms."

"No husband?"

"Her last husband passed a year ago. She's been married twice."

"Really?"

"For the Kalash, the woman chooses her mate. If she's unhappy, they are free to leave and find a new partner."

"How does that work? Do they date?"

"There is social interaction, but not exactly dating. They get to know the man, much in the same way I'm talking to you now. Then they make a decision. Typically, they write a note to the man they choose."

"Not very romantic."

She pursed her lips, contemplating his statement. "I suppose it depends on what the note says."

"What would it say? 'Congratulations, you have the privilege of being my mate?'"

"It is a privilege, isn't it? To be asked to spend your life with someone else? The letters are usually private, but I imagine it would be a bit more poetic. Something along the lines of 'I choose you. You belong to me. I offer you my heart and soul and all the love in this body. Let's walk together, side by side, in this life and all the lives that follow.'"

"Okay, so that's better than what I said."

He wanted to ask her more, but the fragrant smell of fresh bread wafted through the small hut. Soon, they had hot walnut bread and a dish of potatoes that Farah explained was made with an apricot sauce. "You stir the tea with this," she said, holding up a piece of rock salt. She demonstrated for him. "It's salted tea. There is very little sugar here."

He followed suit. The tea was strong and rich. He enjoyed it.

Farah closed her eyes as she sipped it. "I love this tea."

Every time he took a sip, Asmaar Auntie refilled his cup. Every time he took a bite, she added more to his plate. He looked around the barren hut. The children stared at him as he ate. Then realization dawned on him. He was an idiot. There were no other plates. They had not expected company, and this was the family's supper. He slowed his pace to a crawl and pretended to be full.

The woman spoke to Farah, a huge smile on her face. She held out her hands, one too stiff to uncurl. Farah massaged it. "She says the vines are getting harder for her to cut down."

"May I try?" Tristan asked, gesturing to the axe.

Asmaar Auntie shook her head and said a few quick words. Farah translated. "She says you are her guest."

"I insist. At least to repay the generosity."

The children showed Tristan the brambles. The tiny woman named Asmaar, who had to be twice his age and a quarter his size demonstrated the proper way to swing an axe for him. Farah cupped her mouth to hide her giggles.

"You think this is funny?" he asked.

She bit her lower lip. "A little, but more than that, I think it's sweet with a dash of charming."

He bowed. "Well, thank you."

He worked for a few hours while Farah tutored the children on their English. He didn't want to take advantage of this family's kindness. They had so little and gave it so willingly. Plus, swinging the axe provided a great distraction. He craved a physical diversion from Farah.

She had lied.

She was a thief.

She had stolen his senses.

# Chapter 7

Farah tried not to stare at him too much on their walk back, but it was like asking a hummingbird to stop flying. On the way back to the hotel, they were both hungry so they stopped at a roadside restaurant. She told him all the legends and lore she knew about the Savage Mountain. He laughed and told her a few she hadn't heard.

She wasn't sure when irritation had turned into admiration. Or worse, when admiration had turned into attraction. Yes, he was handsome with his mane of burnished gold hair and his eyes as vibrant as emeralds. That was obvious. He'd been a cover model on a men's health magazine, for God's sake. For most women, that was an accolade in his favor. But not for her.

Yet, there was something about him that drew her, not that she could act upon it. As long as they didn't cross a certain line, she'd be fine.

"So you live in Islamabad most of the year?" Tristan asked when they resumed their journey toward the hotel.

"I divide my time between Hunza and Islamabad."

He gave her that smile, the one that was almost boyish in nature. "Why here? Was it to be close to your whale?"

She frowned. "Don't compare me to Ahab. I didn't come here originally to climb the mountain."

"Then what?"

"I came here to meet my mother's family. My grandfather was a Sherpa. Climbing runs in my blood. I did some smaller expeditions, but I never really planned on something this grand." She gestured at the high snow-capped peaks around them. K2 wasn't visible, but she glanced toward the mountain that blocked it. "After a few weeks of this view, I realized I needed to see it from up there." She was optimistic, but she knew the odds and had experienced them firsthand. "I hope I do it this time."

"What happened the other times you tried?"

She was quiet for a while, trying to put her chaotic thoughts into some type of logical sequence.

"Sorry," he said. "We don't have to talk about it."

"It's all right. I don't mind. The first time we ran low on supplies, the next time we were derailed by the weather. It turned on us as we made the shoulder. The last time I made it all the way to the bottleneck, but we had injured climbers. I had to help them down."

"No wonder you were reluctant to let me join. You almost made it, only to turn around because someone else wasn't able to move on."

"It's not that miraculous, Tristan."

He stopped and faced her. "Don't do that."

"Do what?"

"Make yourself out to be less than you are." He was so close she could smell the clean scent of his soap. He held out his hands. They were big and calloused with long slender fingers—the hands of a climber. She thought he might touch her. Maybe hold her for a moment. But at the last minute he shoved them inside the pockets of his jeans.

"I'm not."

"Did everyone turn around for the injured climbers?"

"Two people made the summit. I decided to head back with the injured." She wouldn't have changed her decision, but it did sadden her that she had to abandon her attempt for the summit after coming so close.

"You see what I mean?

"I'm not Mother Teresa."

He smirked as if he was hiding a secret. "Thank God for that." He muttered something under his breath.

"Pardon me?"

"Where did you live in Europe?" he asked, instead of repeating what he'd said.

She would have called him out on his previous comment except the question took her by surprise. "How did you know I lived in Europe?"

"Rana told me you went to school there." Then he added, "He gave me the lowdown on everyone."

"I went to uni in London. I lived in Switzerland and Germany for a bit too."

"And your favorite place?"

She jerked her head toward the mountains above them, the snow-white peaks glittering against a purple backdrop of golden stars. "What do you think?"

"I would guess a certain mountain?"

"You'd be right."

"What's the story with you and Rana?" His smile tightened for a brief moment before relaxing again. It happened so quickly she almost missed it.

"There is no story. We're friends. This will be our first climb together though."

His mouth crinkled at the corners as if he fought his own smile. "I see."

"What about you? What's your"—she thought for a second, trying to mimic his language—"lowdown? How did you get into this?"

"Not much to tell. When I turned eighteen, I decided to disappoint my dad to pursue my passion. Well, at least that's how he describes it. I ripped up my college acceptance letters, packed a bag, and headed down to Joshua Tree. Lived out of my car for two years."

"How did you survive?"

"This and that."

"Thank you for the clarification."

His laugh bellowed, causing several pairs of eyes to turn in his direction. "Okay, okay. I had a small trust from my grandfather. I saved and scrounged to have enough for the next climb. I used that to establish myself until I made money giving tours. My company originally began offering Denali tours. Then after I climbed Everest the second time, I decided to base myself out of Nepal. My goal was always K2 though, but the government of Nepal is a little easier on foreigners. Is that suitably less cryptic?"

"It will do."

Farah thought the walk back should have taken longer, but it ended far too quick for her liking. She wanted to stretch out this beautiful day and the lovely memory they had made. But they were at the entrance to the hotel already. They lingered there taking in the backdrop of a million stars looming above them.

"What about you? How do you fund yourself?"

She wasn't offended by the question. It was common among the climbing community. Climbing mountains ranked among the most expensive sports in the world. "I take photographs. I've sold to magazines, and some of my work has been purchased by private collectors. It's shocking how much people will pay for a rare shot of a mountain scene."

"So you're an artist and a climber?"

"I never thought of myself as an artist. I'm just in a position to capture the obscure. It's a privilege and a passion."

He pulled open the gate to the hotel courtyard. "I'd love to see your work. Will you show it to me?"

"I have a few photographs in my room."

"Are you inviting me up?" he asked.

What the bloody hell was she doing?

"I don't know to be honest." Her breath caught. She usually made decisions quickly, one time at seven thousand meters, hanging from a sloping serac. She'd stared danger in the face and did not blink. Why was she having a difficult time responding to his question? The answer came, swift and simple. Tristan Sinclair was too dangerous...even for her.

He took a step closer. "Take your time."

She swallowed, hoping the spell would break and she'd wake up. At the same time, she hoped never to wake up. "Tell me what you said earlier, the phrase I didn't catch."

He lowered his head and kicked a patch of dirt. He was nervous too. At least they were on level footing. He looked around before turning toward her. He dropped his voice to a husky whisper. "I said, 'Thank God, you're not Mother Teresa, or the twisted thoughts I'm having would land me a seat at the Devil's dinner table.'"

"That's what you said?"

"Some form of that."

This time, she shuffled her feet. She wondered what it would be like to kiss him. To be held in his strong arms and touched by his calloused hands. To run her fingers through his thick mane of hair. To taste his skin and feel the warmth of his body.

A movement flickered in her peripheral vision.

Tristan shifted his gaze in the same direction. "Who's there?"

"Well, I see you two are getting acquainted. Rana was looking for you earlier." Malcolm stepped out of the corner, a duffle bag on his arm.

She almost screamed. They both jumped back like polar forces reversing...or two lusty teenagers being caught right before an epic kiss.

Tristan recovered first. "Hi Malcolm, what are you doing skulking about like an alley cat?"

"Just getting some air and checking out the view." He turned his gaze on her, his expression one of smugness and contempt. For some reason, it fed into her insecurities. "I see you're doing the same, Sinclair."

Tristan moved in front of her as if he wanted to shield her from the man's cold gaze. "We went out for a walk." His body straightened to his full height, his wide shoulders and solid back impressive. "Not that it should matter to you."

"Just making an observation."

She saw Tristan tense. "Make your observations somewhere else."

She had to remind herself this wasn't England. Tristan Sinclair wasn't harmless either. Amma had once told her that stupidity ran in her blood. That, like her, Farah was susceptible to smooth talk and charm. Even at ten years of age, Farah had never believed that. She had always thought of herself as logical and prudent and smart. Getting involved with a member of her group was about the stupidest thing she could do.

"We just got back." She plied her voice with cheerfulness. Otherwise, he might see how irritated she was. What was he doing, standing in the shadows, all alone outside anyway? "It's been a long day. I should get to sleep."

"Me too," Malcolm said. Clutching his bag, he walked inside the building.

"I don't like him," Tristan said. "There is something off there."

Farah wasn't sure about Malcolm either, except Ahmed vouched for him, and that was enough for her. Most climbers were used to spending long hours isolated. Social norms often fell to the wayside when they weren't practiced. "He's a little odd, but aren't we all? I mean, we're not doing the type of thing a normal person does, right?"

Tristan's shoulders relaxed. He turned to her. "Yeah, you make a point."

"Good night, Tristan." She headed toward the door without looking back.

"Sweet dreams, Farah."

That's exactly where he belonged. In her dreams and only there.

# Chapter 8

She hadn't planned to attend the Polo match, which wasn't really a match at all, but rather a casual game. Instead, she decided to spend the day with a Scottish Highlander or three while sipping cups of tea at the hotel gardens. After all, no real man could compete with her Highlanders. They were the perfect medicine. After a few chapters, the allure of Tristan Sinclair would most likely fall by the wayside. She was sure of it.

She had her books all lined up. She prided herself on her pragmatism, but a part of her could not resist the lure and magic of a good paperback romance. A shirtless man in a kilt... Well, there was just something special about that. She started in on the first book, a story about a laird with a stony disposition and the lass he falls for. Farah never thought of herself as a romantic. Her world had never provided much in the way of love and acceptance. But in the pages of these books, she lost herself to a place where things weren't as bleak.

"Hello, Farah," Tristan said.

Her shoulders tensed at the sound of his deep masculine voice. His shadow fell upon her in the middle a very dramatic action scene—all right, so it was a sex scene.

She glanced up, caught off guard. He was a flesh and blood example of the men inside the pages of her creased paperback novels. He wore a white polo shirt, the first two buttons undone and showing off his prominent Adam's apple. His black trousers fit him well. If gorgeous had a face, she was staring at it. He was tall and regal. Her fingers twitched, yearning to tangle in his too-long sunlit hair. The chiseled planes of his face held a slight smile that was one part cynic, two parts mischief. She tilted her head, doing her best to avoid his green eyes, brilliant as the grassy hills of Hunza. They were a trap she wanted to sidestep.

Too much salt in the tea, she thought. Too many highlanders in her head.

"Hi," she said, her voice meeker than she intended.

He swung an empty chair out and took the seat opposite her. "Good morning." The waiter brought him a cup of coffee.

"Where are you going?"

"The polo field."

"That's right." She buried her nose back in her book, but the words might as well have been typed in hieroglyphics.

"What are you reading?"

"Just a book." She clutched the novel tighter.

"You work for the NSA?" he asked.

"No."

"Then why so cryptic?"

Her face heated and her pulse increased. What the bloody hell was in the tea? She held up the book. The cover featured a bare-chested man clad in a dark green kilt. "Happy?"

"I didn't peg you for someone who would pick that."

"Perhaps you shouldn't peg me at all."

He shook his head. "Ain't that the truth."

"I love them."

"Why?"

He wasn't mocking her with the question. If he had been, she would have finally found a reason to dislike him. No, instead, he seemed genuinely curious to learn more about her. Had anyone ever asked her so many questions about herself? He waited patiently for her to answer.

How could she explain it to him? "I don't know."

"Don't be coy. We're friends, aren't we? You can tell me."

She took a deep breath, wishing he'd let it go. "I like the language. It's poetic."

"Got it, you're a sucker for poetic language."

"I identify with the heroines too."

"You identify with women who lived centuries ago?"

"I do."

"It doesn't make sense."

"Tristan, it's different in Hunza and Islamabad. There are rights I should have no matter where I live, but I don't. Tomorrow night I will not be able to sit at a table with you like we are now. I won't dine with all of you. I'll have my dinner served in my room."

"Why?"

"Women are not allowed in the dining room."

His expression grew serious. "I'm an idiot. I should have been able to figure that out."

She shook her head. "It's okay." She held up the book. "But you can understand why I identify with them now. They had similar rules imposed on them. I like how brave they are. People can impose all the rules they want, but that doesn't mean a woman is powerless."

"I understand." He gestured to the book. "May I?"

She handed it to him. He scanned the back cover. "You have a thing for Scots?" he asked.

"I'm partial to them." And she did have a thing for men in kilts, but that wasn't something she needed to voice right now. Apparently, she rather liked men in polo shirts as well.

"Mind if I read a little?"

"Why would you want to do that?"

"We're going on a long trip. I only brought one book myself so I might want to borrow this."

"Are you patronizing me?"

"Not at all, Farah. I swear on my life I would never do that." He looked so contrite she felt guilty for her assumption.

"What book did you bring?"

"The same one I always bring. *The Little Prince.*"

"The children's book?"

"The very one. Have you read it?"

"A long time ago."

"It's one of my favorites. Made me want to travel to distant asteroids."

Tristan Sinclair's favorite novel was a children's book. Somehow that fit him. When they'd first gotten out of the van in Hunza, she'd seen the look on his face. It had fallen between wonderment and glee, an expression typically reserved for children.

She glanced into the horizon, her gaze shifting up toward the tall rock giants surrounding them. They looked like faraway, exotic lands. "I see the parallel."

"I'll lend it to you if you'd like."

"Then I'll have no choice but to return the favor."

"Exactly." He held up her book. "So, mind if I read a bit of this? I'm curious to see if I will enjoy it."

"Be my guest."

"Thank you, milady."

She swallowed hard. Dear God, he was a quick study. She told him she enjoyed the language, and now he was using it against her. *Play by the rules.* Everything he did made her want to waive the white flag of surrender.

Tristan opened the book to the middle and removed the piece of hotel stationery she'd used as a bookmark. He looked around, as if to make sure they were alone. He cleared his throat. "She lay naked and trembling, waiting for the laird to claim her. His kiss held the heat of a million fires."

Shit. He was reading it aloud. Thank God, they were alone. No one would witness her melting into a puddle. How could one voice be deep and raspy and smooth at the same time? She'd wondered about his accent. When he spoke, certain words had a velvety, slow rhythm that made her heart dance. And now that very voice was reading a favorite scene from a sinful story. She sipped her tea and pretended she wasn't affected by him. A few seconds later she almost choked when he read the passage where the laird stroked himself.

He continued in a low drawl. "She wondered if she'd be enough for him. It mattered not, for she belonged to him. He made her body sing like an instrument in the hands of a master musician." Tristan lowered the book. "I see why you like this."

"You do?"

"Uh-huh." Obviously, the impromptu reading was affecting him, too. "Maybe you should skip ahead."

"Okay," he said. He flipped the page. He skimmed, his brow furling. He skipped a few more pages. He sighed and turned yet another page. "How long is this scene?" He let out a frustrated groan that caused her to laugh. "You sure this is a romance and not a fantasy?"

"The writer is just very…prolific."

"And the characters seem to have a great deal of stamina," he said, passing a few more pages.

"Yes, well it is fiction."

"True." The corners of his mouth curled. She wondered for a brief moment how that mouth might feel on her skin. She clutched the frayed ends of her scarf tighter. His green eyes brightened with a devilish glint. Whatever thoughts he was having were inappropriate, but at least she wasn't the only one.

"Maybe you should stop."

He held up his hand. "Wait, here we go. I found a passage." He cleared his throat. "She wanted to soothe the burns. To take away the pain. Slaying dragons was dangerous work." Tristan looked up, his mouth twisting into a smile. "There are dragons?"

"There are dragons."

"Just when I thought this wasn't for me, then you give me dragons."

She jerked her head to the side as heavy footsteps approached.

"Ready?" Malcolm asked Tristan. He rolled a suitcase in one hand and clutched several shopping bags in the other hand. Ahmed followed him with a suitcase of his own.

Farah's chair scraped against the stone patio as she straightened. "What are the suitcases for?"

"We're moving our extra luggage to the storage area," Ahmed said. "I've made arrangements with the hotel staff, since we'll be coming back this way after we get back."

"Oh, that's good."

"Always wise to be precautious in my opinion," he replied, looking between the two of them with disapproval. She ignored the warning in his expression.

"Rana just sprung this great idea at the last minute," Malcolm said. "I thought we were going to keep a room here for our luggage?"

"Why spend the extra money? The storage will be a much cheaper alternative." He turned to Farah and Tristan. "You two should gather your things as well."

"I'll do it this afternoon," Farah said.

Malcolm unzipped his bag and shuffled a few items. He tried to cram the shopping bag inside the suitcase. The man was quiet, a stony expression on his face, but it was clear the task frustrated him. Surprising, since he had experience packing for expeditions, something that required careful thought and preparation to maximize every centimeter of space.

"Let me help," Farah said.

She bent and took one of the shopping bags by his side. She pulled out a large object wrapped in a bright lime green scarf. The scarf slipped away, sliding across the stone pavement. The object, a snow globe, held her attention. It was larger than most and inside the glass was a replica of the Karakorum mountain range with tiny flecks of snow raining down on the jagged mountain landscape.

"This is beautiful."

"A souvenir for my niece," Malcolm said.

"It's so lovely. Where did you get it? I don't think I've seen anything like it."

"Don't touch it." Malcolm seized the globe from her. It was so large and awkward it almost slipped out of his hand. "I can pack my own stuff."

"Take it easy, man. She's trying to help you," Tristan said, the serrated edge of a warning in his voice.

Malcolm lifted his head. His gave Tristan an assessing stare. Maybe it was the way Tristan towered over him or his own embarrassment, but when he spoke his voice was a bit softer. "I got it at this little shop in the market. I don't remember where. My niece... She collects snow globes."

"That's great," Farah said. "How old is she?"

"She's twenty." This had been the most he'd conversed with her since the start of the trip. Malcolm wrapped the scarf around the snow globe and placed it in his bag. He muttered something about meeting them out front.

"Friendly guy," Tristan said.

Ahmed stared after him. "He is a cold fellow, but there is such a thing as being too friendly." He pressed his lips into a frown.

Tristan stood, his eyes narrowing. "If you have something to say to me, Rana, just say it."

Oh, this wasn't good. They weren't even on the mountain, and there was already strife.

She stood in between the men, plastering a bright smile across her face, one she did not feel. "You should go. The match will be starting soon."

Ahmed sighed, but his shoulders relaxed. He even smiled at her. "If you wish to attend, I've made special arrangements for you to sit in the women's section."

She should have politely refused and stayed at the hotel. She was heated enough. Watching Tristan mount a horse and gallop across a field was probably the stupidest thing she could do under the circumstances

She opened her mouth to thank Ahmed and politely refuse, but the words rushed out without the benefit of thought. "Let me get ready." Stupid. Stupid. Stupid.

An hour later, she was seated on a rickety bench, the temperature about thirty degrees hotter, even in the shade. He rode on a white horse. Of course, he did. He galloped gracefully across the field. All he needed was a green tartan kilt and a few dragons to slay. There was a moment when the men were first assigned horses and the teams were going over rules when Tristan gently patted the animal's head and leaned against him, whispering something. What did he say?

Was he making the horse fall for him, too?

If he were just handsome, her emotions wouldn't be as vested. After all, she'd thought he'd be superficial based on the things she'd read.

Bloody hell. She could handle the physical attraction. It was not an issue in itself. It was all the other things about Tristan Sinclair that weakened her resolve. Yesterday in that tiny hut, he seemed so grateful for the experience. He instinctively knew without her telling him that he should not eat more than a few bites and was genuinely interested in learning about Asmaar Auntie.

She'd brought her camera to take a few shots of the game. Somehow, his tall profile made it into every photo she snapped. On the way back to the hotel, she walked with Ahmed. Tristan walked ahead with Malcolm. The physical activity seemed to have mellowed the men, and everyone was in good spirits.

Ahmed walked so slow the distance between the two groups expanded. "You hardly watched the game," Ahmed said, his voice low with a hint of accusation.

"What do you mean? I watched all of it."

Ahmed shook his head. "All of it or just him?" He reached for her camera. "I bet your pictures will reveal the real story."

She took back the camera. "I don't have time for riddles."

"Attraction for people like us is dangerous."

"Don't lecture to me."

"I would never presume to tell you what to do."

"Why is it I have the feeling you're about to do exactly that?"

"When we're high up in the clouds, make sure your thoughts are grounded. I've seen mistakes made when the heart competes with the mind."

"I'm a professional."

"I hope so because, understand this, if I feel things are getting out of control, I will kick him out."

Her blood boiled. What right did he have to impose rules on her? She wanted to tell Ahmed off. But she didn't.

He was right. There were too many external dangers on the mountain. Only a fool would create an internal one too.

"You have no reason to worry."

# Chapter 9

Tristan finally understood why the brightly painted trucks in Pakistan often had the words *Good Luck* etched on the back. A person needed a whole lot of luck when maneuvering these roads. He'd figured the next part of their road trip couldn't possibly be as bad as the first leg.

He was dead wrong.

Their porters were in the truck ahead, ten men crammed into one vehicle, several of them hanging off the sides and the roof as they veered around sharp curves. It might have resembled a clown car except there was nothing comical about it.

A torrent of glacial water fell on both trucks, the muddy water coming in through the open window soaking them all. Farah clutched her seatbelt. Tristan tried to remember his rosary. The driver and Rana repeated *"inshallah"*—the Arabic expression for "God willing." It seemed to fit because the only way they were getting off this road was if God willed it. In fact, every time they hit a bump or section of particularly treacherous road, the driver atoned *"inshallah."* It became so frequent, all the passengers joined in. Fairly soon, the entire van broke out into a chorus of *"inshallah."* Tristan honestly believed the single word protected them. After all, they made it safely.

When they arrived at Askole, everyone got to work, strapping on packs and heading out for the long hike ahead, wanting to take advantage of the last few hours of daylight. Tristan loved these hikes. He used them to reflect and appreciate the nature around him. In a way, they were like active meditation. He'd always been an overactive kid, his teachers constantly complaining about his distracting behavior in the classroom. It wasn't until he learned how to harness his energy into hiking and later climbing that he'd been able to focus. Ironically, he found a sense of peace in some of the most dangerous places in the world.

Today was especially difficult. His focus kept shifting to the girl beside him. She had a serene look on her face, one that said, *Leave me alone, I'm in deep contemplation. Yes, that means you, Tristan Sinclair.* He tried to pry his gaze from her. After all, any diversions were exponentially more dangerous on a journey like this.

Farah Nawaz was a study in duality. Her features were delicate and feminine, but she had a strength that rivaled most men. She laughed like a child, but had a sense of wisdom about her. She was open and free, yet she guarded herself too. Maybe not everyone could see that, but he could. He sensed very few people scaled the walls she put around her.

One thing was for sure—he hated coco butter. He'd decided its sole purpose was to torture him.

Not that it mattered. That would change after a grueling hike.

He spent the next twenty kilometers of solitude remembering excerpts from *Look Homeward, Angel*, and recalling famous chess openings. He replayed the game with Elliot. He realized his crucial mistake occurred about four moves before he'd originally thought. He breathed in pure mountain air and made idle chat with Lino and Bjorn. The men were life-long friends and climbing partners. They were complete opposites though. Lino was short and stout with leathery skin. He'd often pause in conversation as if measuring his words, whereas Bjorn was jovial and quick-witted. Even physically he resembled an Appalachian mountain man with his white beard and hearty laugh.

"I knew my Isabella was the one and only when she accepted my mistress," Lino said.

Tristan almost choked on his water. "Your wife accepted your mistress?"

Lino laughed. "She did." He pointed to their surroundings. "The mountain is my mistress, no?"

"Yes, I understand."

Through all the conversations and solemn thoughts, one thing stayed consistent. Farah still smelled like a fucking chocolate bar. It never changed, not that night or the coming days. Or maybe it did and Tristan didn't notice because he stank, too.

Ignoring him didn't change either.

At least he had the others to keep him company.

Malcolm had brought along a small travel chess board. In the evenings, Tristan, Malcolm, and Ahmed would play a few games in their downtime.

They all had to get along for the good of the climb, but Tristan didn't really care for Malcolm.

He couldn't pinpoint it until he heard the change of tone when he spoke to Farah. It differed from the tone he used with the others and was slightly demeaning. Tristan fought the urge to step in more than once. But each time he did, she would give him a look that said, "Back off. This is my fight." Reluctantly, he honored her wishes.

The dynamics of a climbing group were always precarious, though this expedition seemed troubled from the start. She made it clear she could handle herself. Still, Tristan watched and waited for Malcolm to cross any lines.

When they gathered after the long days of hiking, setting up camp after camp, Farah would often go for a walk on her own, taking along her camera and a dog-eared paperback. He longed to follow her, but stopped himself. She wanted to be alone. He would not intrude on her privacy, but he checked his watch so often while waiting for her to come back that Rana told him to chill out a few times.

He learned a lot about her during their hikes. Most of their time was spent in silence except for the sound of their slow, steady breaths and the crunch of rocks beneath their boots. He'd found during the silent moments you could learn the most about another person.

He stole glances at her, gradually learning the small nuances that were part of her makeup, like figuring out a complicated recipe one ingredient at a time. She paced herself well, knowing when she needed to push harder or slow down to conserve energy, a trait even the most experienced climbers hadn't mastered. When she got frustrated, she blew out a solid breath, long and hard enough to lift the wisp of curly hair that fell against her forehead. She gestured with her hands often. Her fingers, long and slender, were elegant despite being calloused by ropes and rough surfaces. He longed to talk with her as they had back to Hunza. But he decided to let her set the pace. He never initiated conversation.

When they did speak, it was often about the route they were taking, the rough terrain ahead of them, or their previous climbs. Once, he caught sight of the way her heavy pack cut through her skin, leaving a mark on her shoulders. The Savage Mountain was not a place of chivalry. He had to remind himself, when it came to K2, she had more experience. She would be insulted if he offered to take on some of her load. So instead he just placed a few of the cooking utensils she usually carried in his own pack. When she asked where they were, he made it seem like an accident. An accident that happened every day.

They crossed rickety manmade foot bridges over raging water and rock. The structures swung violently, creaking and groaning as if they might snap at any moment. She managed to keep her balance better than him. When they came to a glacial river, one of the porters, an older man with a white beard, offered his back to her so he could carry her across. She'd politely refused, insisting on doing it herself. Tristan stayed close to her. The waves rolled with such force he almost wiped out a few times. But she managed just fine.

He didn't approve of the way his mind wandered to her. He did his best in the coming days to keep busy gathering firewood, looking over weather reports, kneading dough, and checking supplies. When someone asked for a hand with their tools, Tristan was there. When one of the porters became ill, it was Tristan who carried the man over the rickety foot bridge to safety. If they had to scout out a new camp, Tristan volunteered to go. He needed a reprieve from her too.

Rana's warning rang in his ears. *She's not for you.* Some of that had to do with the man's own feelings for Farah and his jealousy, but the accusation in the statement was a truth Tristan could not deny. He wasn't staying here. The last possible thing he was searching for or needed was someone like her. He knew that, just as he knew how to attach rope to a wall of ice so he could scale it or use the crampon points on his boots to get leverage when climbing the side of a mountain. But knowing something and acting on it were two different things. Emotion had a way of clouding judgment. When it came to Farah Nawaz, he had emotion to spare.

Today, he hiked with Bjorn and Lino. The three of them told stories of other climbs. Lino boasted of his wife's pasta, going into long descriptions of sauce made from sweet garden tomatoes and stirred for hours. Tristan could almost taste it. Finally, he demanded a topic change. He was craving carbs like an addict looking for a fix. Bjorn spoke of more pragmatic issues. Mainly his finance business in Sweden and the time he spent as an expatriate in Brazil.

Edelweiss, Rana, and Malcolm were behind them while Farah and the porters were far ahead. As usual, she'd packed up early, hoping to get some still shots. She was just a small figure in the foreground surrounded by men twice her size. She spoke to them like old friends, gesturing wildly with her hands.

"So, what are your feelings on taking the south-southeast pillar?" Tristan asked, using the technical name for the Magic Line.

Lino shrugged. "I fought against it and lost. I've been on other expeditions with Rana and was the first one to sign up. A few months ago, he sent an e-mail saying there was a change of plans for our route. I won't lie, it came as a surprise. Who changes direction after the route is set? Especially here?"

"Why did it change?" Tristan asked. He jerked his head back. "Does it have to do with the burial service on our agenda?"

"Rana says that's not the total reason, but the fact remains that it's where Edelweiss's ancestor's corpse happens to be," Lino said. "At least we have the exact location."

It wasn't uncommon to find remains on the mountain. Hell, they'd found George Mallory's remains seventy years after his death on Everest. Still, the thought of it haunted Tristan. "So Rana took this way to appease Edelweiss?" Tristan asked.

Bjorn shook his head. "He is paying more than the rest of us combined. This means a great deal to the man. Rana is right. The other route has not proven successful. At least not for him. We'll be making history in a way."

"I'd rather make the summit and not risk it with monetary decisions."

"It's not about money," Bjorn said. "Rana is not a greedy man." He dragged a hand across his beard. "This isn't about the summit either. I trust Rana. He is a good man and a strong leader. Do you know he has four sisters?"

"I did not."

"Three of them were in France at medical school. One of them wanted to marry a man above her station."

"Why are you using the past tense?" Tristan asked.

"Dowries and tuition cost money. Rana lost his father ten years ago. He's been shouldering everything. He takes care of them and his mother. Last year, when his equipment took a hit, they all lost their dreams. He's been kicking himself since. He feels he gambled with their futures. This trip is meant to set things right. I worried about the route myself until I really studied it. If anyone can do it, Rana can pull it off."

"Yes, that's true," Lino said.

Tristan adjusted his pack. "Rana is a strong climber. I'm not questioning that."

"I'm glad we agree," Bjorn said, taking out his thermos of water. "I'm not so sure about everyone else though."

Tristan shook his head. "You're worried about Edelweiss? Rana will watch him."

"His weaknesses are evident. We'll see them easily and be able to act. I'm not worried about him. Not in the long run." They resumed their hike. Bjorn's eyes fixed on the path before him.

"Is it Farah's you're questioning? She's stronger than she looks."

Bjorn and Lino both laughed, suggesting they'd had this conversation before. "Not her," Lino said. "She knows what she's doing. She's smart and methodical."

Tristan agreed with the assessment. They respected and admired her the same way he did.

Bjorn stopped in his tracks and turned to Tristan. "It's you, my boy. We're worried about you."

Tristan replayed his words. "Me? Why? I'm the most seasoned climber here."

"Indeed you are, but I doubt you heard me just now."

"I heard you. It's not about money for Rana. I get it."

Bjorn shook his head. Clearly, Tristan had gotten the lesson wrong. "I also said it's not about the summit." He pointed toward all the peaks. "It's about this moment. About the process, not the end result. Edelweiss's grandfather got that wrong. The mistake cost the man his life. He was so determined to summit he refused to descend with the rest of his group. It's true what they say—you never know who will flourish or fail at eight thousand meters."

"Yet you predict I will fail."

"Young man, I fear you want this too much."

"Is there such a thing?"

"Yes, there is. There is a difference between passion and obsession. That is not always obvious."

Tristan wanted to argue with him, but the man had more experience when it came to matters of life.

"I'll keep my wits about me."

"That's all I ask," Bjorn said.

"While you're at it, I suggest you keep your wits off her," Lino said, jerking his head over the crest where Farah had just been. "This is a mountain, not a nightclub. She is strong and capable."

"I know that."

"Then why do you look as if you want to carry her up the mountain when she has two perfectly good legs?"

Shit, his thoughts had been so obvious he might as well have spoken them through a megaphone.

He read the message loud and clear. Tristan gritted his teeth. "Understood."

# Chapter 10

On the third day of hiking, they came around a bend. Everyone halted. Most of them shrugged off their gear and stood in silent awe. Edelweiss sniffed, holding back tears. Rana let out a holler of excitement. Lino and Bjorn spoke at once, alternating between three or four languages, no doubt trying to find words to describe the sight. But there were no words in any language for what they were seeing. Farah fell to her knees. From the smile on her face, it clearly wasn't exhaustion but gratitude and joy. Even Malcolm managed a smile. They had reached Concordia. Tristan was afraid to blink. He'd seen this very sight in photographs and videos, but no artificial lens could do it justice. The group stood before an enormous hub of ice where the Upper Baltoro and Godwin-Austen glaciers collided. Broad Peak and Gasherbrum I, II, and III, four of the fifteen tallest mountains on earth, surrounded them. The weather was clear today, a good omen. They had their first glimpse of K2 directly to the north. It filled up the entire sky, a gleaming giant, looming above them, breathtaking and intimidating. It beckoned every one of them. *Come closer. Kiss the sky.*

He extended his hand to Farah. She took it and rose to her feet. "I don't think I'll ever tire of this view. It's almost as if my eyes can't take it all in." Farah's voice was so quiet and soft Tristan felt as if he was intruding on the conversation.

He'd thought this moment would be all about the mountain. That he would be transfixed by it, and he was. But he was having a similar dilemma staring at the woman beside him. She looked at the pyramid of ice and rock with such reverence. What could he say to express this moment? He couldn't. So he shut up.

Her dimples resurfaced with her smile. "Ever had chapatti on an open fire, Everest?"

"I have. I can make it, too. It's one of my specialties."

"You cook?"

He smacked his stomach. "I figured out a long time ago if I wanted to eat right, I better learn how to make stuff for myself. I hear we're going to have a feast tonight."

"Yes, that's the tradition." She looked like she wanted to say more. Instead she walked past him without another word. He didn't dwell on it. Rana called him over for a group meeting so they could all go over the maps once more. They divided up the tasks for each leg of the climb.

Most of this trip would be done in true alpine style with fast climbs and few supplies to weigh them down. Everest was carefully plotted out with fixed ropes and ladders along the beaten-down routes to help climbers reach the summit, but K2 still had unknowns, and it tested every muscle in a climber's body, especially the brain.

The Korean team was setting up not too far from them. They decided to all join for dinner. Setting up the tents shouldn't have been so difficult, but everyone was acclimatizing to the lack of oxygen, which made the simplest task take longer. Once they got a hot fire going, an excitement filtered through the air. The good vibes and adrenaline were in large supply. They would begin their ascent the next day. They dined on heaping plates of lentils and thin chapatti bread, trying to get their carb overload. In the nights to come, they would mostly eat protein mixes and freeze-dried, packaged foods.

Tonight, they were all in fine spirits. A few bottles of Hunza water were passed around. The drink made from fermented juniper berries tasted like gin. Well, maybe what gin would taste like with an acetone mixer. It caused even the strongest men to cough and sputter. Tristan was no exception.

The porters clapped their hands and sang. They played music that sounded as old as the mountain itself. They taught them a dance. Lino, Bjorn, and Tristan did their best to imitate the high energy moves, but it was no use. Tristan had the same level of grace as a stampede of sloshed bulls. Exhausted and exhilarated, he took the seat next to her. The other men continued dancing and drinking spirits. Tristan was thankful for a brief reprieve.

Maybe it was the liquor. Maybe it was his own weakness. Or just how much he missed talking to her. Really talking. He wanted to break through the wall between them. She stared at the crackling fire. She wore a long wool sweater, shelling a pistachio and popping it into her mouth.

"You plan on sharing?" he asked.

"Not sure. I'm protective of my pistachios." Her smiled inched up into dimple range. "But since you danced, I suppose you deserve a few." She passed him the bag.

He took a handful. "That's a workout," he said. He chugged on a bottle of water and crunched on a few nuts.

"You looked like you were enjoying yourself."

"I was."

"Have a good night, Tristan." She closed the bag and stood.

"Why are you avoiding me?"

She paused for a moment, her entire body tensing, before turning back to him. "What? You're being silly."

"Am I?"

"Yes."

"Prove me wrong." He patted the seat next to him. "Sit with me just for a few minutes. Pass the pistachios, and let's have us a real conversation."

She sat and handed him the bag. He cracked open a shell. "Tell me what's bothering you. Maybe I can help."

"I doubt it."

"Try me."

"You bother me by being you."

"That makes sense." He threw a pistachio in the air and managed to catch it in his mouth.

"It does?" she asked.

"Sure, if we were in the third grade."

"If you really want to do something for me, you can tell me one bad thing about you. Something that will make me dislike you just a little." She pinched her fingers together.

"Why would I do that?"

"Because you're handsome and sweet and kind and funny. I like you too much for my own good. I need your help to let this go. So if you want to help me, tell me one bad thing."

His heart constricted. He knew this attraction between them skirted the line between bad and terrible choices. He missed their talks though. He missed her company. She, being more level-headed, had called it out for what it was. "I can't stand cats, not even cute little kittens. I think of them in the same category as large rodents."

She chuckled. "That's a shame, but it's a preference. I can't hate you for a preference."

"We're going straight for hate, are we?"

"A dose of hate would be brilliant right now."

If he was honest, he'd admit she was right. Rana was full of disapproving looks these days. Not that he cared what the other man thought, but his feelings for Farah were causing a riff in the group. They both needed to stay strong and focused. "I enjoy your company, but you are not my type, Nawaz. You're too aggressive and strong. I prefer a woman who is demure and subtle. I'm not attracted to you. Oh wait, that's a preference, too."

Her lower lip trembled. "No... No, that's perfect and exactly what I needed to hear." Her voice cracked.

He wanted to punch himself. "Farah...I was—"

"Don't. I shouldn't have assumed anything." She stood. "Good night, Tristan."

"Wait. Sit for a second longer." Everyone always said he was an overachiever. "You're not even going to return the favor?"

"What?"

"You have to make me hate you too. At least a little or maybe a lot. That's only fair."

Realization flickered across her face. She caught on to the game at hand and sat down. "You need a haircut."

"That's all you got? Weak."

"If you think that I'm attracted to you, then I have an authentic, one-of-a-kind painting I'd love to sell you."

He reared his head back and laughed. "Better."

They were on land covered in rock and shale and snow and peaks that rose like giants from the earth. He now understood what Bjorn had meant in their conversation about appreciating the journey and not just looking for the summit. This moment was special, one he wouldn't trade for anything.

The porters played another song. Everyone appeared in high spirits. Even Rana had stopped glaring at him. The Hunza water and having K2 in their sights had elevated everyone's mood. Roughly five and a half miles straight up to the sky separated them from the summit.

Rana took out a well-worn guitar. He strummed a soft tune. "Might as well get some use out of this." He jerked his head toward the mountain. "I won't be taking it up there."

The riff was familiar and brought a smile to Tristan's face. "You gotta be kidding me."

"Feel free to sing along, brother," Rana said.

They were so out of tune they might just cause an avalanche. No one would mistake them for Led Zeppelin, but "Kashmir" never sounded so fucking good. It was the strangest of ironies, since they were actually in Kashmir.

# Chapter 11

This morning they had bid their porters good-bye at base camp. Tristan, with Rana's permission, had given each man a bonus. Farah had embraced each man and doled out gifts. The packages contained just three items—a small picture book for their children, a warm wool scarf for their wives, and a bottle of aspirin to cure minor aches and pains. The men's faces lit up when they saw the aspirin. It may not have seemed like much, but in an area where doctors were scarce and a toothache could literally kill a man, it meant the world. They had regarded her with suspicion and uncertainty at first. But by the time they left, the men had nothing but gratitude and respect for this woman. The younger men referred to her as "sister" while the older men called her "daughter."

Now, it was just the seven of them and the huge monolith before them. Even though it was out of the way, they hiked to the Art Gilkey Memorial. Making their way there, Tristan took in the miraculous views. If the Minister of Expeditions was here, he wouldn't need to ask why Tristan chose this life.

Tristan had read and seen footage about K2 since he was a kid. It was the neighboring peak from his Everest, but the differences between the mountains were as vast as the topography of the sun and moon. From Everest Base Camp, a climber could walk a few hours and be lounging in a grassy area with an ice-cold beer in his hand, drinking with other trekkers as they watched the yaks go by.

But K2 stood on its own, completely remote and barren. Even getting to the damn thing had been near impossible. The area, an imposing pile of impressive rock and solid ice surrounded by clouds and storms, resembled Mar's surface more than that of the Earth's. Hell, one of the reasons the mountain was commonly known only as K2 was due to the remote location. While other mountains had been renamed for the people who first surveyed them or by locals, K2 had kept the geological notation as its name because so few people had seen or lived close enough to give it a proper identity. It loomed, a fierce, tall, and unnamed giant. He could not explain it, but it was beautiful to him. It made him feel more alive to be here, standing at what felt like the edge of the world.

The climbers stood in silence to pay their respects. Art Gilkey was a climber and geologist from Idaho who had died on K2 back in '53 despite a heroic rescue attempt by his group. The memorial was erected in his memory. Since then, it had become tradition for climbers to place tin plates with the names of friends, who perished on the Savage, on the piles of rocks. Tristan read the inscriptions. Many of them had died on the descent. That wasn't surprising. Most climbers gave the ascent their all. So much so, they ran out of energy and steam for the way back.

The memorial had grown and stretched. It was meant for one man, and now hundreds of names covered it. Gilkey himself died in an avalanche. Some said it were as if the hand of God swept him off the mountain. Not far from him was a prominent plate with Allison Hargreave's name. She had managed to summit, but passed away when a gale-force wind plucked her straight off the summit along with the five others in her group. There was a German climber named Grohs who had slipped and fallen to his death while pushing to the top.

It was more than just an erected memorial. The pile of rocks and tin plates served as a stern warning that surpassed any words of caution. The seduction of K2 was not without consequence. Many times, the ultimate consequence.

The wind howled today, screaming from the apex of every surrounding summit all the way down like the chorus of a million men emptying their lungs. Yet nothing about the sound felt remotely human.

Tristan glanced at the plates once more. Drew's name should be up there, too. The thought brought raw pain. Tristan couldn't give the feeling a name. It was too fresh, a wound that still bled. He had not cried when his brother died. Or his mother. He had refused to let the pain and guilt consume him. He would not start today.

Edelweiss took out a plate for his grandfather and placed it among the others. The man had died prior to the memorial being erected. They all removed their hats and bowed their heads while Edelweiss said a prayer.

"His name was Fritz Ditel?" Farah asked Edelweiss when he stepped back.

"We have different surnames."

"Fritz Ditel," she repeated. "May he rest in peace."

"If we find his body, he will."

Tristan didn't like the idea of looking for bones. The climb was dangerous enough without sacrificing themselves to bury a man who had been dead for decades.

"Relax, Sinclair," Rana said as if reading his mind. "We're not going to take any unnecessary risks."

That didn't make him feel any better.

Rana retreated down along with the other men. They were heading back to camp. He remained behind, wanting to spend a few more minutes with the ghosts of K2. Farah stayed too.

"Do you feel them?" Farah asked.

"Feel who?"

She gestured to the memorial. "Them. I feel them every time I come here."

"Yeah, it's some kind of powerful, all right."

Some of the plates were made of expensive stone, the words written in neat, elegant script. Others were done by punching holes into tin plates with rudimentary tools. They were written in English and Urdu and Arabic and just about every language in the world.

One thing was clear, K2 might be too simplistic of a name, but the mountain definitely deserved its nickname.

The Savage Mountain fit perfectly.

# Chapter 12

In the coming days, the chess board got more use. "Let's make it interesting," Malcolm said on one of their rest days.

"You want to wager?" Tristan asked. "I didn't exactly bring money for gambling."

"Some things are worth more, especially up here." Malcolm pointed to Tristan's pack. "If I win, I get your binoculars." They were a brand new pair and cost him a fortune.

"And if I win?" Tristan asked.

"I'll give you my snack rations for the next week." He held up the bag of chips he brought. "Smuggled these in from the States. Just the right amount of salt." He opened the bag. Tristan could smell the sour cream and onion aroma. Malcolm popped one into his mouth, the crunch of it loud.

Even though he was craving chocolate like crazy these days, the chips made his stomach grumble.

"Hardly seems fair."

"Giving up one of the few luxuries we have is a big deal."

It was a huge deal.

"I mean it doesn't seem fair because I'm gonna win. I've been winning most of our games."

Malcolm laughed so loud it echoed. "So make the wager then."

Tristan held out his hand so they could shake on the deal. They set up the board. They moved their pieces. He saw Farah in his peripheral glancing up from the book she was reading. One by one, the other climbers watched them too. Farah finally marked her place and came over.

Rana even added some commentary as the game progressed, explaining the moves to Farah. "Tristan is taking many risks," he said.

"That doesn't surprise me," she responded.

Tristan grinned before cutting them a warning look. "I get this is the only entertainment for a hundred miles, but if the peanut gallery could keep it down, I'd appreciate it."

Rana frowned. "What the hell does peanut gallery mean? Is it an art installation for peanuts?"

"He means you guys need to shut the hell up," Malcolm said. He moved to capture Tristan's rook.

Tristan studied the board. The game was close to ending.

"Even at this altitude, I can smell the bullshit," Tristan said.

"What do you mean, Sinclair?" Malcolm feigned innocence. He sucked at acting.

"You're probably a Grand Master."

"Not quite."

"You're definitely much better than you lead on." Tristan moved his queen out.

"Maybe. Sorry, I couldn't refuse the chance to hustle a silver spoon like yourself."

"A silver spoon?"

"C'mon, Sinclair, you come from wealth. You're a pretty boy."

Ah, smack talk, one of the best methods of intimidation. Too bad Malcolm underestimated him.

"I'm here because I'm an experienced climber."

"Sure, sure, but you're also a pretty boy. I've never really cared for hotshots like you. Where I come from, if you're dumb enough to fall for a hustle, you deserve the lumps." Malcolm took another of Tristan's pawns. "Care to resign?"

"Never." Tristan moved his knight.

"Don't worry. I'll take care of those binoculars."

Tristan rubbed his chin, hoping the board would talk to him. It did. He made his move and looked up at Malcolm. "Don't think I didn't suspect. There is something off about a man who brings a chess board on a trip where every inch of space has to be accounted for and then claims he doesn't know how to play very well."

"What does that mean?" Malcolm moved, almost too quickly. His cockiness would be his downfall.

"It means, don't get too comfortable."

"Why not?" Malcolm asked.

Tristan leaned in. "Because you're not the only one who can hustle. I'm better than I led on too." He slid his queen into position. "Checkmate."

Malcolm's eyes narrowed as he stared at the board. "I didn't see the surprise attack."

"I believe that's the point of the surprise attack." He grabbed the chips from Malcolm's hands and popped one into his mouth.

The others laughed and clapped. Grams had once told him gloating was the weak man's prize. Tristan held out his hand. "Good game, really." He offered Malcolm a chip.

Malcolm pushed the bag away. "Enjoy them."

"Sore loser," Tristan muttered when Malcolm left, leaving him to put away the board.

Farah took his seat.

"Do you play?" Tristan asked her.

"Not yet. I've seen matches though, and I'm intrigued so I'm going to learn."

"Oh yeah? When?"

"Now." She started setting the pieces up again. She had a few in the wrong spots. He corrected them.

"Who's going to teach you?"

She looked around, then back at him. "You. You seem a capable teacher."

"I don't know about that, but I won't argue with you. All right then." She held out her hand. "Pass the chips."

# Chapter 13

If she wasn't surrounded by earthly beauty, she might have noticed Tristan Sinclair more often. She might have studied the ways his muscles bulged against his shirt. She might even have chanced a few long looks of his backside and broad shoulders. Or observed how often he dragged his hand through his thick hair when he was frustrated or gritted his teeth when he was angry. Surely, she would have wondered a thousand times what the band of black with tiny roman numerals tattooed around his left forearm meant. It was a date, exactly one year ago from today. Did that have anything to do with why he was acting so somber?

But everything else was too beautiful, and she was far too busy so she just didn't notice. And if she kept telling herself that, she might just start to believe it.

She was doing the cooking tonight. She stirred a kettle of soup and studied the landscape. They were at Camp II. They would be upon the serac soon, a solid ridge of glacial ice. The days would be colder, leaving less time and energy for wayward thoughts. Their days were filled with hiking, setting up supplies, and acclimatizing. Each time the group reached higher ground, they had to settle in and get used to the thinning air for several days. Otherwise they would risk exposure, pulmonary edema, or possible aneurysm. The human body had to adjust to the physical changes.

Ahmed and Tristan discussed the routes they were taking over the next few days. In a big ice climb, there was usually a ratio of ten to one between planning and actual mountaineering. Tristan suggested they leave behind more supplies so they could reach higher elevation earlier. Ahmed was quick to agree.

Tristan had the kind of presence that turned heads. The few women she'd noticed at the Shalimar when they had dinner had paused in conversation to drink him in. Men seemed to affirm and favor whatever direction he gave. His confidence never shifted toward arrogance, though. Tristan Sinclair was wisdom interlaced with wit. A methodical explorer whose crooked smile made the air at these high elevations even thinner.

She quickly looked away when he glanced at her. This was getting ridiculous. How could hormones live and thrive at six thousand meters? The way he gazed at her, sought her out during hikes, and sat next to her at meals left little doubt the feelings were mutual. That didn't make them any less dangerous. He released both the calm and the chaos inside of her. If she gave into those feelings, it would result in a tragic storm.

Being the only woman in the expedition meant she had to remain professional and distant. There were strong expectations placed on her, and her failures would be judged more harshly. She had always listened to a tune that others didn't hear. It had been a difficult road for her, especially when non-conformity was often confused with disrespect. But she had endured the struggles to carve out a life she loved. She wasn't about to throw away all those years of hard work and a chance to summit for a stupid crush.

"So what does someone need to do to get a cup of coffee around here?" Malcolm asked, jerking his head toward the fire.

"Make it," she responded. "I could use a cup of tea myself. Thank you for offering."

Malcolm laughed good-naturedly, a pretty rare occurrence for him. Except for Ahmed, she hadn't known the others in the expedition very well when they started out. They'd had a few meet-and-greets via video chat set up by Ahmed. But the days of hiking and camping had caused an easy camaraderie among the team. Even Malcolm seemed less grouchy.

Ahmed still narrowed his eyes whenever Tristan and she talked, but he never repeated his warning to her. Then again, she and Tristan had remained friendly, always edging that symbolic line in the sand, the one that had a huge sign posted *no trespassing*. They had both drawn the line out of necessity. Neither of them crossed it, like an unwritten pact.

Everyone took their seats around the campfire for the evening meal. As usual, Malcolm and Edelweiss sat together. Tristan sat next to Ahmed. Farah sat between Bjorn and Lino. Lino was teaching her phrases in Italian, a language far too beautiful for her course tongue.

"You and Malcolm met at Kala Patthar last year, right?" Tristan asked Edelweiss. "My uncle hiked it too."

"Yeah, it was nice," Malcolm answered. "My brother bailed on me at the last minute. I met Edelweiss there, and we decided to climb it together.

We discovered we were both interested in K2. Edelweiss because of his gramps and me because... Well, because it's always been a dream."

"What happened during your grandfather's expedition?" Farah asked.

Edelweiss removed the breathing apparatus. "He was with a horrible team that left him to rot and die." Bitterness coated the man's voice. The others used oxygen masks intermittently when needed, except for Farah and Tristan. Edelweiss, though, wore his mask all the time now, removing it only to speak and eat. Tristan didn't respond, but Farah could see the disapproval in his expression, not over Edelweiss's statement, but most likely for the amount of oxygen he consumed on a daily basis.

She pulled up her legs and wrapped her arms around them. "It's hard to imagine climbing the mountain so long ago without the technology and tools we have."

"Yes, but there were still summits," Ahmed said. "Never underestimate a man's will." He laced his boots, making sure each knot was tight. Soon, they would get into the colder climates and have to rely on their warmer clothes, leaving behind the lighter items at one of the camps. The higher they got, the heavier their garments and the lighter their packs needed to be.

"I don't remember ever hearing of a summit bid in 1940, or even in that decade," Farah said. She'd studied every summit, pored over the volumes of text, internet articles, magazine spreads, and even personal journals of the climbers who had made the journey before her. She had wanted to read everything when it came to the subject of K2.

"Yeah, well, not everything was recorded, especially back then," Malcolm said.

Edelweiss took another helping of soup. "It wasn't a well-known expedition, just a few men who wanted to test their limits on the Savage Mountain. They didn't want notoriety like so many climbers today. It was a special mission of sorts to test their strength. They didn't summit, but my grandfather paid the ultimate price." He leaned forward and dropped his voice as if relaying a secret. "He was a bit crazy, you know."

"From lack of oxygen?" Farah asked.

Edelweiss shook his head. "Before that even. He believed in the occult and thought this mountain had its own spirit, one who was both good and evil. He thought summiting would rid him of a curse." Edelweiss gestured up to the sharp peak, so high the clouds obscured it. "He called K2 his own Koh-i-Noor."

"After the diamond?" Farah asked.

Edelweiss nodded, his eyes lighting up. "He thought the only way to kill a curse is with a curse. You know the tale of the Koh-i-Noor, dear?"

"Of course," she said. "The nickname makes sense to me. K2 is carved from two tectonic plates crashing." She angled her hands, touching the tips of her fingers together in a pyramid. "It is the ultimate diamond in the rough. I believe Koh-i-Noor is Persian for 'mountain of light.'"

"Hate to break up this theater of the macabre before Act Two, but let's discuss our route for tomorrow. Sinclair, have you mapped it all out?" Malcolm interjected.

"I have." Tristan jerked his head toward Farah. "What is the story of Koh-i-Noor?"

"Everyone knows it," Malcolm said, not hiding his irritation.

"I don't," Tristan said, his eyes narrowing on Malcolm. "Can someone enlighten me?"

Farah looked at Edelweiss, but he gestured back to her "Please, you tell the story."

"We should be focusing on our route tomorrow," Malcolm said, the familiar scowl appearing on his face.

"We need time to relax, and a little entertainment wouldn't hurt," Ahmed said. He gave Farah a smile of encouragement.

She'd always thought the stories behind the Koh-i-Noor were interesting. As a child, she'd read the book about the mystical gemstone from cover to cover many times. "First of all, it's not a fable. It a real story about a real diamond. I would argue it's the most famous diamond in the world, even more so than the Hope Diamond. The legend says it came from India, excavated from the first diamond mine that ever existed. It weighed almost eight-hundred carats."

Ahmed let out a low whistle. "I had no idea about the eight-hundred carats. That has to be over a hundred grams."

Edelweiss tapped the fire with a long stick. "Closer to two hundred, and about a third of a pound. It's been cut down and polished several times. Now, it weighs closer to one-hundred carats. Still, quite large by any measure." He nodded toward Farah. "Please continue, my dear."

"Well, over the centuries, kingdoms have been won and lost by this single gem. It has caused a great deal of bloodshed. In the seventeen hundreds, when the Persians conquered India, the Indian Emperor hid the Koh-i-Noor in his turban to keep it for himself. The jewel made even the wisest men greedy."

"Was the man's name Gollum?" Bjorn asked.

"No." Farah crossed her arms and pretended to be annoyed.

"I'm sorry," Bjorn said.

She smiled and wiggled her fingers at Bjorn. "But it was everyone's precious," she said in her best imitation of the Lord of the Rings' character. "Anyway, the Persian leader had been warned about this. So he insisted the two leaders take part in a tradition where they exchanged turbans to symbolize their new-found friendship and peace among their lands."

Ahmed clapped his hands. "The old turban trick."

"Not the old turban trick. That was where the trick originated." She loved telling stories. The best ones were plucked from the history books in her opinion. The team seemed to agree, since they were hanging on her words. That was everyone except Malcolm, who had a permanent frown on his face. She ignored him, focusing on the other faces around the campfire. "When the Persian ruler unwrapped the turban and first laid his eyes on the large brilliant stone, he proclaimed 'Koh-i-Noor,' which roughly translates to 'Mountain of Light.'"

"So what happened to the diamond?" Tristan asked.

"The diamond traveled from India to Persia to Afghanistan to Lahore. Finally, when the British placed their flags on Lahore and the Punjab was proclaimed part of the British throne, the diamond was presented to her majesty. It still resides as the centerpiece of her crown today. Of course, it's a point of great debate as both India and Pakistan claim rights to it, which the throne refuses to acknowledge. There is a Hindu curse on the Koh-i-Noor that states any man who owns the diamond will own the world, but they will also come to know all its misfortunes. That knowledge will ultimately destroy any man. Only God, or a woman, can wear it without punishment."

"Are you bullshitting us, dear girl?" Bjorn asked.

"I swear I'm not," she said.

"She speaks the truth," Edelweiss confirmed.

She took another spoonful of her soup before it went cold. When she looked up, they were all staring at her with rapt attention. "What?"

"Why God or a woman?" Tristan asked.

"Not exactly sure, except maybe because women aren't slaves to power or something philosophical along those lines. The curse actually held true for all the men who claimed the gem. They all amassed amazing power and conquered many lands, but they all died horrible deaths."

"Sounds contradictory," Tristan said.

She shrugged. "Legend and logic are rare bedfellows. In a way, the Koh-i-Noor is both a talisman and curse."

"The ultimate corruption of power," Tristan said.

"Exactly," she agreed. "Strangely enough, if a woman possesses the diamond, it is said to protect her. Maybe that's why the queen's crown is the best place for it."

"How do you know all this?" Tristan asked.

"I studied history at university. Folklore has always been my passion."

"Like the legend of Maiden Shina?"

A heat crept across her face, but she wasn't exactly embarrassed. His smile, boyish and full of light, was contagious. "Yes, like that."

"Maiden Shina?" Ahmed asked. "Tell us that story, Farah."

She shook her head. She was content to let that lie as a private joke that lived somewhere between here and Quebec. "Another time."

"My dear, your knowledge of Koh-i-Noor is impressive," Edelweiss added.

"Thank you. But how did your grandfather think climbing K2 could rid him of a curse?"

Edelweiss paused for so long she almost repeated the question.

"Who cares?" Edelweiss said, dismissing her question. "As I said, he was crazy."

Malcolm laughed. "Curses, huh? For someone who feels unlucky, the last thing they ought to do is attempt a mountain referred to as 'killer' and 'savage.'"

"Indeed," Edelweiss agreed.

Questions rose to Farah's head like bubbles rising on a steaming pot of water, one after the other until the whole pot almost boiled over. But the wind picked up. It echoed and howled around them, an ominous warning of the long night to come. Rocks started to hurdle across the terrain along with their tools and equipment.

"Secure the supplies," Malcolm said, jumping to his feet.

They yelled orders at each other. The shouting became necessary to compete with the wailing wind. The group scattered in different directions. Farah put out the fire and gathered the cooking utensils. They needed to secure their tents with more anchors so they wouldn't blow away in the night. They had to shelter the supplies and tie everything down as best they could.

Things changed at lightning speed on the Karakorum, especially weather. It took approximately five seconds before the wind sped up to the roar of a plane engine. Pots and pans and supplies were picked up and scattered. Everyone scrambled to grab hold of their objects and seek shelter inside the tents. She managed to catch her pack, but her camera bag was lighter and blew from her grasp. She tried to chase it down, but the wall of wind physically blocked her from moving forward.

She fell to her knees, curling into a ball, trying to keep herself low, centered, and attached to the ground. She said a silent prayer that she not become another object for the mountain to whirl and toss at its will. She lifted her head, trying to focus on where she was. She watched in disbelief as her tent ripped from the ground and flew like a bright yellow parachute until the night sky swallowed it whole. A canopy of stars illuminated its flight right over the edge of the precipice and into the dark. It resembled a flapping dress, a sari to be exact, yellow silk with a golden boarder. She heard Amma's laugh, smelled the rose and vanilla of her perfume, and felt the warmth of her hug. *Remember child, you have my blood and his. The blood of queens and whores mingles inside of you. You have to decide which one you are. You can be either.*

*I don't want to be either, Amma. I choose none of them.*

Panic flooded her veins, pumping as fast as a tidal wave. The fear consumed her entire body. She could not breathe. She could not think. She could not even cry for help. Her feet and hands scraped along the rocky dirt without her permission. The wind pushed her in the same direction as her tent, bit by horrific bit. She would spiral into the dark abyss.

*I'm dying,* she thought. Death wasn't calm and serene with a white light in the distance. It was overlapping memories and quick flashes of regret and insanity intensified. It was pleading and fighting and struggling to breathe. Most of all, it wasn't quick and short like the flutter of a hummingbird's wings. No… It was long, so bloody long that time stretched like an elastic band, growing larger, and then larger still, until it finally snapped.

She let go of all her yesterdays and forgot about all the tomorrows. There was only this moment. This moment where she would die. Something popped in her ear. The elastic band maybe? She heard the call pulling her back into the now, away from the abyss. She felt something. An arm wrapped around her waist. A man screamed in her ear, calling her name, his hot breath spilling onto her skin.

"Farah. Farah. Farah. We have to get inside." She could feel his presence and the vibration of the words against her body, but his voice barely cut through the howling echoes. The mountain cried like a wounded animal.

She broke from her paralysis. "My camera!" His arms tightened around her before she could escape and go after the bag that contained all the photographs of the expedition, which amounted to a large percentage of her wages for the next few months.

"Leave it. It's gone."

He all but picked her up, his arm secured around her as they fought against the storm and battled the strong forces of air, bit by bit. He pushed her into the tent. She sputtered to catch her breath as he zipped it up. For a moment, it was just the two of them in the dark, breathing hard and coughing as they struggled to get air into their lungs. He clicked on a flashlight. She blinked, her eyes adjusting to the brightness.

"Look at me," Tristan said, his voice much calmer now. "Are you all right?"

"The others?" she asked. Her voice came out ragged and choppy, each syllable requiring too much strength. She pressed her face to the windowed flap of the tent, but it had grown too dark to see. It had happened so quickly. Did they lose someone? Her heart began beating so hard it pounded in her eardrums. Or maybe that was the wind. She placed her hands over her ears and closed her eyes, trying to block it out. But she could still hear the horrible sound. She could still see the haunting image of the yellow tent flying across the night sky and diving into oblivion.

He held her upper arms. She opened her eyes. He looked composed. How could he be this calm in the face of chaos?

"Breathe with me."

She did, fast at first. She focused on his eyes. Her heart stopped jumping and her lungs only had a dull pain now. "Did we lose anyone?" She was afraid to hear his answer.

"They all got inside."

She swallowed, but her throat was dry and parched.

"Drink." He unscrewed his water bottle and handed it to her. "They are safe. I saw them all get inside, except for you. I went to look for you. What happened out there? You froze."

"Are you sure?" she asked. "Where is Ahmed? Edelweiss?"

"Safe, Farah. They are all safe. I promise you."

She took a deep breath and wrapped her arms around herself. A shiver ran down her spine, one that had nothing to do with the weather. Had she been inside her tent, she may have blown away with it, right off the mountain's edge. Just one more spirit doomed to roam the Savage for an eternity.

"Shhh," he said. "You're okay, Dimples."

She'd been through these close calls before. Why was this different? Her reaction wasn't normal. She didn't want to think of the reason, but no matter how hard she tried to block it, the razor-sharp memory pierced through all her shields. The yellow tent reminded her of that day in Islamabad when her mother slipped on the marble staircase of the Jat's mansion. Amma had worn her favorite yellow silk sari, the one with the tiny pink flowers embroidered into a sparkling gold border. The material was so soft Farah imagined it was spun by angels.

At ten, she'd watched in horror as her mother tumbled down the stairs wearing that sari. Amma never screamed, not once. But Farah did. At least she thought she did. The shrieks echoed in her ears for weeks. Her throat would dry up and she'd start shivering even on the hottest days. The shiver followed her, invading her body without warning, no matter how much time and distance had passed. She had become paralyzed then too, helpless and hopeless in that moment. Her mother's body lay limp, a pool of crimson circling her head like a halo as it seeped onto the pristine, white stone floor.

"Farah?" he whispered, rubbing her shoulders. She barely felt it through the thick material of her coat, but she realized it wasn't the first time he'd said her name. She gazed at him. He looked concerned for her. "I keep losing you. Stay here with me. Where do you keep going?"

"I... I don't know." She wanted to beg him not to ask her more. Dear God, was she having a panic attack? She hated being vulnerable. Hated the way he looked at her now as if she needed rescuing. She straightened her shoulders and sat up so she was looking him in the eyes. "I'm fine. I'm fucking fine, Tristan."

"Okay."

"I am."

"I believe you."

"I just really loved that tent." She cursed the way her voice cracked.

He looked perplexed for a second, but maybe he sensed what she needed because he smiled. "Yeah, it was a nice tent. It really sucks."

She wanted to back away, but his arms felt too warm and comfortable. "I'm tired."

"Me too. Let's rest." He opened the sleeping bag for her to climb in.

"There's only one. We have to share."

He nodded. They had to sleep on their sides so they could both fit. Outside, the wind sounded like a million screaming women, full of grief and agony and despair. She wondered if the Goddess of the Mountain was warning them to turn back. She squeezed her eyes shut and covered her ears.

"It'll pass," he said.

She hated how weak she'd become. How did one single memory have the power to transform her back to the scared child she once was?

She thought about other things, trying to force her mind to shift focus with images of chocolate cake with whipped butter cream frosting, the laughter of her students, the sun setting over Hunza Valley...the man lying beside her. Of all the odd things in her head, she remembered the photo of him in the magazine. The cover had clearly been a staged shot. But inside the article, there was a picture of him hanging off a long, jagged piece of vertical rock in the Rocky Mountains. He was shirtless, his pants covered with chalk, a dozen carabineers looped around his waist. His fingers griped the tiniest handhold in the rock, his head tilted toward the sky as the high sun shone in the background. Not a woman in the world could have resisted a second or third look at that photo. He was attempting a complicated climb, but he had a genuine smile on his face. She'd seen him smile that way a few times on this trip.

"Why aren't you sleeping?" he asked her, his voice low and edged with concern.

"Just thinking."

"What are you thinking?"

Bloody hell. She could hardly tell him about her lusty, inappropriate thoughts. "Why did you start climbing?"

"I figured out a long time ago that I'm the happiest when I'm on the mountain. It's as simple and as complicated as that. What about you? Is it really just about proving the world wrong?"

"I can't explain it, not even to myself." She doubted she'd ever been so honest.

"Try."

"There were obstacles all my life. Politics and social rules and things I couldn't see, but I felt them. At least up here, I know the challenges I'm facing. They're not whispers behind my back or judgments made my bitter people."

"I understand," he said. "I admire your strength."

Strength was the last word she would use to describe herself right now. She wanted to ask him about the ink on his bicep, but she wouldn't risk bringing him into a dark place too. She had no inclination to talk about herself. "What supplies do you think we lost?" The real question was if they would be able to move on with the journey.

"Don't worry about tomorrow. Tomorrow will take care of itself. Tonight, we need to take care of each other."

Each other? As far as she could tell, it was only him taking care of her. But she didn't have the right words to voice her gratitude. "Okay."

The wind howled outside, pushing against the tent. But their shelter gave them a reprieve, almost as if they were in their own little snow globe. He put his arms around her. "Don't worry, I secured the tent with more anchors as soon as the storm started. I just didn't have enough time to get to yours."

"I'm surprised you had time to do any of them."

He frowned. "Farah, it was at least forty minutes from the time the wind started to when I got to you. I thought you were already in your tent, and when I couldn't find you, I went in search."

How had so much time passed with her being stuck in a trance? "I'm sorry. I should have helped. I'm better than this."

"Don't be sorry, not with me."

She wanted to say more, but the words didn't materialize. He seemed so calm when faced with chaos. She wanted to know how he was able to keep his wits about him. "Tristan, what is your weakness?"

"My weakness?"

"What makes you mortal? I've done this trip with some of the best technical climbers in the world, but even they would have a hard time coping with what happened."

"I have a lot of experience, not that I don't have my fair share of weaknesses too."

"Give me one so I know you're real."

"Go to sleep."

She sighed and shut her eyes. Her eyes felt heavy. The wind didn't sound as ominous, or maybe she had gotten used to the sound. Everything had gone quiet. She felt his breath against her skin. He whispered her name slowly, the raspy cadence of his voice filing her up like a balloon. She didn't stir. Her mind was creating another illusion. This time, she wasn't sure if she wanted to wake up.

"The girl with violet eyes and a dimpled smile. The one who captures me with her stories. She talks with her hands, and she's incredibly strong with enough grit to keep a man on his toes. She…she is my weakness."

# Chapter 14

Supplies were lost during the storm, but not as many as they thought. Lino and Bjorn had gathered many of the loose supplies, while the others had secured the tents. Sadly, she'd lost her professional camera and the digital photos she'd taken, but at least she still had her less-expensive camera. Most of all, she still had her life, thanks to Tristan. When she woke in the morning, she tried to thank him, but he shook his head.

He locked eyes with her. The intensity of his gaze, sharp and penetrating, left little room for coherent thoughts. "Are you able to do this? Or do you need to turn around, Farah? There is no shame in heading back. Just tell me, and I'll support you."

"I can do this, Tristan."

"Then we don't need to say anything else. If you need to talk about it, I want all of it, not bits and pieces. Until then, there's nothing else to say."

She understood that also meant the words he whispered to her. Exploring those ideas would cause a fissure that could not be mended. So she didn't reply.

The weather had cleared. In fact, the following days were warm. So they continued on. He'd offered her his tent and bunked in with Ahmed. He never mentioned her breakdown or made her feel uncomfortable in any way. He didn't tell the others either. She was relieved for that.

They made it to Camp III, an area known for avalanches. This would start the most technical part of the climb. Lino and Bjorn were going up to bring supplies to the next camp. Tomorrow, it would be Malcolm and Ahmed's turn. They had stayed at Camp II longer than planned. The storm had left them surprised and in need of recharging. Securing ice screws was dangerous and back-breaking work. They needed more rest at the end of each day as well as to acclimatize and get their bearings. They were already at seven thousand meters, though. The summit was in their sights.

She'd decided to go for a hike to capture some more pictures. Tristan joined her. Usually, he walked like a man with purpose, but at other times, he looked as inquisitive as a young boy, especially when they came upon an amazing view.

"I think there should be a rule that every climber should be a poet," he said. He swept his hand across the sky. "It's a shame to get to see things like this and not be able to put it in words."

"I don't think words could do it justice, even if you are a professional wordsmith. This is a view only birds and adventurers get." She understood his feelings. It was probably one of the reasons she started investing in photography equipment and educating herself. The money supported her climbs, but it seemed a shame not to capture some of God's greatest work for posterity when she had the chance. She lagged behind today, trying to snap photos of the brilliant afternoon sun casting a glow upon the silvery snow caps. Tristan stayed back with her. She hoped it wasn't because he feared for her, but rather because he enjoyed being with her.

"Can you stand in the frame?" she asked.

He dragged a hand through his hair. "You want me to pose for you?"

"Well, you are a professional cover model."

"Very funny, smartass."

Come to think of it, a shot of him might just increase the dollar value. "Actually, I was looking for some perspective."

He moved in front of her, his figure creating a focal point, even amidst the backdrop of sharp snow-covered peaks and blue sky.

Even the heavy mountain gear couldn't mask his muscular form. They both wore dark sunglasses to protect their eyes from the sun's harsh glare, but his glasses highlighted his strong jaw and sensual mouth. She snapped a few pictures, both with and without him. He made a show of flexing in one of the frames, causing her to laugh.

"How's your perspective?" he asked, a mischievous smile forming.

"Getting foggier by the minute."

"It's a clear day," he said.

Shit, she hadn't meant to say it out loud. Of course, he was looking at her with complete sincerity.

"Have you heard anything?" he asked.

"No." Unlike at ground level, talk about the weather was a topic of great importance and debate up here. She ignored his amused smile. He was probably replaying her statement. "We've been lucky." She snapped a few more shots. She could not get the night they spent in the tent out of her head. But she knew she had to try. A different, more turbulent storm was happening inside of her. The tall man beside her was the cause.

She pointed to the other climbers, almost a kilometer ahead. "You can go on. I have a feeling when the sun hits the horizon, it's going to cast everything in a soft glow. I want to wait for that."

"I don't mind waiting."

He looked as if he might say something more, but instead he just leaned against the mountain wall next to her. He watched over her shoulder as she scrolled through her pictures.

"I'm sorry you lost all your other photos."

She shrugged. "I'm actually getting some amazing pictures." Neither had brought up that night until now. He'd told her not to unless she was ready to talk about all of it, but how could she keep silent? A conversation was long overdue. At times, she felt his eyes on her, a gaze that bore through all the layers of clothing and those other layers she'd put up to protect herself.

"I never thanked you for what you did. That was very impolite of me."

"No need to thank me."

"Of course, there is a need. I'm sorry I froze. I don't know what happened."

"I think you do, Farah. You don't want to tell me though. But for God's sake, don't apologize. Everyone has their own version of dark. Sometimes you just need someone to flip on the light."

That is what he did for her. He acted as a light when she needed one the most. Maybe he deserved to know what triggered her darkness. She wanted to explain herself.

"My mother fell down a steep flight of stairs when I was ten years old. I watched her tumble and fall and hit her head against a marble floor. She landed at my feet. I don't remember much. I thought I screamed, but they told me I didn't. I guess I was silent the whole time. Almost paralyzed. I didn't speak for weeks. For whatever reason, the yellow tent flying across the sky reminded me of that moment. She wore a yellow sari, you see." She choked out a sound between a laugh and cry.

His expression, compassionate and sincere, made her feel better about sharing the story. A story she never told.

"I'm so sorry, Farah. I can't imagine what it was like witnessing such a horrible accident, especially so young."

She bit back the emotion before it tore away at her. She needed every shred of composure. "I suppose I lost it for a moment, but you did more than shelter me from that wind—you pulled me out of that place. Thank you."

"It was nothing."

"It was very much something."

He put his hand on her shoulder. She wished he wasn't wearing gloves and she wasn't in a huge coat with three layers underneath, including a special material to keep her body insulated. A rather stupid wish considering she would freeze to death.

"What about the fig tree?" he asked.

She blinked her eyes. Oh God, had she talked about the fig tree?

"When I first got you into the tent, you were screaming about it. You don't remember slapping me, do you? Telling me to leave you alone?"

She shook her head, embarrassed by how she'd acted. "I'm sorry if I did that. I didn't mean to."

"You didn't know it was me. It's okay," he said. "We don't have to go there. But if you need a little light, you just let me know."

"Why did you call me Dimples?" She knew it was a weak attempt to change the subject. Thankfully, he went with it.

He titled his head as if he was confused by her question. As if she wouldn't remember him calling her by that name. Then again, she had no recollection of hitting him.

"In the tent, you called me Dimples. I remember some of it."

"When you smile, you have these two predominate dimples. I've been calling you that in my head. I guess it just came out that night."

She tried to tame her smile, but she might as well have been wrestling a seal in an oil bath. Amazing, she could smile at all considering she'd been near tears a moment earlier.

He grinned back at her, cocky and self-assured. "And there they are." He took off his gloves. His thumbs grazed over her cheeks. Her breath hitched. She struggled between leaning in and falling back.

As if he sensed the danger of the touch, he dropped his hands. "We should catch up with the others."

"Right."

They began to work their way toward the group. The snow was getting deeper. In the next few days, they would need to start using their ski poles for leverage.

"You don't believe in oxygen either." The way he asked made it clear it was an observation, not a question. With the rest of the group starting to use oxygen regularly, Tristan and she were the only two who refused.

"I've always felt that if I can't climb with the body I was given, then I'm not meant to be this high. But I have nothing against someone else's choice, unless it causes a danger to the group, or if they choose to leave behind their empty canisters and pollute my mountain." She'd already had a stern talk with Edelweiss on that point. "Anyway, it's a promise I made to myself. It's the reason I know this will be my last time on K2. This body is capable of some amazing things, but I know its limitations."

"I feel the same." He adjusted his goggles. "My clients use it on Everest. In fact, we provide it to them, with close monitoring of course. I never wanted to depend on it though. Just curious, do you think someone is hitting the O a little too hard?"

She didn't need to ask him for clarification. Clearly, he referred to Edelweiss, who ran through his oxygen canisters as if they grew out of the ground.

"I noticed. I don't think he should go much farther. He'll be a liability." She didn't trust Edelweiss to secure screws into the ice or attach fixed ropes.

Farah tuned in the direction of the other climbers. Something was happening ahead. They were all standing around Edelweiss, who flapped his arms wildly. "What do you suppose is happening up there?"

"Think he found his gramps," Tristan said.

She focused the lens of the camera to the scene. Edelweiss was more animated than she'd seen him during the whole trip. He pointed to an area, waving his arms up and down as if he was calling out directions. Ahmed and Malcolm were collecting rocks and clearing a path in the snow. Edelweiss carefully moved a body. Tristan was right. She zoomed in as Edelweiss took the pack off the man.

"We should catch up," Tristan said.

They both picked up speed. They were at the shoulder, the last expanse before the climb turned vertical. For once, he did sound short of breath. By the time they caught up, Malcolm and Ahmed had gathered a layer of ice and rock in a cairn.

"There you two are. Can you help?" Edelweiss asked.

Tristan helped the other men with the preparations. She had seen dead bodies on K2 before, but she had never gotten used to the sight. Nothing decomposed quickly at these temperatures. Dead bodies resembled unfinished wax figures, the frames intact, but part of their features missing. Farah took in the partial skeleton with the snow shoes at his feet. Little spikes poking out of the shoes acted as crampons. His ankle twisted away from the rest of his body. Her gut rumbled. She looked away before she lost the contents of her lunch. But not before she caught a glimpse of the small insignia on a patch of fabric on the dead man's arm. A red angled cross with intersecting arms, the symbol of hate and tragedy. Nothing good could come of this.

She hugged herself, a mixture of anger and disappointment and betrayal hitting her at once. This was not right. "What was in there?" Farah asked, pointing to the battered leather pack Edelweiss clutched.

Edelweiss tightened his hold. "Supplies."

She took out her camera to snap a picture.

Edelweiss moved in front of her. "No pictures. Have some respect for the dead."

*Have some respect for the living*, she thought. She stumbled back. "I was going to take a picture of his supplies, not the body."

Tristan stood next to her. "Everything okay?"

"Fine."

Tristan scanned the body. His eyes widened. The shock turned to disbelief before it transformed to rage. Farah understood it. She felt it herself.

"Edelweiss, I can't help you bury this man."

"Why not?" he asked.

"You should know why. You should have told us. We deserved to know." Edelweiss waved his hand. "The dead are the dead. They deserve respect."

"Not all dead," Tristan said. He grabbed his own pack and moved forward. Farah went with him.

Edelweiss turned to Ahmed. "Before you raise an objection, I suggest you remember the premium I'm paying." He smiled widely, his black and gray beard making him appear almost menacing. "Koh-i-Noor," he said.

# Chapter 15

Ahmed was supposed to set up the next camp, but he'd sprained his foot during the hike and needed a rest day. Bjorn and Edelweiss suffered from attitude sickness so they stayed back too. The others thought it best to wait a few more days. Wanting to stay on schedule, Tristan said he'd forge ahead to the next camp. She volunteered to go with him. She wanted to prove her usefulness to the group and to herself, but the need to be with him was so strong she questioned the logic of her decisions.

Climbing K2 involved setting up camps along the route. The team would head to one camp and get used to the climate. They would hike for a day and head down to a previous camp. They did this several times until they acclimatized and could stay at the higher camp.

They left behind whatever supplies they could once they left each camp, trying to get lighter each time. The camps would be used on the way down too. Each day, they hiked for long hours, taking in the most beautiful views. They checked and rechecked the food stocks every day. It would be easy to misjudge and run out of food. Everyone ate enough to be productive, but they all lost weight.

Tristan had been unusually quiet since they discovered the body. He barely made conversation. There was a current of unease and distrust that strained the whole group. Their decisions took longer. They disagreed on the paths they needed to take, the division of duties, and even the way they rationed their food. The only one who seemed in better spirits was Edelweiss, who had slowed down on his supplemental oxygen and was acting more like a leader than a follower these days. It wasn't unheard of for climbers to suddenly find their stride, once acclimation took hold, but the quick shift seemed strange. The whole group dynamic had changed. Finding the body had been a bad omen in Farah's mind. It all felt wrong. Farah wondered if they had angered the Goddess of the Mountain by uncovering buried secrets and disrupting bones that were laid to rest decades ago.

She worried for Tristan most of all. He'd lost his playfulness along the way. His spirit was that of a true explorer, but the man who read a children's adventure book for inspiration was dormant now. She wanted nothing more than to flip a switch for him and bring light into his world too. She recognized this personal time with him was a gift of sorts. They were in the most remote place in the world, yet this was one of the first times they were alone.

The weather was becoming frigid as they reached higher elevations. The awesome expanse around them made for some beautiful photographs. Today, she woke to find Tristan gathering garbage from the treks that had passed this way before them. Without a word, she started picking up the rubbish too. The previous group had littered the landscape. The mountains had survived a million years, but now they had a serious predator—humans.

The two of them soon had a pile of paper, clothes, and used oxygen canisters. Farah sighed in defeat. It would take a hundred years for the clothes and paper to degrade at this altitude, but the canisters were even worse. The canisters would never decompose and remain for an eternity.

"There's so much," she said, shaking her head.

"We can bring this down to a lower elevation, maybe?" Tristan said. "Possibly, Ahmed has porter contacts he can hire to clear the site if we can't carry it all back."

"I believe he does. That's a good idea. I can carry a few more kilos back. I can't believe people left all this behind."

"I wish I could say the same, but nothing surprises me anymore." He went into the tent to retrieve the butane stove. "How about a fire, milady?"

"That would be nice."

He frowned as she added a few more items to the growing pile.

He lit the fire a distance away from their growing heap. "I always inventory all our supplies on treks. I like to confirm that everything we brought up with us has come down. We weigh everyone's pack before and after. All of my clients pay a non-refundable fee if they leave garbage behind. It covers the costs to hire Sherpas to bring it all back down. Luckily, I've never had to keep anyone's deposit. Guess whoever was in charge of this expedition didn't feel the same."

"That's a brilliant solution."

He shrugged off her compliment. "It worked well."

She laid out a sleeping mat. She pulled her legs up and wrapped her arms around them, warming herself by the fire. "I'm sorry," she said.

"For what?" He sat beside her.

"I misjudged you and your company." She pointed to large pile of refuse. "Obviously, you're not like others."

"I don't blame you for being pissed. This is ridiculous."

They were silent for a while. She leaned her head against his shoulder. Everything inside her told her not to do it, but it was so comfortable there. He put his arm around her. She stiffened from his touch, but he pulled her closer. His hair had grown and his beard was full. If he had a kilt and sword, she was sure he could slay a dragon.

She stood before they stepped over any boundaries. She walked over to the northeast edge of the mountain. He followed her.

He broke the silence. "So who would have guessed Edelweiss's gramps was a Nazi? Did you know?"

Irritation flickered through her. "Of course not. If I had, I would not have agreed to go looking for the man."

"I'm sorry. I have a lot of angry feelings toward the whole thing. This feels so wrong."

"To me too. I feel stupid. I should have figured it out."

"How?"

"I could have put the pieces together, especially with my background. I've researched the history of all the mountains in Karakorum, especially K2. When I think about it, it's probably the reason why that trek was covered up and not in the official records. I read somewhere that Hitler wanted to prove Germany's superior athletic ability across every sport, especially mountain climbing. After all, planting a Nazi flag on top of a mountain is the ultimate sign of an alpha race. Alpinist clubs were the first to ban Jews. I know the SS sponsored many summits in the Alps. I just didn't know they did it here too."

"That's true. Never thought I'd come face to face with evil like that. Not up here."

"I hope we can just move on and put it behind us now."

"Me too," Tristan said.

"I'm happy I'm here with you, Tristan."

He didn't respond, not verbally anyway. He embraced her instead. She would not move away this time. Her body longed for his touch.

She turned her head toward the sky and then shrieked. "Don't move."

"What?" he asked, searching around, no doubt looking for an avalanche or falling serac.

She pointed. "There. Do you see it? I never thought I'd see one in my whole life. It's a Specter of Brocken. Do you know how rare that is?"

They both stared in awe. A Specter of Brocken was like a rainbow to the millionth power. It was an extremely rare phenomenon where the play of light magnified a climber's body, casting it into a cloud surrounded by brilliant colors. She thought it was similar to looking at her own shadow, except the shadow was illuminated in the sky. Mountaineers could climb all their lives and never witness the event. This was even stranger because it wasn't just one of their images being cast, but both of their silhouettes were inside the cloud looming high above them and frozen in the sky. She felt blessed.

"This is some real Harry Potter shit, Nawaz."

She laughed. "We should be still. It might dissipate if we move."

"You sure you don't want to try for a picture? It's gotta be worth a great deal to capture a Specter of Brocken on film."

"No. I just want to enjoy this moment with you." The day and this image was something she refused to share with anyone.

He held her close. Neither of them moved, afraid to disturb the image. "We look like giants," he whispered.

"I think it's more ethereal. Like we're spirits," she said.

"That last bar of the rainbow, it's the same shade as your eyes."

She stiffened, realizing just how close they were. Her heart raced. She felt his muscled body pressing against her. The image dissolved into the skyline. He tucked a strand of loose hair behind her ear.

"Tristan, we shouldn't."

He frowned. "You don't feel this?"

She moved away from him. "It's not that. This isn't the right time."

"It seems like there will never be a right time for us."

As happy as seeing the image had made her, she felt the loss of something she never had—him. "I wish I could say that wasn't true."

"Can we be somewhere else today, Farah?"

"Where else would we be?" she asked.

"Let's pretend we're normal people. Just for today. What do you say, milady?"

Each time he called her by that term, her toes curled. Not an easy motion in heavy climbing boots. The endearment should have made her laugh, but instead her heart did a jumping jack inside her chest. "Your normal and my normal are two different things, Tristan."

"Well, here we are, about as far away from civilization as we can get. We're at the top of the world, girl. What better place to find common ground?"

"What is normal for you?"

"I don't know anymore. Except you make me feel normal. Is that strange?"

"Not to me." Was it the thin air or was he the reason she was struggling to breathe? "You make me feel normal too." Normal and completely abnormal at the same time.

"Will you go out on a date with me?"

It felt so surreal, sitting on a cliff, miles above the ground with his arm around her. She wondered if this was a dream. She laughed and begged herself to stay asleep a while longer.

"I wasn't joking," he said.

"I accept. But only if you promise to remain valiant and noble."

"So that would mean what? No third base?"

"Is that a football term?"

"Never mind. I promise I'll be a complete rake."

She punched him. "Tristan!"

"Sorry, I got my terminology wrong. See, if you'd lent me the book, I would know these things."

"It's disrespectful to the mountain for us to do anything up here."

"Are you serious?"

Yes, she was serious. When it came to K2, the scales were already tipped out of their favor. Tempting fate would be the most foolish thing they could do. She tilted her head. "There are many superstitions. Remember the story I told you back at the shop?"

"Maiden Shina, how could I forget?"

"The story was true. They say the Goddess who lives on the mountain is jealous, especially of lovers. I don't think we should draw her attention." She shut her eyes. "Not that we're lovers."

"No, we're not."

"We have today though, and this."

"I promise I'll be a gentleman." He took her hand. "May I have the honor of your company, milady?"

"Why do you call me 'milady'?"

"Because it means noblewoman. And you, Farah Nawaz, are the noblest woman I know."

She didn't believe his answer, but it was so romantic and sweet she didn't question him further. "Where are you going to take me?"

"You let me worry about that. I'll pick you up at your tent around sixteen hundred hours. Be ready to go."

"But I have nothing to wear."

He laughed now, the sound rumbling out of him. "You'll figure it out."

True to his word, he arrived outside her tent at exactly the time promised. Deciding it was a wasted effort to make herself presentable, she put on a warm knit cap. She unzipped her tent. God help her if he didn't stand so tall and sure and beautiful. He took her hand.

"I made us soup," he said.

"That's my favorite." She held up a small bag. "I brought pistachios."

"Perfect." He gazed down on her snowsuit as if she wore the most dazzling gown. He tucked a loose strand of hair behind her ear. "Farah Nawaz, I believe you're the most beautiful woman I've ever seen."

"That's a lovely thing to say, but it might have something to do with the high altitude and the fact I'm the only woman you've seen in the last forty days."

"Doesn't matter. The words are true." He held his arm out for her.

She took it. Even though there was a chill in the air, a powerful heat stirred within her. It could go no further than holding hands. Even then they would have their gloves on, but there was something so intimate about the moment. For the first time, she shed her inhibitions and allowed herself to get swept up under his intense gaze.

He'd arranged his sleeping mat next to a fire. They sat. The pungent aroma of juniper hung heavy in the air. He poured them steaming mugs of soup. They shared slices of freeze-dried apple.

"The view is amazing," she said, gesturing to the snow-peaked caps around them. She took a bite.

"It is," he said, looking straight at her, his expression lusty. He grabbed her wrist and ate the rest of the apple in her hand in one bite.

She almost choked.

"Are you all right?"

"No," she said. "This is how you do a first date? Are you trying to kill me?"

"Sorry." He shook his head. "Too strong?"

"Any stronger, and you'll end up on the Richter scale. Do you woo every girl this way?"

His lips curved into an amused smile. "Woo?"

She crossed her arms. "I said 'woo.' Get over it. Now tell me."

He laughed. "I've never wooed anyone."

"I find that hard to believe."

"Farah, I swear, you're the only girl I've ever tried to woo. So please forgive me if I do something wrong. Or if I come off cheesy."

"I would not call you cheesy." He was far too good at this. He could break through every chain she put around her heart with a single word, a stare, a careless caress.

He reached into his pocket. "I got you something. Hold out your hand."

She removed her glove and held out her hand. He deposited a shiny, round pebble on her palm.

She stared at it, turning it over in her hand. "A rock?"

"Not just a rock, sweetheart. I picked it out myself. Just for you." He leaned his forehead against hers. "Normal would have been to get you flowers. That's probably the right thing to do. I wanted you to have flowers. But in my defense, it's pretty barren around here and most florists don't deliver. The only live thing is the prickly vines that grow on the edges of the glacier. I wanted better for you than a prickly vine. So I found the best rock I could. I even shined it up. In the end, I figure it's better than flowers. Flowers die." He placed the pad of his finger over the pebble and moved it around her palm. "This will last. It will be a reminder that you were here. That I was here. The two of us held hands on top of the world. We had this one day. This magic memory. It will live in my heart forever, just like this rock."

She choked back a sob. "You're really going to have to work extra hard to make me hate you after this."

"I snore."

"You don't. I've slept next to you, remember?"

"I'll think of something. I have a lot of faults."

She shook her head. "It's okay, I already know one bad thing about you. I've worked it out for myself."

"What's that?"

"You're a liar. You told me you weren't a poet. Obviously, you are."

"You must be my muse."

He'd wooed her.

Without a second glance, she stepped across the imaginary boundary she'd set for them.

# Chapter 16

They never told anyone of the Specter of Brocken. It was their secret. The day of normal had made things better in many ways. It had changed things too. Their feelings ran deeper now. They could not go back to avoiding each other.

The whole group had learned to live on the ice. To walk on it, scale it, make water from it, and sleep on it. The whole day had been spent hiking, the rhythmic puncturing of hard snow with their crampons and poles making the only sound. They all wore goggles to prevent ice blindness. Being this close to the sun created its own perils. Edelweiss seemed quicker in his steps and relied less on the oxygen, as if burying his relative had released a dormant strain of energy within him.

Farah on the other hand was exhausted. She climbed into her tent ready to sleep for ten bloody days. Sometimes she thought of what it would mean to have more days of normal with Tristan Sinclair. Even in the most rugged and isolated environment, he managed to be a gentleman. She found herself feeling inside the lining of her pocket where the stone he'd given her lay.

Today, she and Tristan were setting the last of the ice screws. It was supposed to be her and Edelweiss, but Tristan insisted on taking his place, claiming he had more experience. Edelweiss didn't put up an argument. Farah had a feeling Tristan was carving out more time for them to be together. She was grateful for it. Every moment she got to spend with this beautiful man was a precious gift.

Tomorrow, they were going to attempt the summit, the very last one-thousand feet of their journey to the top of the world. The weather, except for that intense windstorm a few weeks back, had been kind to them. She prayed it would hold out so they could secure the summit. It had to be done in one day. A solid four hours of climbing uphill and then descending back to camp, all in a day's time. There was no place to camp that far up, and the temperatures would plummet so low a man could turn into a block of ice just by sitting idle.

She craned her neck back, taking in the sight of what lay ahead. She adjusted her helmet, making sure it was secure. The sharp granite pyramid cut through the clouds. They were at a slope, their ice axes providing one point of contact and the crampons on their boots securing the other. He swung his axe into the ice, easing in at first, testing the integrity of the structure with the adze. Once he was satisfied, he'd take one of the twenty-one-inch screws and spin it around until the teeth bit into the solid mass of ice. A climber needed to become intimate with the ice. If the screw spun too easily, it meant there was too much air. He had to find areas in the ice with the right amount of friction. The work was both dangerous and precarious. If he struck into rotten ice, he could lose his grip and fall from the dangerous angle. If his axe hit the wrong way, a chunk of rock could come loose and hit one of them.

Below him, she performed the same ritual, careful to vary her screws so they would not be linear to his. If the ice cracked, the fracture would follow any easy patterns and cause them both to tumble. She normally lost herself in the tedious work. But today, she kept looking up to check on him.

Seeing him above her like that, she understood Ahmed's fear.

Her feelings for Tristan made the task more difficult. When she met his eyes, he was already staring at her. They were checking on each other constantly, reassuring themselves the other was safe. It prolonged the job.

Wasn't this the danger Ahmed had warned of? With the adventure of the conquest, she was always prepared. She understood the risks and accepted the possible consequences. Somehow, the risks had just grown exponentially without her permission.

But Ahmed was wrong too.

If anything, knowing someone she cared for so deeply was depending on her made her more cautious.

She hummed to herself, something that helped to ease the chaotic thoughts drifting carelessly in her head. She was surprised when he added the lyrics, his baritone voice echoing through the icy canyon.

"You know the song."

"'Landslide'? Yeah, it's one of my favorites. But it's probably not the most appropriate song right now."

"When have we ever been appropriate, Sinclair?"

"You make a point."

She continued to hum, the sound of their ice axes acting as background music. She focused on her task. When she finished, she tilted her head up. He was already looking down at her. "Do you think we're safe?" he asked.

*Not in the least*, she wanted to say. There was nothing safe about Tristan and her.

Except he was referring to the ice screws.

"Let's see." She dug her feet into the ice until she felt a solid hold. Then she leaned back, testing the rope. "It's solid."

Tristan climbed backward until they were even. He turned around, leaned back into the snow, and removed his gloves. He adjusted his helmet. He checked hers too. "Just making sure it's secure."

"It is."

The work had taken its toll. They were both exhausted and all her muscles ached.

"Thirsty?" he asked.

She nodded. He uncapped his drink bottle and passed it to her.

"You ready to kiss the sky, milady?" Tristan asked.

Her heart pounded so hard she checked the horizon for signs of an avalanche. He must have felt it too because he leaned in just a fraction.

"Kiss the sky?" she asked.

"When we summit, we'll be kissing the sky."

"I've never heard that expression." It occurred to her she had never even kissed him. She could count the number of times their bare skin had touched without using all her fingers on one hand.

"My brother, Drew, used to say it all the time."

"Does the sky kiss back?" she asked, passing him back the thermos.

He took a long sip and wiped his mouth. "If you're lucky."

"You never talk about your brother."

"I guess I don't."

"What happened to him?" Back in Concordia, Ahmed had told her about Drew.

"This isn't the right time."

Of all the intimate things they shared, he still sheltered parts of himself. She saw turbulence and pain in his emerald eyes. "It might help you. It's not just our packs that weigh us down."

He inspected the rope next to her and lowered himself another yard. "Who says I need help?"

"I think you carry more than your fair share, Sinclair."

He shook his head. "We're all carrying the right weight for our size."

She kicked down with her crampons until they were face to face again. "I don't mean on your back." She placed her palm over his heart. "I mean right here."

His cynical laugh took her by surprise. "That's rich. I know what you meant. Just let it go, okay?"

"The tattoo on your arm. It's an arm band of mourning. The roman numerals are the date he died."

"You're quite the detective, Nawaz."

"You're doing this for him, aren't you? Why?"

"You're a hypocrite, you know that?" he said, not taking his eyes off the rope.

If they weren't in this precarious position, perched at a 45-degree angle, she might have stomped off in a huff. But right now, storming off wasn't an option. They had to work together and track each other's movements to come down safely. This was quite possibly the worse time for an intense conversation. "What do you mean?"

He titled her chin so she was facing him. "Where did you go that night, sweetheart? Tell me about the fig tree."

"I told you already."

"I don't think so. I haven't mentioned it. We never talk about it. I never push. You went somewhere in your head though. For a few frantic minutes, I thought you'd stay there forever. I have a feeling it was very dark and cold there."

"Tristan, stop it."

"Sure, I'll stop. Because we can do all the pretending we want, but we can only go so far with each other, right? We are never going to be normal, you and I. But I have been careful with you, haven't I? Can you extend the same courtesy to me?"

"I'm sorry I intruded."

They continued to work. He lifted his hands and double-checked all their screws. She followed after him, doing the same, tugging on each anchor to make sure it was secure. Once their feet reached the ground, he yanked off his helmet and dragged a hand across his hair. "Let's head back."

She nodded. "Tristan, are you okay?"

"Fine."

They walked several steps. Then he kicked at the snow and let out a harsh sigh. "I don't want to tell you because it will give you a real reason to hate me."

She placed her palm on his face. "I can never hate you. Not even a little. Trust me, I've given it my level best. It's an impossible task."

Tristan was quiet for so long she thought the conversation might be over. "Drew was a dreamer more than a climber. We both got the bug early." Tristan laughed, almost to himself. "We cheered for Ed Viesturs to become the first American to climb all fourteen eight-thousand-meter peaks as much as we rooted for our Panthers. We were such nerds."

"You root for panthers?"

He looked perplexed, until understanding flickered across his face. "The Panthers are football," he explained. "American football."

"I see." She could imagine him then as a young boy, his hair a little too long for convention with a streak of mischief in his emerald green eyes and the kind of smile that could thaw a glacier.

"Our father wanted us to go into the family business."

"What business?"

"He's an attorney turned politician. Talk about dangerous work. But neither of us could sit still long enough to fill out an application, let along run a business. Hell, a life of bureaucracy and red tape? We'd die a slow, painful death. We were restless by anyone's standards and even reckless according to some. All I know is life called to us in an atypical way. A call most people would disconnect.

"So Drew and I made a pact when he was ten and I was twelve that we'd climb K2. We had this oath, you see. We swore on all fourteen eight-thousanders by naming them off. Drew knew them better than me. I'd stumble on the names. Last year was supposed to be our year, but a journalist wanted to trek with me on Everest. The exposure would create positive publicity for my business. I backed out of K2 at the last minute. Somewhere down the line, I forgot why I climbed. The passion that used to make me feel alive became a business. Drew tried to convince me. He argued with me like crazy. We'd made all the arrangements and gotten the permits. Hell, we'd been planning it since we were kids. Somehow, even doing something I loved made me greedy. Drew called me out on it. We got into a big fight over it. I told him we weren't kids anymore. I hung up on him, Farah.

"He wasn't good enough for this climb. He didn't have the experience. We both knew that. I was supposed to come here with him. He made it a little farther than where we're standing. They ran out of supplies before they got to the top. He didn't die on the mountain though. He made it down. He had an aneurysm three days later. Isn't that fucked up? He survived the Savage Mountain only to die a normal death. The elevation probably triggered it."

She wrapped her arms around him. "I'm sorry, Tristan. You may not have been there, but he knew how much you loved him."

"Did he? I'm not sure. When I spoke to him on the phone, I could tell something was wrong. He wasn't coherent. I should have recognized the signs. Signs I'm paid to recognize. If I had made him go to the hospital in Islamabad, they could have treated it. But I didn't. He got some treatment in Askole, but I think it made it worse. He made me promise I'd climb K2 with him the next time. He said if we went together, we'd summit for sure. He started to name the eight-thousanders. This time he couldn't finish. I've replayed that conversation a million times. It was only nine minutes long, but there were so many clues I missed. How was I so stupid? I've seen what happens to men when their brain swells. A doctor could have relieved the pressure and saved him. Hell, even a shot of dex might have helped him. He would still be alive if I had thought of those things."

"You couldn't save him whether you were here or not."

"That's a question that's above both our pay grades, wouldn't you say?"

"Don't put it on yourself. We all know the risks. No matter how much you think you know, you can't predict what never happened. There are no winners in a game of what ifs."

"My mother begged me to go with him, and I refused. She's gone now, too. I sat at her bedside for the last few months while her body deteriorated and she mourned over Drew. She never said, but she blamed me. I didn't kill him, but I sure as hell had an ample opportunity to save him."

Farah shook her head. "She didn't blame you, Tristan."

"How do you know that?"

"Because no mother would put that on a child. This burden isn't yours to carry."

"It's my duty to him." His voice became thicker before it trailed off. He stopped and became very still. "I'm here to fulfill my promise the only way I can. I know no one else understands my reasoning, but I don't care."

"I understand it." She reached up and took off his goggles. She wanted to touch him just then. Jealous Goddess of the Mountain be dammed. She needed to feel his skin on her fingertips. To hold him. She took off her glove and gently placed her hand on his cheek. He leaned into her palm. She wiped away his tear. "Let it go," she whispered.

His shoulders shook. He buried his head inside her neck. They stayed locked in the embrace for a long time. In those moments, the connection between them grew. She absorbed his anger, guilt, depression, and hopelessness. It was him in the dark place now. The emotion came in wave after turbulent wave, raw and painful.

Then it eased. He backed away. He tilted her chin to meet his bloodshot eyes. He inhaled a deep breath. "Thank you. I feel lighter." He took her hand and pressed it over his heart. "Right here."

"I wish I could make things better for you."

"What makes you think you don't?" He pressed his lips to her forehead. "We should head back."

"Yes, we should. It's getting dark. We need our rest."

They were quiet on the walk back, each lost in their thoughts. When the lights of base camp came into their sights, he took her hand to stop her.

"You were humming that song the first time we met at the shop in Islamabad."

"The song?"

"'Landslide.' I kept trying to place it."

It seemed like such an inconsequential detail. "How do you remember that?"

"Because there is nothing about you that's forgettable, that's why."

She'd read once that falling in love with someone made you feel like you were on top of the world. Since she was quite literally at the top of the world already, she wondered what would happen to her.

Would she just float away?

She had no idea.

All she knew was that tomorrow they would both kiss the sky.

She was sure of it.

# Chapter 17

They woke early, before the sun even made an appearance. *Today was going to be a good day*, Tristan thought.

They would stand upon one of the highest places on earth. Tristan described himself as a spiritual cynic, a man who meditated but never prayed, but he thought he might just be close enough to heaven that he could catch a glimpse of Drew and his mother.

They would have to be quick and efficient to make the journey from Camp Four to the apex and back before dark. Once the sun faded, it would be difficult to find their way in the dark, cold night. He hoped all the weeks of preparation had paid off.

"Weather?" he asked Malcolm, who was in charge of getting the reports from their forecasting company.

"It's clear."

Edelweiss clapped his hands, the sound echoing across the serene landscape. "Well then, gentlemen…" He turned to Farah. "And lady, let us depart."

"You're in good spirits," Tristan said as they geared up.

"I've done my duty to my bloodline."

Tristan frowned. He'd kept his distance from the Edelweiss fiasco. He would not let the man ruin this day.

"I wasn't planning to summit today," Edelweiss said. "But I'm feeling quite well and Malcolm convinced me. I'm so close it would be a shame to stop now."

"You shouldn't come if you have doubts," Tristan said.

Edelweiss fixed him with a steely gaze. "I have no doubts."

Edelweiss had seemed to get a second wind during this leg of the trip. He wasn't even relying on the oxygen that much. Tristan decided not to waste his breath or energy on the man.

Farah smiled at him. "Safe travels. I'll see you at the top," she said, adjusting her goggles.

"Same to you."

He focused on the climb. Uphill climbing was the most difficult and labor intensive. The thin atmosphere made it difficult to draw in deep breaths. Energy was at a premium, and they could not waste it with idle chitchat. They focused on their task, each lost in their own thoughts. He scaled it, one step at a time, each rise growing more difficult, his limbs getting heavier as the air grew thinner.

They had decided the night before they would place the most skilled climbers in the front and back to keep the line moving at a decent pace. Being the fastest, Ahmed led them with Farah behind him. Malcolm, Lino, Bjorn, and Edelweiss followed. Being the strongest, Tristan anchored them. It gave him the unique vantage to spot trouble up ahead and call an audible if needed. On the way back, they decided they would change up the order, letting Malcolm lead and Rana anchor. They used the fixed ropes Tristan and Farah had anchored into the ice to guide them.

He thought about Bjorn's advice and his wise words earlier in the trip. The man was right. It wasn't the summit. It was all the beauty that surrounded him and the moments he spent with a passionate girl that he would hold in his heart. Now that he was close, though, he had to fulfill his promise to Drew. The promise he's made to Farah too, when she allowed him to join the group. He said he would get both of them to the top. He intended to make good on the vow. The thoughts diminished as he got closer. His senses took over and his body relied on instinct. Still, he watched her, a small figure in orange high above him.

*I love her, Drew. I love her so much.*

*I know, bro. Just wondered when you'd figure it out.*

*Keep her safe for me.*

*Will do.*

He heard Ahmed call out when he took the final steps onto the summit. Each climber joined him one by one. Most of them fell to their knees after they took the final step to the apex. Tristan didn't turn his attention to the ground though. He looked toward the sky. He noticed Farah did the same. She had tears in her eyes.

"We're here," he said, wiping her tear with his glove.

"You promised me we'd get here, and we did. And guess what?"

"What?"

"The sky does kiss back," she said. "I felt it."

"Yeah? Good kisser? Should I be jealous?"

"Maybe." Ice clung to her hair and she smiled, almost wide enough for the dimples. He knew every bone in her body rang out in pain and joy and relief. He knew this because his body was reacting the same way. The elation was something that couldn't be described in words. They were in the place where heaven and earth met. He held her, the woman he loved. That made the moment perfect.

Lino and Bjorn hugged. Malcolm let out an exuberant scream and actually did a whole I'm-the-king-of-the-world DiCaprio impression. Lame. Rana was solemn. Edelweiss cried. And Farah. Well, Farah did what she said she would. She tilted her head and closed her eyes. She prayed.

Adrenaline pumped through his veins, rushing harder than the Ganges during monsoon season. They stood at the cruising altitude of a 747. Goddamn, if it wasn't the most amazing feeling in the world.

After the initial shock of being on top of the world, the climbers began documenting the summit with their cameras and notebooks. Farah snapped several pictures. Each of them posed on top of the mountain with the flags of their respective countries. Malcolm and Tristan held the stars and stripes between them. Farah and Ahmed held up the banner with a white crescent moon and a five-pointed star on a green field that was the Pakistani flag. Bjorn stood with the Swedish Flag and Lino with Italy's banner. Hell, they looked like a consortium of United Nations delegates… but with less fighting.

Tristan took his camera and angled it at her. He snapped shot after shot of her taking in the amazing sight without her knowledge. He wanted to remember this moment. The way her hair whipped wildly around her face, strands of it crystallized from the snow. Her cheeks had a reddish glow. The perfect O of her mouth. The triumphant smile complete with dimples. She took off her goggles. Her violet eyes shined bright and fiery. God help him, if she didn't rival the view.

"What did you pray for, milady?" Tristan asked.

"Why do you call me 'milady'?"

"Cause it fits you." That wasn't the right answer, but how could he really explain something he didn't understand himself? "Answer my question."

She took a few breaths before answering him. "I thanked the Goddess of the Mountain for letting us see this. I prayed she will be merciful to us on our way home."

She was right to pray for it. They no longer focused on climbing. They focused on surviving now.

He was reminded of the Gilkey memorial and how many of those mountaineers perished on the descent. Many of them had stood where he was standing, but they had not made it home to tell their tales.

Tristan adjusted her goggles back over her eyes. At these altitudes, being so close to the sun, it was possible for a person to go blind.

"We should head back now," Malcolm said. "We're running behind."

Tristan gestured to them. "You guys get started."

Malcolm pointed to the skyline. "It will be dark before we know it. We're an hour behind."

How had they lost a whole hour? Tristan looked at the sun, still at a high arc. "I'm right behind you."

Malcolm gestured to Farah. "Ready?"

"One second," Farah said. She held up her camera indicating she wanted to snap a few more photos.

"I'll start down," Rana said.

"I'm leading," Malcolm responded, shaking his head. He turned toward Tristan and Farah. "Let's go."

"I need a bit," Tristan said.

"I say we head down right now."

"What does it matter?" Rana asked.

"We already decided this," Malcolm said. "I'm lead on the descent."

Rana grimaced. "That is your position on the climb. I am the leader of this group."

"You know what I mean. We're losing time."

"Just start already." Rana sighed or maybe he took a deep breath. Tristan wasn't sure anymore. "He's right." Ahmed clapped Tristan on the back. "See you soon, Sinclair."

Tristan hugged the man. "Thank you for getting me here."

"You're welcome, brother."

Tristan didn't have the appropriate words to express his gratitude. He made an oath to thank Rana properly and give him a bonus to use for his sisters' tuition payments and dowries.

"You're a good man, Sinclair. I could not have chosen a better man."

"Same to you, brother."

"Let's go," Malcolm said as he grabbed on to the fixed rope.

Tristan almost growled. Maybe he would have if he could have caught his breath better. "In a few minutes. I can take care of myself."

"Fine." Malcolm turned to Farah.

Tristan said, "She can take care of herself too."

Malcolm looked unsure, like he wanted to argue with Tristan, but his breathing had grown stiffer. In the end, he took hold of the rope and moved down. Wise choice.

Ahmed began his descent. Edelweiss, Bjorn, and Lino followed him, each of the men bidding a short good-bye to the summit. Farah took a few more pictures before she lowered the camera. "Do you want me to stay?" she asked.

"I have to do this on my own."

"Do what you came here to do, but don't be long." She pointed to her watch. "Tempus fugit."

Just when he thought she couldn't be any smarter, she hit him with Latin.

He took her face in his hands. This was the perfect moment to tell her how he felt, but he could barely form words, let alone the right words. If he could, he might tell her how his world was better because she was in it. Instead, he smiled and pressed his lips gently to her forehead. "I'll see you soon."

She grabbed a hold of the fixed rope and followed the others down. The sunlight dimmed too quickly for his liking. He rifled through his pack, searching for the small canister he'd carried every day of this journey. Carefully, he unclasped the jar.

He didn't speak aloud, but said the words in his head. *We made it, little brother. I'm so sorry I wasn't here for you when you needed me the most, but I thank God I can fulfill your final wish. I don't know if you can hear me, Drew, but I think you can. I feel very close to you right now.*

He turned the jar over. The dust swirled in the air before settling in the snow. "Earth to earth. Ashes to ashes. Dust to dust." Tristan could see straight through the clouds. Nothing but mountaintops and dusky sky surrounded him. "You're gonna have the most amazing view."

He repacked the empty jar and then walked to the edge. He saw the others descending at a steady pace, at least a hundred yards below him. They were making quick time. He turned and buried his crampons into the ice to begin his own descent. A combination of exhaustion and elation, the likes of which he'd never known, surged in every fiber of his being. He looked for the fixed rope.

He blinked his eyes, searching. Where the hell was the rope?

That's when he heard it.

The scream sounded distant at first, so distant he thought it was a trick of the elevation, a raspy wind echoing through the rifts. But it wasn't. The sound was human. A man's scream. No, scratch that. The scream of several men.

And one other.

Farah.

# Chapter 18

Reflexes took over. Tristan worked his way down. He used his ice axes and crampons to lower himself. Something had gone terribly wrong. He craned his head back. He couldn't see them. They shouldn't be that far down he couldn't see them. He yelled for them, calling each of their names, drawing out the syllables in Farah.

No response.

He descended faster, ignoring the burn in his legs and arms. The mountain was too slick and steep to rush down. He would break his neck if he fell. But he went as fast as he could without letting gravity have the upper hand. Thoughts jumbled in his head. Had a serac fallen on them? It had happened before. Surely, he would have heard it. Was it an avalanche? Did someone simply slip and take the others with them? A million possibilities occurred to him. With each prospect, his heart beat so fast he thought it might rip out of his chest. But he already knew the answer. The damn rope had come loose.

"Farah!"

Nothing. Not even the fucking wind responded.

He came to an area with punctured ice and the empty holes where the screws he'd put in once stood. He turned on the headlamp on his helmet and looked below him again. He saw nothing but ice and snow and rock.

As an experienced climber, he didn't let panic overcome him, but he felt it on his heels, at the back of his neck, in the grip of his hands. In the painful aching dread building in his gut, so raw and intense he could not define it.

*Please God, not her.*

"Farah," he called out, unsure if he'd actually said it aloud.

He heard a sound, but it was too far away to be Farah. Maybe it was the Mountain Goddess laughing against the wind. Or his mind playing cruel tricks. Time was a funny thing at high elevations. It could create fake landscapes just like a desert mirage. It could have been minutes or hours or days that passed while he tried to find his group. The light grew dim.

He called her name again.

She sounded closer this time.

"Is that you? What happened?"

Nothing but a faint cry.

Tristan descended the last few feet until he was level with them. Farah lay on the snow at an odd angle, hanging onto her ice axes. Malcolm was a few feet lower, some rope tangled around his feet. "The screws gave out," Malcolm said. "They all fell."

She was parallel to him, her head buried against the ice, her body slack, a trail of blood around her.

The angle was difficult. If someone lost their grip, they could easily fall right off the edge. He saw her, parallel to him, her head buried against the ice, her body slack, a trail of blood around her.

No. No. No. No.

"Farah, look at me."

Then the slightest movement from her released what felt like a million pounds of tension. He struggled to grip her, the tilt of her body awkward and unsteady. "Give me your hand."

She lifted her head slowly, as if the weight was too much for her. She reached her hand out. He grabbed her arm and pulled her against him.

"Where are you hurt?"

"I'm okay," she said, almost like a question rather than a statement.

The hell she was. With one hand on his ice axe, he loosened her helmet and took off her goggles. He needed to assess her injuries. She had a small gash on her head. A rock must have hit her.

"The others?" she asked.

"We have to get lower," he said, not knowing how to answer her question. He thought she might have a concussion.

He looked down at Malcolm again. "Malcolm, can you move?"

"The rope... It caught my leg. Fuck, I think it's broken."

He might as well have said he died. Tristan took a deep breath. Even through the thick layers of clothing, he felt Farah shaking. Her hot tears cooled as they made contact with his cheek.

She was thinking about the others. Mourning them. She'd heard their screams as they plunged. Maybe she'd even seen the succession of them falling, arms grasping as the darkness claimed them. She was coming unraveled.

He leaned closed to her ear so she could hear him clearly. "Farah, I need your help. If we're gonna make it, we have to work together. Focus on me, on where we are, and what we need to do. Can you do that for me?" Although the thoughts came fast and frenzied, somehow, he had found the energy to make his voice calm. Calm for her.

She pulled her head up and nodded.

"Say it."

If he heard her speak, he could be sure.

"Yes...yes."

The sun began to set. He worried she might have snow blindness. He reached up and twisted the light on her helmet so it activated. "Can you get your grip?"

Her hand shook, but only for a second. Her ice axe swung up before plunging into the ice wall.

"Good. That's good. Do you have rope?"

"No."

"There's some here. I'm tangled the fuck up in it," Malcolm called. "Get down here."

Snow fell and swirled around him. A storm was coming in. "How far down are you?" Tristan asked.

"I don't know. Maybe twenty feet. I slid part of the way. The rope stopped me."

"We need to work our way down to Malcolm. If one of us is on either side of him, we can bring him down with us. Do you understand?"

She didn't hesitate in her reply. "Yes, I understand."

He hated what he was asking her to do. It meant she had to move a few feet farther away from him. She would be out of his reach. If she fell, he would not be able to save her. She did not question him though. It was the only way he could think that would allow all three of them to have a chance.

They worked their way down, each foothold becoming more precarious. Snowflakes as large as saucers fell against them. He locked eyes with her as they moved. It became a reassurance each step of the way. "We got this, Dimples."

Something stopped his foot. Tristan kicked at the air, trying to get it loose, before he realized it was Malcolm's hand gripping his boot.

"About fucking time," Malcolm said.

They flanked him. The man bellowed out in pain when Tristan unwound the rope tangled around his ankle. "You can use your arms, right? You have to use your arms. I can't carry you."

"Yeah," Malcolm said.

The snowflakes grew in size and force. They clouded the skyline, making it difficult to see. Tristan turned on his headlamp and looped the rope through Malcolm's harness. Farah took one end and Tristan the other. He didn't have to explain it to her. She knew. They both looped the rope around their waists. This was a very dangerous technique, but they didn't have much rope and hardly any choices left. They had to work in unison. This way if Malcolm lost his grip, Farah and Tristan could pick up the slack. But if either Farah or Tristan lost their grip, all three of them would likely fall.

They moved down the mountain, one excruciating step at a time. Minutes turned into hours. The last rays of sun disappeared, leaving them in the oppressive dark. Wet snow pelted them, making it difficult to grip their tools.

"Keep talking, Farah."

He needed to hear her voice to keep his own sanity.

"I feel stronger now," she said.

"That's good. Really good. You're doing so good."

"Say something besides good."

He chuckled. "Great. You're doing great."

"We both are."

Tristan heard something rumbling from above. He held his breath. *Please, not an avalanche.* The rumble stopped. Thank God.

He took a deep breath. Then a rock slammed into his right hand. He lost his grip on the axe. He still had three points of contact on the ice wall with his feet and left hand. He would have been fine. Three points would have held him up. That was if Malcolm had hung on. But Malcolm chose that moment to let go too.

Tristan twisted in the air and landed on his back. He could feel himself slipping down the edge. He tried to push the spikes on his boots into the snow to stop his fall, but between his awkward angle and the steep grade, he could not get purchase. He spun several times, rotating with each turn, so he didn't know which way was up. He kept sliding, all the way down to the edge of the mountain. The rope went taught, burning into his skin. He stopped just short of the precipice. Half his body dangled off the cliff, but he was still on solid land. He was still alive.

Malcolm screamed in pain.

Tristan let out the longest breath of his life. "Fuck."

"Tristan?" Farah called.

"I'm okay. I'm okay. I'm okay. I'm okay." He said it aloud four times, maybe to convince himself of it. The fourth time was when he heard the ice fracture. The crack sounded like a long piece of rough cloth being ripped into shreds. This was the melody of death, he thought. He closed his eyes. "I'm so sorry, Farah. I cannot save us."

"Tristan!"

The mountain was going to eat them. Swallow them whole. "Crevasse," he said, right before the world fell from under him.

The rock beneath him disappeared into an abyss. His body swung, back and forth, a bulky pendulum of flesh. A dull roar echoed in his head. A warm gush of thick liquid rolled down his face. He heard his name. The angels called for him.

*I'm dead, Angel. I'm dead.*

Except, he wasn't dead. His heart still beat. His lungs still yearned for air. He could feel the blood on his face. The pain was too real for him to be dead.

"I can't hold on much longer. You have to pull yourself up, Tristan."

He looked up and saw Malcolm's boot at the edge of the crevasse. He hadn't fallen over yet. It clicked. She saved him. Farah, who was half his size, was holding onto the ice, supporting his weight, with the rope tied around her waist.

Hope bloomed for a brief second before it shriveled and died as the dark realization set in. "I can't climb up."

"No," she cried out. He reached into his pocket and pulled out the blade. The sharp silver edge glinted against the night. He held it against the rope. "You will survive, Farah. I know you can do this."

"What the hell are you doing?" she demanded.

"I'm cutting myself loose."

"No! Pull yourself up."

"There is nothing for me to hold on to but air."

"There's a fucking rope. The one you're dangling from. Climb it."

Was she crazy? He was the worst kind of weight. Dead weight. Not to mention the weight of his pack. He'd pull her straight down.

"I swear to God if you die, I will kill you. Do *not* leave me."

The statement didn't even sound ironic. With those words, he knew he had to try. He took a deep breath and stuck the knife his mouth. He pulled himself up; his hands slipped at first, the rain and material of his gloves making it impossible to get a grip. He considered taking them off, but he'd risk the chance of frostbite setting in and his fingers freezing against the rope. The rope swayed.

"Fuck." He growled in frustration and tried again. This time he managed a grip. Using brute strength that didn't come from rational thought, but deep inside his soul, he pulled himself up, inch by painful inch. He saw it then. The edge of the mountain almost within his reach. He swung back, trying to make contact with the rock. He did it again. Each time, she let out a scream. Not quite a scream. Later, he would call it something of a battle cry. A sound of pure adrenaline expelling itself.

He made purchase with the rock, sinking the sharp points of his crampons into it. He exhaled, dropping the knife in the process. He'd lost his ice axes. He used his fingers to find holds in the rough exterior. He stopped thinking, relying on instinct and training. He found his way up the side, until he was finally on the surface again. She was a few meters higher, her ice axes plunged inside the snow. Her arms had to be ready to fall off.

"Milady."

"You're safe," she said, more of a statement than a question. She must have felt the relief as the pressure of his weight disappeared.

"I am." Tristan took off a glove and put his fingers against Malcolm's neck. "Malcolm passed out from the pain, but he's still alive." He put his glove on again before the cold air destroyed his skin.

"*Inshallah*," she said.

Tristan swung his arm over the man and pulled him closer. "We need to make camp."

"Here?" she asked. The elevation was too high and cold for any reasonable camp. They might freeze to death. But if they kept moving down, they would risk the possibility of another crevasse. They would not be so lucky the next time.

"It has to be here. We'll have to bivouac. Work your way to the left."

"All right."

"Keep talking to me, sweetheart. I can't see you right now. I need to know where you are so keep talking."

"I… I'm too tired." Her voice sounded weak. "I can't think."

"Sing with me then."

His voice cracked on the song, the familiar song that reminded him of ice cold beer on a hot summer day. Her voice, soft and distant, joined his. Tristan dragged Malcolm, checking his pulse every few minutes to make sure he was still breathing. He made his way up to her while dragging Malcolm as she worked her way down. They would meet somewhere in the middle.

It took twenty minutes to find a flat surface where the three of them could sleep without slipping off the mountain. At least he thought it was twenty minutes. Time no longer seemed linear. They had sung the song three times already. When she reached him, he pulled her against his chest. He buried his head inside her neck. He rubbed her arms. He felt down her padded clothes, inspecting her for sore muscles and broken bones.

"Farah," he said, his voice cracking as he held her. God, her arms had to be on fire. But they'd found each other, stumbling through the dark without any hope. But this… This sense of safety was false and dangerous. After all, they were still on the Savage.

"You're a horrible singer," she said. "Anyone ever told you that?"

God help him, he laughed. "Yeah, I've heard that before." He groped around her. "Where's your pack?"

"I don't know."

"It's okay. I have mine and Malcolm has his." He undid his pack and Malcolm's. He rifled through both, searching for any supplies that would be useful. The temperature plunged at a rapid pace. He turned off her light. "We have to conserve."

He took inventory of the measly items in their pack. There were several bags of trail mix, two space blankets, and a bottle of water they'd have to share. He put his extra pair of gloves over her hand. Her own gloves were shredded to pieces. He found his small first aid kit and put some gauze over the wound on her head. He didn't bother with antiseptic. It would freeze her skin off. Besides, germs could not survive at this temperature, but he wasn't sure if they could.

He turned his attention to Malcolm next. He took one of his poles and aligned it next to Malcolm's leg. He wrapped gauze around it to create a temporary splint. He doubted Malcolm would make it through the night. He looked at Farah as he held up one of the blankets. Neither of them said anything. She took the other end of it and secured it around Malcolm. Dedicating any of their meager supplies to him would jeopardize their chances of survival. They both knew this, but…

Maybe they would live, but how would they live with themselves if they didn't help him?

He picked her up gently, surprised how light she felt even now. He positioned her so her back was against his chest. He pulled the other blanket around them. She rested her head against him. He put his arms around her and held her close.

"You saved my life," he said.

She yawned. "Good night."

# Chapter 19

As a little girl, she loved eating fresh figs from the huge tree in the Jat's garden. Mr. Jat was her mother's employer. She liked him. He always smiled at her and bought her dolls. Once, he'd brought her a scarf all the way from France, a country where they ate a lot of fruit.

She wanted to visit France one day. But her favorite place would always be her spot inside the fig tree. She'd discovered the tastiest fruit rested at the very top of the tree. She had reasoned, in her eight-year-old mind, that it made sense the most delicious fruit would be closer to the sky and sun. Today, she had to be stealth, since everyone was home. Mr. Jat listened to one of his western albums. He had a record player and a CD player, but he preferred the record player. He'd attended university in America in a place called Ohio. The word sounded a bit magical to her. Today, she heard one of her favorite songs, the song about climbing mountains. She took it as a good omen as she climbed the tree. She pulled herself up on creaking branches, her mouth watering for the sweet fruits that awaited her.

Every chance she had, she climbed the tree, trying to get higher and higher in search of the perfect fig. If Mrs. Jat caught her, she would make her stand in the empty room, her face pressed against the cold stone wall for hours. Sometimes, Mrs. Jat would find a vine from the tree and drag it across her back. It didn't hurt when she dragged it, but Farah knew she was toying with her, the way the cat pawed at the rubber ball. She was the rubber ball. Once she got used to the feel of the soft wood against her skin, Mrs. Jat would pull it back and slap her. The noise of slicing air and breaking skin made her gag. She pretended it wasn't her skin though. That helped. She told herself the figs were worth any punishment. She would not give the woman her tears.

Besides, Mrs. Jat didn't hurt her too much. It was the Jat boys who frightened Farah the most. They looked for reasons to torture her. The nauseating tang of grit in her mouth resurfaced every time she thought of them. One held her arms back while the other rolled a ball of mud in his chubby palms. She could see the bugs on it. He called her the name, the one that meant "bad woman." But she wasn't a woman. She was a girl. He pushed the ball into her mouth. They laughed and laughed.

"You're worse than the worms," one said.

"You're nothing but a maid's daughter. Beggars eat dirt."

"You have witch's eyes. We're going to gouge them out so you can't curse us."

"This is our tree. You are a thief. The next time we will give you a thief's punishment and cut off your hands."

"She's a whore. There are other things you should cut off a whore."

The experience should have kept her away from the tree, but it did the opposite. She felt the tree was put here by God. Therefore, she had as much right to it as those stupid boys. The fruit it bore was the sweetest thing in the world. At least in her world.

Finally, she reached the top. She plucked a fig. She'd figured out figs were the only thing that could mask the flavor of dirt. When she'd told Amma about the incident, she'd gotten the blame. Amma said it was improper for a little girl to climb a tree.

She found a place to rest, nestled high in the branches.

Why was it improper for her? The men of her tribe had climbed mountains, or so she'd been told. Didn't the same blood flow through her? She didn't want to be a queen or a whore. She wanted to be an explorer.

She sat, hidden inside the branches, savoring fig after delicious fig, careful to hide the pits inside the knot of her dupatta so they would not fall to the ground and betray her location.

She hated the Jats.

She hated the two boys of the house, who tortured her every chance they got.

Hated Mrs. Jat, whose beady eyes and sour face followed Farah's every movement. The woman rarely smiled, and when she did, it didn't fit her face, as if real joy could not live in her expression. The only time Mrs. Jat's smile resembled anything human or genuine was the moment right before she slapped Farah's face or put raw chili peppers on her tongue.

The peppers had burned off her taste buds for months. She thought she would never taste sweet things again until she climbed up the tree and found the highest fig. Then she thanked God and swore to never take sweet things for granted again.

She wondered why they had left Hunza and come here. For that, she hated her mother. Amma said she'd get an education here and an opportunity to marry above her means. A chance for a future. What use was the future when they were miserable in the present?

The only person she could tolerate was Mr. Jat, who punished his sons for their cruel behavior. He asked her not to climb the tree because it would be dangerous for her, not because it was improper.

None of them understood her reasons, though. Sitting high up, inside the branches of the tree, with the dappled sun warming her skin, she felt like herself. She floated in the air, living closer to heaven than earth. It was a place that existed just for her.

Her conscious mind was aware he was holding her in his strong arms. He whispered to her, soft words ripe with concern. But she did not hear him. She stayed in the tree. She ate figs. She hid the pits in little knots she made in her dupatta. She would not throw them to the ground. That is how they caught her last time.

"Farah, please."

What did he want from her? She was cold. She was tired. She chose death. He should respect her wish.

"Farah," he said, his chapped lips brushing her temple. "Stop it. You have to keep talking. You cannot go to sleep."

"I'm dreaming." Had she said it aloud?

"Okay then, fucking dream, but wherever you are, I need to go too. Let me be in the dream with you."

"There is no room for you. You'll break the branch."

"I won't. I promise. What branch? Where are we?"

"High up in the fig tree."

"I like figs. Tell me more. Please baby, keep talking."

"They taste like sugar, don't you think?" She felt cold, wet snow against her face. It landed and melted on her skin. Or maybe that was the dream, and the fig tree was reality.

"Yes, sugar. What else?"

"We made her angry, Sinclair. She's not going to let us go now."

"Who?"

"The Goddess. We made her jealous with our love, and now she's going to kill us. I'm going to sleep now."

"No!"

"Good night."

"I will not let you go. Do you understand? No one is going to kill us. We are survivors, you and I. Do not fucking surrender on me. No. Sleep. If you sleep, I'll sing to you again. Is that what you want? I'll bounce on the branch." Sure enough, he started on a god-awful tune that would cause stray cats to gouge their ears. His body shifted as if he were bouncing her.

Dear God, did she laugh? How was that even possible? "No, not that."

"If you like Fleetwood Mac, wait till you hear what I can do with Santana. Now talk to me. We're in the fig tree, you and me. We're eating figs so sweet they taste like spun sugar."

"I don't…. I don't know what to say." Every word made her weaker.

"Tell me what else you prayed for when we were on top of the mountain."

"My mother."

"Why?"

"I prayed she was happy. She wasn't happy on earth. That's why she killed herself." His arms tightened around her. She felt safe and free. The same way she felt nestled inside the fig tree.

"I'm so sorry, Farah."

She thought she'd seen the dark. But the lack of color behind her eyes gave a new name to darkness.

"She died when you were young. Who did you live with? Tell me." Desperation tinged his voice. He was trying so hard to keep her talking. "Does it hurt to talk about?"

"Yes, it hurts."

"Good."

Good?

He kept talking, close to her ear; the sound of his voice and the warmth of his breath circled around her like the branches of the tree. "The pain cuts you on the inside. It makes you feel. You need to feel so you don't go numb." He stroked her hair, his fingers twisting in the strands. "C'mon, tell me now."

"Mr. Jat said I couldn't live there anymore. He had to send me away. He paid for me to go to the best schools. I met the sons and daughters of kings and politicians. I learned to speak different languages. How to be a lady. I got to make choices for myself Amma never had. I had more education than even his sons. He spared no expense on me. He'd visit me too. During school holidays, he took me places. France a few times. Germany once. He wanted to find me a husband. It was expected I should marry, but I didn't want to. I wanted to see everything. Do everything. He didn't hold me back. When he died, a package arrived at my London flat. He could not leave me an inheritance in the traditional way. Instead, he saved up in a secret bank account. He wrote a long letter and told me to use the money any way I wanted. He'd hoped I'd use it to finish my education and for my dowry, but I used it to climb a mountain instead." Her small throaty laugh turned into a cough.

He rubbed her back until it subsided. "Here." He held the water bottle to her lips. "Drink slow."

Even in this half-awake state, where every cell in her body cried out from exhaustion, she stopped drinking when she realized she was taking more than her fair share of their rations.

"It sounds like he cared for you."

"I cared for him too. I didn't do it to spite him. I did it because I needed to be closer to heaven than earth."

"I'm not thinking that. Why would you do it to spite him?"

"Because it wasn't what he wanted. He never told me, but I knew it in my heart. I probably knew it from the time I was eight and I fell out of the fig tree. He carried me inside the house and called a doctor for me. He told me stories of Hunza and how he'd visited many years back. The way he looked at me, I knew it right then. No one had to tell me."

"Tell you what?"

"He was my father. I was his bastard child."

"Your mother was his maid?"

"She was a girl he met on a business trip. He was already married and had two sons when I came along. Afterward, he found out about me. He didn't want me to grow up with that stigma. So when he brought us to Islamabad, he kept my mother as a maid. She told me my father had died before I was born. I think she loved him, Tristan. It drove her crazy to live in that house. His wife knew who I was. His sons did too. They treated me badly, but every day they stole a piece of my mother's soul until the world went dark for her. Dark like it is now. So dark you'll never find the light again."

"You'll find it. I'm going to help you find it. Just don't fall asleep. Keep your eyes open."

She thought her eyes were closed this whole time. She blinked, realizing she was wrong.

"You must hate him."

"Who?"

"Your father."

"I should, right? I tried to, but I can't. I loved him. He tried to make a better life for me. He blamed himself for her death. He gave me choices. I want to hate him for all of it, but I can't. I come from him. His blood is my blood. I'd have to hate myself too."

# Chapter 20

She didn't remember everything they'd talked about, but the stars started to disappear. The black sky turned dark gray with bits of red. Eventually, it grew to a dull, cloudless white. They were still alive.

"Take some food," he said. He held his hand flat, revealing a few handfuls of granola.

Her stomach churned with a hunger so fierce she could have eaten her own hand. She went to reach for it, but her gloves were clumsy. She would have knocked it over if he hadn't closed his palm.

"Just open your mouth. Chew slowly."

He fed her. After three handfuls, she stretched, her muscles protesting each movement. "It's morning." She honestly didn't think she'd ever see another morning.

"We have to get going, Farah. If we make it to base camp, we can radio in for a rescue."

Still cradled in Tristan's arms, she turned her head to the man wrapped in the thermal blanket beside them.

"I just checked his pulse. He's still alive."

It was incredible that all three of them survived the night. "Really?"

"We don't have time to appreciate miracles. Not when we have a few more to go. We should move while we still have energy left."

She stood. Her legs turned to rubber and she almost fell, but he caught her. He put a hand on each of her hips.

"My body..."

He leaned his forehead against hers. "Your body is strong. Don't you for one second think you cannot do this. This body?" He held her tighter. "This body managed to latch on to the slickest ice while holding up the weight of two full grown men in the middle of an ice storm. You have the strength of a million angels."

She believed him. He said exactly what she needed to hear.

Tristan rolled Malcolm inside the blanket. He tied the length of rope around Malcolm to secure the material and wrapped some torn pieces of clothing as a second layer. She wondered why he was leaving so much rope loose on either side. Then she realized his intention. He took the two ends of rope and tied them around his waist.

He handed her a set of poles that must have been Malcolm's. He used his set. They had slept under an overhang that had kept the snow off them, but she realized now how deep it really was. It came up past her knee.

They started their long walk. Their progress was slow. Malcolm's body dragged behind Tristan.

"When we get back, I'm going to eat a whole chocolate cake by myself," she said.

"You won't share?"

"You can have a bite."

"Only a bite? That's cold."

A trickle of sweat rolled down his face. His breathing had turned harsher. Of course, carrying the burden of Malcolm by himself was taking a toll on him.

"Give me half."

"What?"

"Give me the other half of the rope."

"You can't be serious."

"I am."

"I can do it by myself."

"Chivalry is going to get you killed. I'm better now. You can see that, right? Give me half. I can carry my fair share."

"It's not chivalry. This isn't your fair share. It's mine. All mine."

"Why?"

"What happened up there, Farah?"

"The rope broke."

"How did it break? Did the screws come apart?"

"I think so."

He closed his eyes. "The skin on his foot has been exposed. He's probably going to lose his leg even if he does live. We need to get him down."

His voice had the sharp edge of anguish. How did she not notice the rigid way he held his jaw? Last night, he'd saved her from herself. This morning, she had to return the favor.

"It's not your fault." She saw the whole sky in the mirror of his glasses. "We have to keep going. We don't have time for a therapy session."

"Funny, when you're comforting me, it's a partnership. When I'm trying to do it for you, its therapy. I'm not sure if it's chivalry or misogyny now."

"Whatever it is, you really suck at this."

She moved in front of him to stop him from taking another step and get him to listen. "You blame yourself. Why? Because they were the snow screws you put in? But Tristan, I was there, remember? I put them in too. I checked and double checked each one of them. We did good work up there."

"I let myself be distracted. I should have checked them myself."

"You did check them. They were secure. Every climber knows not to put your full weight on the fixed rope, but even if they had, they were secure."

"Then how the hell did it happen, Farah? Four men are dead. Malcolm is almost dead. You… You almost died."

"I don't know what happened. This is bloody ice, Tristan. It changes and contracts. When I looked down, Malcolm wasn't even using the fixed rope. I have no idea how he got tangled in it or how the others fell the way they did. But I do know one thing, if you give into this guilt, it will consume you." She bent to the ground and scratched against the snow.

"What are you doing?"

"Looking for something."

"Are you going insane?"

"No. Just shut up." She dug until she got past the layers of snow to the surface. She stood on shaky legs. She held out her palm. There lay a perfectly round pebble.

"What is this?"

She unzipped her jacket and reached into her pocket. She took out her own pebble, the one he'd given her that day they were normal. She took off his glove and placed the pebble in his hand. She put her finger on top of it and rolled it around his palm. "It's a reminder."

"A reminder of what?"

"A reminder of the time you saved my life by making me talk to you all night. The time you attached a rope around your waist and dragged a man through yards of snow. The time when a maid's daughter from Hunza and the son of a politician from the West survived the Savage together."

He stared at his hand.

"Say something."

"What? You couldn't get flowers?"

She smiled, feeling hope for the first time. "Give me one end of the rope."

He pocketed the pebble. "Have it your way."

She bent down while he untied the rope from his waist. He put the pebble in his pocket. He tied one end of the rope around her. He hugged her. "I would kiss you right now, but it's so fucking cold, our lips would probably stick together."

"Yeah, that wouldn't be smart."

With the weight dispersed between both of them, they could move faster. They got to lower ground. The breathing became easier. When camp came into sight, Tristan untied the rope. He told Farah to get to the radio. He carried Malcolm the rest of the way.

The helicopter could not land at their location. It was too high, but they were able to make contact. Rescue workers arrived. They took Malcolm in a special stretcher. Tristan and Farah walked the last twenty kilometers to the helicopter. They both collapsed onto the cushioned seats, sighing as if they were on a king's lux throne.

The pilot and another man checked Malcolm's vitals. Both Tristan and Farah expelled a sigh of relief when they confirmed he was still breathing. Part of her had wondered if they were so desperate to believe he was alive they imagined his pulse. The men loaded Malcolm onto a stretcher at the back of the aircraft. Tristan grabbed a water bottle. He twisted off the cap and offered it to Farah first. She saw there were other bottles there, but she took a sip from the one he offered her. They took off their jackets, goggles, and gloves. She collapsed into his arms.

She leaned her head against his shoulder. "Can I sleep now? Or is this a dream?"

"Sleep, milady. We survived. We saved each other. We're safe, high up in the fig tree now, you and I."

His heartbeat sounded as rhythmic as a lullaby, perhaps the only thing rhythmic about Tristan Sinclair.

She took the tiny stone from her pocket and closed her hand around it. The reminder they survived. The reminder of how strong this man was. The reminder of the day she fell in love with Tristan Sinclair.

He made her feel closer to heaven than earth.

They had looked into the eye of the beast and survived.

It was going to be all right.

Yet, she had a sinking feeling the beast wasn't ready to let them go.

# Chapter 21

They were taken to the nearest hospital. Malcolm was already awake by the time they reached there. The doctors wheeled him into surgery. They would need to amputate his leg.

"Sinclair, can you bring me my pack?" he asked.

"Now?"

"I have my camera in there. I need my bag from the hotel too. I have no clothes."

Tristan knew he was in pain and on all sorts of medication, but God help him, a part of him wanted to punch the man. He hadn't asked about the others who'd died. He hadn't even asked about Farah and him. "I'll bring it to your room."

The doctors checked their wounds. In narrow hospital beds, Farah and Tristan slept for a few hours hooked up to IVs to help with dehydration. Finally, they were discharged.

"She might need a cat scan," Tristan said. "She hit her head."

"We don't have the equipment," the young doctor said.

She took Tristan's arm. "I feel fine, Tristan."

She'd read his mind. He was thinking of what happened with Drew. Still, he watched her closely and vowed to take her to the hospital in the next city if she showed any signs of distress.

A nurse brought them bowls of soup and bread. When they finished, she laid her head on his shoulder as they waited. Once Malcolm made it out of surgery, they headed to the hotel. Tristan fetched their bags from the hotel storage and paid a porter to bring Malcolm's items to the hospital. They checked in to separate rooms on the same floor, so they would not alarm the man at the front desk. But there was no way they were sleeping in separate rooms. He refused to be away from her. Tonight, he needed to hold her in his arms.

"You're staying here with me," he said.

"I wasn't planning on leaving."

"Good."

Everything they did took a very long time. They moved slower, each step requiring an absurd amount of effort. The soup had just made him hungrier. He ordered a seven-course meal for them. They sat on the bed and ate heaping bowls of rice and spiced chicken. It was probably delicious, but he could not taste it. The spoon-to-mouth motion was rudimentary and merely survival instinct.

"I need to shower," she said. She looked toward the bathroom with longing as if trying to conjure the energy for the trek.

He took her hand and helped her up. She tugged on his shirt. He pulled it off. He removed her long sweater and the layers of protective garments she wore underneath. He unclasped her sports bra. She unbuttoned his pants. Layer after layer of clothing found its way to the ground until they stood in their truest form. This went beyond sexual desires. He needed to take care of her. He needed her to do the same for him. He led her to the bathroom.

They stood against a spray of hot water, leaning against the wall for support. Finally, he lathered some soap in his hand and rubbed down her body. He fell to his knees and worked on each of her feet and then her long legs. He took more soap and worked up her curvy hips and thighs. She had a beautiful body, the body of a Goddess. He lathered across her belly and over her breasts. He wanted so much to worship every inch of her, but right now, he wanted to keep her safe even more.

"Lean your head back." He washed her hair. She returned the favor and washed every inch of him too. They only stepped out of the shower when the water turned cold. They brushed their teeth three times each. Her hair was dripping wet. He took the towel and dried it. Neither of them could summon the strength to go through their luggage for clean clothes.

He stared into her mesmerizing eyes. "Let me look at you." Inspecting her body, he took note of every bruise and mark. He winced when he saw the rope burn around her waist and hips, the area where the rope had tightened when she'd held him. How much time had passed while he tried to climb up? Five minutes? Fifteen? Carefully, he traced the angry red welt slashed across her beautiful brown skin.

"I'm okay. How are you?"

"Better now." He took her hand and led her to the bed. They didn't say a word as they fell into it. They had almost died. They had saved each other. They had shared all their darkness until they found the light again. The ordeal they experienced had been far more intimate than their naked bodies. They had bared their souls to each other.

He grabbed a bottle of arnica cream and gently rubbed the area across her belly. She sucked in a sharp intake of breath as his fingers applied the salve. "Am I hurting you?"

"It's not that."

"Then what's wrong?"

"I didn't think about it in the shower, but this is the first time you've touched me like this. We've never kissed."

He traced her lips with his finger. "We really need to fix that." He cupped her cheek and kissed her. He tried to be gentle. Everything hurt, and her lips were chapped. But he couldn't help himself. She parted her mouth. The kiss became more aggressive and needy. Thank God, she didn't push him away or recoil. Instead, her fingers threaded through his hair. He tasted the mint of fresh toothpaste and her sweet, sweet mouth. He pulled away before he lost himself.

"Tristan?"

He leaned his forehead against hers. "There is so much I want to do to you right now, but our bodies need time to recover."

She nodded. "We need sleep."

Then he slowly spread the ointment across the rest of her body, gently rubbing it into every muscle. She moaned against his touch.

When he was done, he laid his head back. She took the ointment from his hand.

"What are you doing?" he asked.

"It's my turn."

She rubbed his shoulders and back. She worked her hands into the muscles of his legs. When the container was empty, she laid her head against his chest. She ran her finger over the band of black on his left arm. He rubbed her back and looked out the window as the afternoon sun gave way to stars.

He wrapped his arms and legs around her, holding her in a tight embrace, a position that should not have been comfortable, but he could not imagine sleeping any other way. Then they slept. Really slept in a heavy, dreamless sleep on a warm bed with their arms folded around each other as if they were part of the same cocoon.

# Chapter 22

When Farah awoke, she was alone. She stopped the panic from settling in. She wasn't on the side of the Savage Mountain fighting for her life. She was in a warm room on top of a comfortable bed. He was close. She could feel his presence. She turned her head. There was a single stem next to her with a folded scrap of hotel stationery on his side of the bed. She unfolded the note, taking in his neat script.

*Milady, I ran out to visit Malcolm and to get us some sustenance. I had the hotel launder our things. Naturally, they put your clothes in your room. My clothes are on top of the bureau. Please help yourself. This morning, I saw you sleeping and it felt so normal. I thought about doing a crossword puzzle with you and brunch. I don't think I've ever had brunch in my life. Anyway, it occurred to me, it might be nice if you woke up next to a flower. I was trying to locate the perfect bloom for you, but the markets aren't open yet. As you know, pot seems to grow in wild abundance around here so here's a cannabis stem. It's not ideal, but it is fragrant. Figured you could chew on the seeds till I get back. Love T.*

She pressed the note close to her heart.

She stood, stretching her aching limbs. She walked to the bureau and found a T-shirt of his that came just above her knees. She washed up and brushed her teeth. When she came out of the bathroom, she glanced at the stem he'd left for her. It was nice, but she'd always treasure the pebble.

The pebble.

She searched around the room. Where was it? How could she lose it? She searched for her pack and then remembered she had lost it. But she carried the pebble with her. Where were the clothes she'd worn?

"Farah," he said, his frame taking up the whole doorway. He held a bag in his arms. "What are you doing?"

"Looking for the pebble. I lost it."

"It's just a rock."

She wondered if he had a concussion. "How can you say that? It's my rock. The one you gave me and now I've lost it."

"You didn't." He set the bag down on the small table and walked toward the bureau. He opened the first drawer. Inside was a small open box. Both of their stones rested next to each other.

She expelled a long, happy sigh. "Brilliant."

"I found it in your coat pocket this morning."

She hugged him. "How is Malcolm? I would have gone with you."

"You were sleeping so peacefully, I'd feel like a total ass waking you up. Malcolm is fine anyway. Ornery as fuck, but fine. I would say he asked after you, but he didn't, the ass."

"He's been through a lot."

Tristan arched his brow. "He's been through a lot?"

"We all have."

"You're right. I'm cutting him some slack and hoping it was the morphine talking. We'll go later. But I did talk to the doctor."

"And?"

Tristan's smile was so full of relief she felt a blanket of tension slip away from her body. "He should be able to get around in a month or two with wheel chair. He won't be climbing mountains, but he will live."

"Thank God."

"Hungry?"

As soon as he said it, her stomach cried out. "Starving."

She sniffed the air. She almost licked her lips. "What is it? It smells so good."

"Chicken kabobs with jasmine rice. Warm chapatti and lentil soup. Oh, and a surprise for you."

"Surprise?"

His smile turned impish. "Yeah, but only if you share." He lifted a large white box out of a bag. He cut the string and opened it. With a flourish, he took off the lid and bowed. "A whole chocolate cake."

She did lick her lips this time. "I'm eating that first, and it's all mine."

"Only if I get to feed you." He set it in the middle of the bed. He slid the fork down the side of the moist cake. He spooned some extra frosting. As promised, he fed it to her. She closed her eyes. The decadent dessert melted in her mouth.

He let out a frustrated growl.

She looked up at him. "Tristan, I was joking. Of course, I'll share. Have some." She gestured to the cake.

"It's not that."

"Then what?"

He narrowed his eyes. "Eat faster."

# Chapter 23

They finished their food. She threw away the last of the plates. Tristan gazed at her beautiful form, taking it all in, her dark curly hair, her soft skin, the sway of her hips, and her long, lean legs. As good as she looked wearing his T-shirt, he wanted her out of it.

He crossed the room in long determined strides and hooked his arm around her waist, pulled her against his chest. "I like the way you look in my shirt, but I'm about ready to rip it off you." He kissed her and coaxed her mouth open. She tasted like chocolate cake, decadent and rich and delicious. "Does this feel wrong for us to do? Because if it does, you need to say something and I'll stop. It'll be the hardest thing I've ever done, but I swear to you I'll do it."

She kissed him, soft and slow. "We're not on the mountain anymore, Tristan. We're safe. I'm less superstitious at this altitude." She sat on the desk and unbuttoned his shirt. "To answer your question, nothing about us feels wrong to me."

He buried his face in her hair. "I promise I'll be gentle." He planted slow kisses along her jaw.

"Why? Do you like it gentle?"

"You're not tired?"

She shook her head. "We slept for over twelve hours."

He laughed against her neck. "You're not a virgin, are you?"

"No."

"Forgive me, my misogynistic thinking ran away with me. Sorry for my assumption."

"Does the idea of me being innocent appeal to you, Tristan?"

He gave her a coy smile. The first time his smile had ever been coy. "I don't know if there's a right answer to this. It feels like a test."

She threw off his shirt and kissed his chest. "Just be honest with me. We've been honest with each other so far. I'm curious to know your thoughts."

She moaned when he caressed her breasts with his large hands. Even through the T-shirt, her skin fired up. He whispered in her ear. "You turn me on, Farah. I like you as you are. To me, you're perfect. If you have experience, that's even better because I know I won't be hurting you. I just want so much to make you feel good everywhere."

"You make me feel good everywhere." She pressed a finger against his lips. "Do one thing...."

"What's that?"

She gripped a hold of his shoulders. Her mouth hovered close to his ear. "Don't be gentle. I'm not fragile."

"That much, I already knew."

Her teeth grazed his earlobe. "I want to feel you inside me even when you're not."

"Now... That's new information." Something clicked as if a switch had been flipped. He picked her up. Farah swung her legs around his waist.

He covered her in hard, wet, hungry kisses. He threw her onto the bed by her hips. She bounced. For a second, he worried he'd hurt her, but the look in her eyes quieted his fear. He grabbed the box he'd picked up while he was out. It wasn't easy to find the item. It definitely was not easy to convey what he wanted in a language he did not speak.

She shook her head.

"We need birth control, Farah."

"I'm on the pill, Tristan. I had a full physical before this trip. They did every type of blood test. What about you?"

"Same. I've been tested for STDs."

"Then put the box away."

He threw it across the room. He unzipped his jeans. They met the same fate as the box. He moved onto the bed, covering her body with his. She reached between them and touched him. He closed his eyes and grunted. It took every ounce of strength to maintain his control and not come undone right then. There was something feral about this moment. She had become a basic need for him—he wanted her in a way that was completely primitive and wild and difficult to rationalize.

Physically, it was just sex. Mentally, it was so much more.

He kissed her neck and worked his way down to her nipples. He pinched her breast while he flicked his tongue over her sensitive flesh. She fisted her fingers through his hair, pushing him lower. He loved how she wasn't shy. He went farther down, lowering his head inch by inch. She didn't squirm or shy away from his touch. He held her hips and traced the welts around her stomach with his mouth. He went lower still.

She moaned when his tongue penetrated her. "Tristan...please."

"Shhh." He held up his head and locked eyes with her. "You know how you ate that cake? Like it was the best thing you've ever tasted? Well, that's what I'm planning to do to you."

He explored her until she quaked around him. She whispered his name, her fingers tugging his hair. Her one leg draped over his shoulder, her back arched.

He watched her, mesmerized by the way her mouth parted and her eyes widened. The soft throaty moans that escaped her lips. He moved up to swallow the last of her moans. He entered her in one swift motion. She was so wet. Her legs twisted around his hips like a vice, pushing and pulling in sync with his thrusts. Fuck.

Maybe he was the virgin because sex had never been like this for him. He rolled onto his back, bringing her with him. She rose up. Her damp hair swung back and forth as her hips undulated. She had rhythm, this girl. While she danced, each pulsing, intense move drove him deeper to the edge. He pulled himself up and grasped her hips. This time he led and moved her where he needed her.

He sank his teeth into her shoulder. She scratched his back. Then he felt himself slipping. He could not go there without her. He pushed her on her back. He clasped her ankle and angled her leg over his shoulder. He thrust fast and hard, each time causing her to gasp his name. He leaned his forehead against hers.

"I need you to do this for me, Farah."

She moaned louder as he said her name.

"Farah. Farah. Farah. Please come. Please let me come."

She let go then, the last shreds of her will dissipating. She cried out his name, her body shaking in waves of pleasure. He followed her there.

She collapsed into his arms. He was exhausted and spent. And feeling good all over.

# Chapter 24

Sensing the absence of him the next night, she blinked herself awake. They'd gone to see Malcolm today. Tristan seemed different—his shoulders stooped and his smile didn't hold the same joy. He kissed her with the same passion, but he was more distant. His eyes were darker, his smile not as bright. She sat up on the bed. Tristan was on a chair by the open window. The moonlight bathed his muscular, naked body. He drank from a clear open bottle.

"Tristan?"

"Sorry, did I wake you?"

"What are you doing?"

"Just thinking. Come here."

She got up from the bed. Cold air grazed her skin. She wrapped the blanket around her and walked the few steps to him. She curled up on his lap and placed her head against his chest. He put his arms around her, much the way he had on the mountain the night they almost froze to death.

He offered her the bottle. She took a sip and then sputtered and coughed. The gin was strong and acrid, but it felt warm going down. "How can you drink that?"

He rubbed her back. "It's an acquired taste."

"What's wrong, Tristan?"

He kissed her on the forehead. "Just thinking."

"Remember when you asked me to take you to where I was?"

"Of course, I remember. We ate figs in a tree high off the ground."

"You saved me."

He kissed the tip of her nose. "You saved me."

When she cupped his face, he leaned into her hand. "Take me where you are now. I need to be there with you."

"It's all so surreal."

"I know."

"I keep thinking about them."

"Me too. We haven't mourned them properly." She leaned her head against his chest. The rhythm of his heartbeat had become a familiar sound. It comforted her.

He rubbed his thumb across her wrist. "Rana and you were close."

"We were friends. I will miss him."

"He was in love with you, Farah."

She wiped a tear. "No, he wasn't."

"He had his reasons for wanting us to keep apart, but that was chief among them. You never caught the way he looked at you."

She pulled her head away and sat up. "We had mutual admiration for each other. I know that. He proposed to me once."

The bottle hit the table with such force she thought it might break. "That would signal more than friendship, don't you think?"

"You don't understand how it works here."

"I've lived in Nepal, Farah. I understand plenty."

"It's a completely different culture, Tristan. Ahmed and I had only met once when he asked me. He thought we'd be compatible because we were both climbers and had similar backgrounds. I never had those feelings for him. He didn't love me, not in a romantic way. Maybe he thought we could cultivate those feelings, but I didn't. That's all. Not that it matters."

"It matters."

"You still blame yourself?"

"I just keep thinking it doesn't feel right."

"It doesn't to me either. I didn't tell you this when we were up there, but I heard the screws come loose. All of them."

"So it was my craftsmanship."

"I put them in too, but that's just it. I don't think it was. Ice is almost a living thing. The topography of it changes. We both know that's why it's so difficult to climb. But it doesn't change in one instant. The ice we had going up the mountain should have been the same ice we had coming down. I could understand one screw coming loose or the ice shifting. But every single one of them? That's got to be as rare as a…a Specter of Brocken."

"Not a great example, milady. We saw one of those on this trip too, if you recall."

"How could I forget? But it is weird, right?"

"Yeah, I agree. You reacted well."

"Only because of my position. I had enough warning and heard the sound of the screws coming loose. If I hadn't heard it, I wouldn't have unclipped. I yelled to the others, but it was too late."

She shivered and buried her face against his neck. The realization hit her again. How many ways had they almost met with death? She tried to choke back a sob. He held her close, rocking her as she came apart. Finally, she wiped the tears and caught her breath.

"Do you love me?" he asked.

The question shook her to the core. She'd been so careful with her heart, guarding and protecting, even keeping it in a vault. She'd decided long ago, freedom and independence had the same definition…at least for her they did. She would not let a man dictate her future. But she'd never bargained for this man who had removed logic from the equation. It became close to impossible to hold back the dam of feelings circling inside of her. Love was a virus. It had to be. What else could affect the head, the lungs and, most of all, the heart in one fell swoop? It swirled around her like a warm phantom wind only she could feel. It left her confused and panicked and emotional. It left her full and happy and dizzy too. Love was the virus. What was the cure?

"Tristan…"

The sound of his heart changed then. The beat sped up. "I know Rana loved you because he looked at you the same way I look at you. As if you are my ground and my sky."

She opened her mouth. He placed a finger over her lips. "I'm not done. I've been sitting here getting a little drunk and thinking about us. You don't have to say it. It's probably better if neither of us says it. I already have the answer. I even know why we haven't said it to each other already or why we never talk about our tomorrows. It didn't feel right when we were almost dying. It doesn't feel right when we're alive and well either. I've been racking my head, trying my damndest to figure out why. I get it now. It's something you said to me once. My normal and your normal are not the same. I can't stay here and you won't leave."

"Don't hate me."

"Never. It's impossible to do." He held her closer. "Sometimes, I think this is all a dream and we're still stuck inside that Specter of Brocken. I'm happy we had that day. I was closer to heaven on that day than the day we summited. I will never regret you, Farah Nawas. Not for one second. But let's be honest. There's no room in the fig tree for both of us after all."

# Chapter 25

Tristan had pleaded with all the gods he knew to prolong their days and postpone their good-bye. But the inevitable always happened. The day had come without his permission and despite all his objections. She came to the hospital with him to visit Malcolm. He would catch a flight back to Islamabad and spend a few days with Elliot before heading back to the States.

Malcolm was in good spirits. He sat in a wheel chair and prattled on about the recuperation program they were putting him through. Farah and Tristan smiled and nodded, but neither was very talkative.

The snow globe Malcolm purchased for his niece sat on the counter along with the scarf and a chessboard. Tristan stared at the snowflakes as they fell against the mountain in the background. There were pink stones in the foreground.

Tristan looked through Malcolm's paperbacks to keep his hands busy. He had a Max Montero novel and a few classics. He had to keep the urge to take Farah into his arms and beg her to come with him at bay. This was difficult enough for both of them. "You're a fan of Poe?" he asked Malcolm, holding up the small book.

"Not all of Poe, but I like that one. 'The Purloined Letter.' Have you read it?"

"A long time ago. If I remember, it has something to do with a letter, as the name suggests. A hidden object, right?"

"Yeah, all these detectives searched and came up empty, except it was hidden in plain sight the whole time. Pretty ingenious."

"Yeah."

Malcolm banged on his table. "Nurse. Take away my plate."

The nurse came over, shooting him a look that could laser through ice. She took his plate and walked away without a word. "Thanks, honey," Malcolm yelled after her.

"Did you leave your manners on the mountain?" Tristan asked.

"They don't understand the language anyway. Besides, the nurses here think I'm a loud-mouthed prick."

"It's not just the nurses," Farah muttered.

"Want to play a game?" Malcolm asked, setting up the chessboard. "No hustle this time. I've been practicing. I'm sure I'll beat you."

Tristan laughed, but it sounded hollow. "Not with the Queen's Gambit."

He glanced at Farah who sat on the metal chair, her expression stoic as she looked at Malcolm. Her fist was closed. Tristan wagered the pebble was inside. His was inside the pocket of his jeans.

He'd made love to her this morning. Scratch that, he'd fucked her. Hard. Until they both lay on the bed exhausted and spent. He'd loved every inch of her with every inch of him. He knew it would be the last time.

Malcolm cleared his throat as if to remind them he was still there.

"Sorry," Tristan said. "I have to get to the airport. I'm flying back to Islamabad today."

"You opted not to take the bus this time, huh?" he asked.

"I don't think I could handle another bus ride on the Karakorum Highway." He spoke to Malcolm, but he could not take his eyes off her.

"What's wrong with you two?" Malcolm asked, looking from one to the other.

"Nothing," Tristan said. "You sure you don't want me to stick around for a few more days? At least until they get you moved to Islamabad?"

Malcolm shook his head. "I'm fine."

"Do you need money?"

Malcolm laughed so loud a nurse frowned in their direction. "What are you? My father? No, I got plenty. Medical is at bargain basement prices on this side of the world anyway."

"I'm really sorry about Edelweiss. I know you were close."

Malcolm gave him a smug smile. "Look Sinclair, you're okay, but let's not pretend we're gonna twine friendship bracelets for each other. We climbed a mountain. Sometimes that bonds people in the short-term. But I'm not looking to bond."

Farah stood, the metal of her chair scraping the floor. "You're a real asshole. Do you know what this man went through so you can sit in that bed right now?"

God, he loved her. She looked so angry she might just throttle Malcolm.

"Would have been nice if he could have been heroic enough to save my foot at the same time."

Tristan stepped between them. He gazed at the girl who owned his heart. He didn't want to taint their good-bye. "Don't waste your breath." He took her hand. "Come and walk with me one last time."

Tristan threw his duffle bag over his shoulder and placed his other arm around her. "See you around, Malcolm," he said, without even facing the man. They made their way down the long corridor.

"He had no gratitude."

"Don't give him any more thought, sweetheart. I don't want him messing with any part of this good-bye. It's hard enough as it is. Walk me out?"

She shook her head. "I have to go back in there."

"Farah, just leave it alone. He'll only sour everything."

"Not him. I left my bag in there."

"Oh."

"Besides, my heart can only break so much. I don't know if it will mend. Remind me again what we're doing?"

"Will you come with me?" he asked. The smallest shred of hope sprouted inside of him.

"I've carved out a life for me. I have things to do here. Students to teach. Young girls to help."

"So there we have it."

"Tristan…"

He knew it wasn't proper, but he held her inside the crowded hospital. "Shhh."

"Should we write?" she asked.

"What do you think?"

She thought about it for a second. A tear rolled down her cheek. She swiped at it. "No. No writing. No phone calls. No visits. Like the Goddess of the Mountain, I'm jealous too. I want you to be happy, Tristan. I'll pray for it every night. But I cannot bear to hear about you falling in love with someone else. It will kill me."

As if she had to worry about that. "It's not possible for me either. I can't keep in touch with you and not touch all of you." He shook his head. "If you're going to be in my life, I need to claim every inch of you as mine, milady."

He kissed the back of her wrist. He would have done more, but they were in public, and such displays were frowned upon. As it was, they were already getting dirty looks.

"Wait," she said. "Why do you call me 'milady'? What's the real reason?"

"I thought you would have figured it out by now."

She put her hand on his shoulder. "Tell me."

"Because it sounds an awful lot like my lady." He hadn't even realized it himself until recently. "*Au revoir.*"

She flashed him a sad smile. "You do know French, Quebec."

He pinched his thumb and index fingers together before turning around and heading down the corridor. He opened the door to the bright sunlight, thinking that his heart breaking sounded an awful lot like a fracture in the ice.

That would have been it.

If not for the pop sound.

Then his heart went still.

# Chapter 26

Adrenaline took over. Everyone was pushing and cramming to get out of the hospital. Tristan was going the other way, driving against the crowd to get back in. People were screaming, shouting, and running. He shoved them out of the way, pushing against the crowd at a full sprint, calling her name.

Then she was right in front of him. He let out a breath. She was okay.

"Tristan," she said.

He held his fingers to her lips and looked around. Where the hell was the shooter? Tristan saw the man first. He wore a black mask and came from Malcolm's room. He was taller than all the people rushing in every direction. He pointed the gun into the air and cocked it. Tristan pushed Farah to the ground and covered her.

"What's happening?"

"We need to take cover."

The bullets fired in succession now. He heard them, over their heads, getting closer. She shook underneath him. He slid them against the stone floor until they made it inside a small room. He closed the door. He knocked into some brooms and mops when he stood. The room contained long metal shelves. It was crowded and hardly big enough for the two of them.

He surveyed the area. A square of light filtered out of the dusty shelves. He moved them, wincing at the creaking sound as they slid against the concrete floor. As he suspected, there was a small window. He looked at Farah and jerked his head toward it. "You can climb up the shelves and through that window." He bent down and interlaced his hands. "Step up."

"What?"

"You can do it."

"I've climbed the tallest mountains in the world. Of course, I can do it."

"Then what's the problem?"

"You won't fit through there."

"I know."

She shook her head. He cupped his hand over her mouth. "Don't be stupid."

She shoved his hand away. "You're not cutting the rope again. I won't let you."

"This is not the time for arguments."

"I'm not leaving you."

The shots range faster now. *Pow, pow, pow.*

He clasped her arms. "You need to listen to me. Either way, if I have to, I'm going to shove your ass out that window, but you'll have a better chance of not landing on your hard head and cracking it open if you go willingly."

Her nod was so slight he wasn't sure if he'd imagined it. Either way, she placed her foot inside his palm this time. She used the metal shelves to lift her higher. Her step was light enough so they didn't groan or move too much. She grunted as she tried to pry the window open.

Shit, it wasn't going to open.

*Pop, pop, pop, pop.*

"Break it if you have to."

She gave it one last shove and almost fell out as it gave way.

"How far is the drop?" he asked.

"Too far to jump."

"Do you have a foothold on the other side?"

"I think so." She led with her foot and dropped down the other side of the building. "Tristan, don't die or…"

"Or what?"

"Or I might just kill you."

He smiled in spite of himself. "Get out."

*Pow, pow, pow.*

He heard her feet hit the ground. She was safe.

"Tristan, there's another window. It's larger, about fifteen meters down. It's probably two or three rooms away from you. Can you make it?"

"Okay. Farah, you have to run away from here and get shelter."

"Promise me you'll make it."

"I promise."

He heard the shooter kicking open doors. If he was going to survive, he needed to get out of the room fast. He leaned against the wall, keeping low. He went past three rooms, opening each door. On the third, he found the window, but it wouldn't open. He pried it with his hands.

*Pow, pow, pow,* the bullets rushed.

He smashed it with his elbow. He was perching on the ledge just as the door kicked open. He came face to face with a man in a crude mask made of black ribbons that covered his face except for his eyes. They widened. He pointed his gun at Tristan's chest. He didn't shoot though. He looked around the room, almost in a panic.

That's when Tristan jumped.

# Chapter 27

The police questioned them for hours. Tristan reiterated he knew nothing. They told him Malcolm had been shot. Despite all the bullets, he was the only fatality. It was the greatest of ironies. The man survived K2 only to face a bullet in the back of the head. Public displays of emotion were frowned on. Farah kept her distance from him, but he found her eyes searching for his often. All he wanted to do was hold her. It was torture not being able to.

Who the fuck was he kidding? How could he even think of leaving her?

Tristan wanted to talk to her, but that was damn near impossible. He didn't trust anyone else with this information.

They separated them for questioning. He asked if he could see her and be in the room with her. Each time, he was told to stay put and they would check. Farah and Tristan had been questioned extensively after K2. There were always questions when there were deaths. Now, they were being questioned even more intensely. The police inspector asked him about every member of the team and their backgrounds. Why would someone want to kill Malcolm or shoot up a hospital?

Three hours passed. Three of the longest, most miserable hours of his life. He experienced a raw panic so sharp it could have punctured him. At least on the mountain, he knew the risks and possibilities. Here, he was working blind and the woman he loved was in danger. They still asked him question after question. They asked him to explain the sequence of events. How well he knew Malcolm. By the time it was done, his throat had run dry and the panic was drowning him.

"I've already told you what I know. Let me see her."

"What is your relationship with her?"

God, how to answer that? She was his ground and sky. "She is my climbing partner," he said through gritted teeth. "I need to see her."

"The request is not possible," the inspector, a thin wiry man, said.

"Let me make a phone call then."

"Not possible."

It wasn't until his third request, he was allowed. He closed his eyes as the phone rang. Please pick up.

"Hello Tristan, I'm leaving for the airport to pick you up now."

"I'm not on the flight, Elliot."

He'd spoken to Elliot the day they had gotten back and told him what happened on the mountain. Elliot had made Tristan's flight reservation.

"We had a deal, Tristan."

"Listen to me. Something went wrong."

Tristan explained the details around the shooting, at least, what little he knew.

"Don't tell them a damn thing. I'll take care of this," Elliot said.

Apparently, Elliot had a great deal of influence. One phone call from him, and the officers changed their tune.

"I'm sorry, sir," the officer in charge said. "You and the girl are free to go."

The officer looked at Farah and back at Tristan. Although his voice was relaxed, he did not hide his disapproval.

"Any news on the shooter?" Tristan asked.

"No, sir. We're ruling it as a random shooting. Possibly an act of terrorism. It's a tragic but not uncommon event here. At least security shot the man before he could kill anyone else."

The statement didn't sit right with Tristan. There were a lot of people in the hallway, and the man shot his gun off several times. Yet, the only person dead was Malcolm...execution style.

"Will you get word to us if any information becomes available?"

"Consider it done, sir."

He doubted the man was sincere. Tristan held his hand toward the exit of the station, gesturing Farah to go first.

"Sir."

"Yes," Tristan said, turning around.

"I'm sorry for your loss. This belonged to your friend. All his possessions are in here." He held up Malcolm's battered climbing pack. "From his information"—the detective held up the pack and read the label—"he resided in Albany, New York. We were going to ship this to his family, but since you live in the US, it may get to them faster if you shipped it once you arrive."

Shit, Malcolm's family.

Ahmed's family.

Edelweiss.

Bjorn and Lino.

He hadn't thought of those things. As a guide, if any member of his tour died, he'd be making the phone calls to the next of kin. Thank God, it had never happened. He had no doubt Rana followed the same protocols, but the man hadn't survived either. He was sure the government offices contacted the families to inform them of the tragedy. It seemed such a cold way to find out about the loss of a loved one. Naturally, they would have questions. He and Farah were the only witnesses to what had happened up there. Although he wasn't 100 percent sure himself, they deserved to at least hear what happened from him.

"You're aware we were with the climbing expedition."

"Yes, on K2."

"Do you happen to have the emergency contacts for the next of kin?"

"Sir, that information would be held at the expedition's office in Islamabad. I'm sure they have a copy as long as you have the right permissions."

"Thank you."

The man not only let them go, but he hailed them a cab to the airport. Once inside the cab, Tristan put his arms around her. They clung to each other. If the cab driver was offended by their actions, he didn't say anything.

"You're all right?" Tristan asked, inspecting her closely.

"Yes, you?" She touched his chest and arms and face.

He took her wrist and kissed the back of it. "I'm fine."

"What happened? Do you think Malcolm was involved in something?"

"Not sure. What do you know about him? You met him before I did."

"Ahmed said Malcolm and Edelweiss approached him for this climb. They had been planning it almost a year out. Lino and Bjorn were already signed up. I was the last to join, and just a few months ago. I wasn't sure if this was my year to go. Because we all lived in different areas of the world, Ahmed created an e-mail loop. We talked about equipment and experience levels. There wasn't much in the way of personal information."

Tristan's expeditions ran similarly. He became the main point of contact. Sometimes strangers in the climbing group became friends and chatted on their own. But it didn't always happen.

"When did you meet Malcolm in person?"

"At the Shalimar about a week before we left for K2. He was pretty quiet. I could tell he did not approve of me coming. I'm not sure if it was because of my gender or age, but I sensed he didn't have faith in my abilities. When we divided up the workload, he always suggested I cook. I thought he just didn't like me until I realized he treated everyone the same. He climbed Kala Patthar with Edelweiss, but even they didn't seem very close." She grew quiet for a minute.

That was true. They didn't exhibit many signs of camaraderie. Farah shivered beside him, her mouth curved down.

He squeezed her hand. "What is it?"

"I can't believe he's gone."

Tristan held her. "I know.

"What about Edelweiss? Do you remember anything about him?"

"He was fixated on finding his grandfather from the start. He paid extra. Ahmed didn't agree at first, but then he realized the Magic Line Route had some benefits. He asked all of us if we'd accept the new route. We all agreed except Lino. Not at first anyway. He argued there were more fatalities on that route and less chance of success. Eventually, he came around too."

He looked at the cab driver. He didn't want to divulge what he knew in front of this man. After all, what if he reported it all back to the inspector?

"When we get to the hotel, we'll figure it out."

She looked out of the car window and back at him. "Tristan, I need to go back to Hunza. I have a class starting soon."

"You're going to cancel it."

"But—"

He shook his head and placed a finger over her mouth. "I'm sorry. I'm calling the shots right now." He winced. Poor choice of words. "We're going to Islamabad. There is something going on that we're a part of. We need to find the answers together."

"So you think the shooter was there for Malcolm?"

And maybe us too, he wanted to say, except that didn't sound right either. Tristan turned to the cab driver then back to her. "We'll talk about that later. But until we know anything for certain, I'm not letting you out of my sight. We stay together. We're better together."

"We are. We keep each other safe."

She had used present tense. They were better together in every way two people could be good for each other.

# Chapter 28

Tristan had scoured the airport, searching every face they passed. Did any of them wish them harm? He hadn't been sure and, therefore, hadn't trusted a soul. They finally arrived back at the Shalimar. Where they had started. God, how different he was now from the man who'd asked a mysterious girl to let him join the expedition a few months ago. They had been too exhausted to dissect the shooting and Malcolm's connection. Instead, they had fallen asleep in each other's arms, just as they did when they returned from the mountain.

This morning wasn't any clearer, but he had come up with a plan to keep her safe. That is, if Elliot agreed to help. Tristan had left Farah at the hotel, instructed her to keep her phone close, lock the doors, and not let anyone in. At least the hotel had excellent security. He didn't want to leave her alone, but he needed to speak to Elliot, and his chances were greater if he went alone.

Elliot paced back and forth across the ornate Persian rug in his office. The vein in his forehead was getting more prominent by the minute. "Let me get this straight. You want me to use my influence, the influence of this office, to obtain a US visa for this girl you just met?"

Tristan stood from the chair. It felt too much like he was in the principal's office getting a smack down. He walked over to the chessboard set up on a round table in Elliot's office. The look Elliot was giving him told him this would be an uphill conversation. In a corner of the office, there were boxes packed. Some were labeled home and others noted the names of other Embassy officials. "I didn't just meet her, Elliot. I've known her for three months."

"Well, three months is a lifetime." Sarcasm dripped from his voice.

"We climbed a mountain together. We saved each other's lives. If anyone can understand our bond, it's you."

"Which is why I think you're acting irrationally and your judgment is clouded. You've been through a set of extraordinary circumstances. You'd feel a survivor's bond, perhaps a survivor's guilt. I've never climbed with a female before, but I can see how feelings can develop."

Tristan's hands flexed into fists. "A female? Are we caveman? She is one of the most capable climbers I've ever met. Do you think I'm so fickle I'd fall for just anyone?"

Elliot held his hands up. "I'm not saying that. You'd feel a certain devotion to anyone whose life you saved. It's human nature."

"She saved my life too."

"Even more reason."

"I'm clearer than I've ever been." Tristan spun the globe on Elliot's sideboard around. He watched the world rotate for a moment. Strange, beautiful fucking world. "I loved her before then."

Elliot's expression softened. "I'm sorry, son. Even if I could help, you're asking for the impossible."

The impossible? Elliot didn't understand. Tristan would move mountains for her. There was no way on this earth he'd go back home without making sure she was safe. "First off, I know you can help. You have a lot of power here. You forget how much I've seen you do. Things like making sure my permit gets declined and getting us out of that police station in Hunza Valley. Your best friend is a US senator. Your father was golfing buddies with the former Secretary of State. Not to mention, you are one of the best lawyers in the world."

"This is different. A visa isn't a climbing permit. Have you opened a newspaper? They're not exactly clamoring to let people enter our boarders right now. Certainly not from here."

"Her passport is active. She has dual European citizenship. That has to help."

He threw his hands up. "Oh well, in that case."

Tristan stared at the pieces on the chessboard. The game was in progress with a Queen's Gambit opening. He felt sick. "So, you'll do it?"

"You have no idea what you're asking for."

"Lucky for me, I have an uncle who is a high-ranking official of the US Embassy to Pakistan."

"Don't joke, Tristan."

It was time to lay down all his cards. "I'm not. Look Elliot, I'm in love with this girl. We've both been through a lot of trauma. We need time to heal. I want to take her somewhere where we can do that. Can you help us?"

"What happened on the mountain?"

He'd called Elliot as soon as the plane landed. He'd given a broad account of events from the hospital, but he was careful not to reveal too much. "I told you. Everyone in our group died except us. Well, Malcolm made it off the mountain but he wasn't lucky for long."

"They say the shooting was a random act. Do you have another theory?"

"No. But I'm not certain, and until I am, I'm going to exercise every precaution possible." He should tell Elliot how the man at the hospital had a chance to take a clear shot of him and didn't. He wasn't sure if that would help or harm his cause right now.

He rubbed his jaw. "An American citizen is dead, and you want me to get a visa? The shooting makes it even more difficult. The shooter came from the tribal areas."

That didn't sound right either. "If you can't do it, then I'm staying here with her."

"Oh no, you won't. You'll go home to your family like you promised."

"Then she comes with me. We stay together. At least temporarily."

Elliot pounded his fist on the table. "Fine, then I'll get her a damn visa. But the two of you leave on the next flight. I'm coming back myself. When I get there on Wednesday, we can get together and discuss next steps regarding this situation."

"You're coming back?"

"Don't look so surprised. I told you I was retiring. Now, anything else I can do for you?"

"We need the emergency contact list for the others in our group. The Expedition Office should have a copy, but I'm not sure if they will release it to me."

"You know it was a rhetorical question, right?"

"I'm sorry. I would not ask if it wasn't important. Men died, and I owe it to their families to make more phone calls."

"The government offices would have notified them."

"It's not the same, and you know it. We were there. Farah and I. The families deserve to know more than where or when."

Elliot's expression turned contrite. "Yes, I do. I'm sure I can obtain the list for you. Let me make a few calls. I'll work on the visa and have my secretary check on flights."

"Thank you. We need to go to Albany first."

"Albany? As in New York?"

"I want to drop off Malcolm's belongings to his family."

"I can arrange it."

"And Elliot?"

"Yes?"

"Do you know where I can purchase some tin plates?"

# Chapter 29

Farah wondered what was keeping Tristan. He'd left hours ago to visit his uncle, instructing her to keep the door locked and stay close to the phone. Finally, the knock came. She checked through the eye-hole first. His frame was so tall she saw only his chest, but it was enough confirmation. Here in Islamabad, they had been careful to keep separate rooms. She peered out the door and checked around the hallway before letting him in. It had been over twenty-four hours since the shooting, and they still had no answers. Only more questions.

He had several sacks in his hands. He laid out all the materials in piles. There were a dozen shiny metal plates, two wooden blocks, two awls, and hammers. He didn't need to explain anything more.

"I'd forgotten," she said, ashamed of herself.

"Me too, sweetheart. But they deserve this. Their names need to be on the memorial."

Traditionally, fellow climbers were the ones who created or commissioned the plates that hung on the Art Gilkey memorial.

"You're right."

"I figured we can spilt up the work. There is a porter I trust. We can pay him to take the plates back to Hunza Valley. From there, a Baljit local will place them on the memorial for us."

"Why so many plates?"

He set a plate over a wooden block. "In case we mess up. I've never done this before. Arts and crafts aren't exactly my thing."

"I have."

He tilted his head. "When?"

"My last expedition. We lost someone. I made his plate."

She took the awl and hammer. "I'll start with Lino."

"I'll do Edelweiss."

They sat on the floor. She traced out letters with a non-permanent marker noting the names of the climber, the date of the death, and the location. Like so many of the plates on the memorial, they all died during descent. Once she had the spacing, she began punching small holes into the plate until they formed letters. The letters became a word. He watched and followed her lead. The work created a much-needed distraction and a chance to mourn each member of their expedition. They talked about each man, exchanging stories. Farah even had some positive things to say about Malcolm and Edelweiss. She struggled with Rana's plate so Tristan helped her finish it.

"How did your meeting with your uncle go?"

"You're coming to America with me."

"What? Tristan, have you gone mad?"

"He's going to work on a visa for you. He'll expedite it. It helps that you've lived in Europe."

"Tristan…"

He sighed and dropped his awl. "Do you not want to go?"

"I didn't say that. Why don't you ask me instead of telling me? You're acting strange."

"Strange? Yeah, well, I've had a pretty intense few days. Is there a protocol when you almost die…twice?" He groaned in frustration as his awl dug too deeply into the plate, ripping a wide hole in the center. He flung it like a Frisbee onto the bed and pulled out new materials. Maybe he saw the fear in her face because his features softened. "I'm sorry." He scooted closer and took her hand. "Here is the situation. I have a feeling that shooter was looking for Malcolm. The shot was too dead-on to be a coincidence."

"I know. We talked about that."

"I also think he was looking for something else."

"Us?"

"I don't think so. He had a clear shot of me, Farah. He didn't take it. But he was going from room to room. There had to be something he was looking for. Maybe it was just an escape route. Or maybe it was us for some other reason."

"Why would anyone be after us?"

"I've been trying to figure it out. Maybe it has something to do with what we saw on the mountain. I don't buy that this was a political statement. Not when he went straight for Malcolm, execution style. Yet he fired all those other shots and missed."

"That could just mean he was a bad shot and support the story he was a villager."

"Not really. You were there. The hospital was crowded. It would probably take more skill to shoot and miss than hit someone."

"You think he was purposefully missing to make it look that way?"

Tristan shrugged. "I'm not a detective. I honestly have no idea. Either way, there is something else going on. My main focus is to keep us both safe. I think distance will do it. So, I want you to come to Albany with me."

"Albany? I thought you lived in Richmond."

"I do. But Malcolm lives in Albany, or at least his family does. We can ask them a few questions and try to get some insight."

"Did you tell your uncle any of this?"

"Not yet, but I plan to. Once we're safe in the States, I'll tell him. Right now, I just want to get us both out of the country."

"So you're whisking me off to America to keep me safe?"

"I would have liked the circumstances to be less dire, but for lack of a better description, yes. Does it sound too archaic?"

"It sounds like you really care about me."

"Is that even a question, milady?"

"We can't hide out forever."

"Just until we figure it out." He took out a scrap of folded paper from his back pocket.

"What's this?" she asked when he handed it to her.

"The next of kin for everyone. Elliot's secretary printed it for me before I left. I need to make some difficult calls."

She took the sheet from him. "We'll both do it. Together."

He kissed her head. "Okay."

"Ahmed's family lives here. I want to go visit them in person." He opened his mouth, no doubt to object, but she kissed him. "Listen to me, I have to pay my respects the proper way. They live close. I'm sure they already know about his death, but I would not feel right calling them."

"I understand why you want to go in person. Let's do it together, though."

"I agree. Do you think Malcolm's family is going to just invite us to visit them?"

"Well, you have photos of him on the summit. They will want those." Tristan patted the battered pack. "Besides, we can also go under the guise that we need to deliver this. Maybe they have no idea what he was involved in, and if that's the case, I don't want to spread any rumors. We'll feel it out and just see."

"I think we're in over our heads."

He laughed and put his arm around her. "You're telling me? I have no clue what I'm doing here. Ask me to ski down the side of a mountain or paraglide across a volcano, I'm your guy. But Jason Borne, I am not."

"That's a good thing."

"Why do you say that?"

"The women in his life always seem to die."

Tristan laughed. He got better with the plates once he focused on the task. When they were done, they piled them on the table. He began putting away the tools.

"Wait." She put her hand on his shoulder. "You have one more to do."

He looked at the plates on the dresser and counted them once more. "We did everyone. We're done."

She kissed him on the cheek. "You are not finished." She handed him a fresh plate. "Make a plate for Drew. He deserves a plate."

He took the piece of tin from her. He didn't have the right words to convey what he felt for her. All he knew was that she made his life better. He had almost walked away from her. Even then, if he had, he knew without a doubt, his life would have been colorless and bland. He'd have come back for her. She was his ground and sky.

She was his normal.

# Chapter 30

Ahmed's family had invited them to dinner. The evening had been emotional, but they had shared all the information they could remember. Ahmed's uncles, aunts, cousins, and friends turned out. There were so many people at his haveli Farah wondered if all of Islamabad had turned out. He was loved and respected by everyone. She'd had the digital photos printed and gave them to his mother and sisters. They smiled through their tears at the sight of him holding up the flag of his country with fierce pride.

Tristan was especially sweet with Ahmed's mother. He told a few stories about her son and said all the right things. The woman barely spoke English, but somehow she seemed to comprehend. Then he handed her an official bank check with so many zeros the woman had to ask if the number was correct. Once it was confirmed, she burst into tears along with her daughters. The money would mean education and dowries and futures for all of them. When they left, Farah asked him how he knew just what to say.

He shrugged with modesty. "Because I've been through it with my mother after Drew died. Besides, grief doesn't have language barriers."

"That was a lot of money you gave them."

"I had enough saved for two trips. Like you, I decided along the journey this would be my only try. I wanted them to have it. Rana was a good man, a hard man, but a good one. He was my friend and your friend. He deserved so much more."

Tristan was a good man too. He had been born of wealth, but wasn't materialistic. He thirsted for adventure and had a heart as deep and rich as the Hunza Valley. She vowed to do everything in her power to keep him safe. They may not have been meant for this life, but she would never have these feelings for anyone else as long as she lived.

They each spoke to the other families on the phone. Bjorn had a sister. Lino had an older son and wife. Farah was grateful none of them had young children. The calls had also taken their toll. They'd had to relive the descriptions and explain the situation. Farah still heard Lino's wife's soft crying. Edelweiss's contact, a cousin, never answered the phone. They had tried numerous times to no avail. Malcolm's next of kin was his brother. He took the news in stride. He seemed happy they were bringing him Malcolm's pack. He suggested he meet them at the airport in Albany, but they were getting into the city late. Tristan said they could drive up to his house the next day.

In the quiet of night, she lay in Tristan's arms, and they would replay that devastating night. Neither one of them wanted to recount it, but they had to put together the facts they knew so they could make sense of the situation. Sometimes, it became too emotional and they had to stop.

Tristan's uncle had come through with Farah's visa just three days later. She wore a scarf over her head, veiling her hair. She clutched it tighter as they headed through the airport. They waited in the long line at airport security until a short, spry man with a bushy mustache approached them. He introduced himself as Mr. Shah, a friend of Tristan's uncle. He explained they were to follow him. He had airport security clearance and could get them through the lines.

People glared at them as they bypassed line after line. The searches through their items were minimal too. She suspected part of the stares wasn't just the line-skipping, but also due to shock and disapproval that she was with Tristan.

"Cold?" he asked, pulling the wool airline blanket from the basket in front of them.

She put her hand in her pocket and felt the small pebble there. For whatever strange reason, it always brought her comfort. Perhaps because, like he had said, it was forever. It would always remain a solid reminder they once had a perfect day. Even more than that, it made her believe there would be many more perfect days to follow. She laid her head against his chest. "I'm fine."

They arrived in Albany at midnight. Tristan rented a car at the airport and purchased prepaid phones for each of them. Tristan called Elliot to give him the number. They checked into a nearby hotel. The early autumn air was balmy.

"Hungry?" he asked, quirking a brow.

She wasn't sure if he was being flirty. He stretched his arms, the fabric of his T-shirt coming up just enough to reveal the finely chiseled muscles of his abs. Her body longed for his touch. The greedy way he kissed her. The way his hands possessed her.

She took a few steps toward him, fluttering her eyelashes and letting her hair fall over her face. She wasn't practiced at the art of flirting. She was the kind of girl who just asked for what she wanted. Right now, she wanted to make his pulse race the same way he did to her.

"Actually," she said, keeping her voice low and husky, "I'm ravenous...for you."

He stared at her as if she'd grown a third eye. Then his cynical laugh echoed through the room. "Did you really just say...ravenous?"

She dropped her hands in frustration. "Is that the wrong word?"

"Very wrong."

"Too..." What was the word? "Corny?"

"Sweetness, that's got more corn than all the fields in Iowa."

She shrugged. "Read it in the regency romance I bought at the airport. I'll have you know when the Duke of Wellington said those words to Lady Amelia, it melted her heart."

"Is that a fact?" He tsked, making his way toward her, his stance predatory. "They aren't exactly a turn-on for me, and I'm definitely not Lady Amelia. By the way, it's kind of emasculating that you're using the guy's lines on me."

"I'll have to think of a way to make up for that." She took off her shirt. For the first time in her life, she wished she possessed a bra that wasn't utilitarian in nature, something with lace and a pretty pattern. But there was nothing in his expression that suggested anything other than lust—pure, unabashed, raw lust. She was sure her expression mirrored his.

His gaze traveled down her face past her neck and over her chest. "That's a nice start," he said. He unhooked her bra. It fell off her shoulders. He circled her nipple with his tongue.

"Just nice?" She slid down her jeans. Then she hooked her thumbs on the sides of her panties and slipped them down as well.

"Real nice." His voice croaked as he kicked off his shoes and pulled off his shirt.

She headed into the bathroom and turned on the water. "I'm taking a shower."

"Uh-huh."

"Are you coming?"

"Only after you." His jeans and boxers came down in a single movement.

Before she knew it, he was behind her, his hands clasped around her waist, his mouth on her shoulder. He twisted her hair and pulled it back.

He sucked her earlobe. She moaned softly as the hot water pelted her skin. His hand traveled lower. He penetrated her sensitive flesh with his fingers. She leaned back against his strong chest and closed her eyes. He kissed down her jaw line and neck. She reached her hands back and roughed through his too long hair. He thrust inside of her while whispering the sweetest words. She turned her head, taking in the intensity of his green eyes, the strong tilt of his jawline, and the firm grip of his large hands. He kissed her, hard and long, except it was more than a kiss. There was no doubt in her mind that he claimed every inch of her with his mouth and fingers and words.

He positioned her hands flat against the tile. "Hold on for me." His voice was deep and commanding. She'd made fun of his singing, but the truth was she could get lost in his voice. When he spoke, it caused a low rumble in her belly. The sound of their passion was a song she'd never tire of, one that called to her in every way. Whenever they were intimate, she felt as if she was discovering something new about him…something new about herself too.

He entered her slowly, letting her get used to the position. He pushed gently at first, building as her moans increased. He placed his hands over hers, covering them completely. He had big, strong calloused hands. She'd never felt dainty or extremely feminine, except with him. She gave into every pulse-pounding sensation that was Tristan Sinclair. The pleasure hit. It drowned her in wave after beautiful wave.

# Chapter 31

Tristan drove them to Malcolm's brother's house the next day. He watched as Farah unwrapped the snow globe and shook it. Tiny pink rocks floated around the mountain landscape. "I don't remember the crystals in here. They're pretty, aren't they? They dance around the mountain like shooting stars."

He managed a half-hearted smile. Only she could find something lovely in the gruesome situation they were in. He loved that about her.

It was a fairly large snow globe, almost the size of a cantaloupe. She shivered. Her mind was probably going back to the nightmares they shared.

"You okay?" he asked, putting his hand on her knee.

"Yes. Just nervous." She folded the scarf. She carefully placed it and the snow globe back into Malcolm's pack. "What are we going to say?"

"I don't know. We'll figure it out when we get inside."

They drove through a suburban area with look-a-like houses where the yards boasted signs advertising window and roofing companies. Tristan had to admit he was angry at Malcolm. The man had put them in danger. Put the woman he loved in danger. Tristan wasn't going to write any songs for Malcolm or give his eulogy, but the man did have people who loved him. They lived here. A young woman, whose uncle had bought her special souvenirs from the other side of the world. Tristan tried to keep that in the forefront of his mind.

"This is it," Tristan said.

He grabbed the pack with Malcolm's belongings and the souvenirs. They had already looked through the luggage several times, searching for anything suspicious, but had found nothing. They hoped to get some answers, some type of clarity. Tristan wanted to believe the distance from the shooting kept them safe, but he wasn't willing to place a wager on that.

An older man with dark hair answered the door after the first knock. "David?" Tristan asked.

David smiled and held out his hand. "Nice to meet you. Please come in."

It had been a long time since Tristan had been in an average American house. The kind of house where photo frames line the fireplace mantle and the China cabinets brimmed with trophies. They followed David to the living room and took a seat on the plaid couch he gestured to.

"Our condolences," Farah said. "We're sorry for your loss. Malcolm was an important member of our team and an impressive alpinist."

Tristan had to commend her for the description. He himself was trying to search for the right words on his feelings regarding Malcolm. Even if he didn't have anything to do with the shooting and it was a random act, the man was gruff, and the few times he did speak, it was to complain. But even if he had been injured and unconscious most of the time, the three of them had struggled in that snowstorm together. The idea he could survive all that and die senselessly from a gunman's bullet left a bitter taste in Tristan's mouth.

David nodded. "It's hard to believe. I told him not to go to such a dangerous country." He shook his head. "Shot in a hospital, for God's sake."

"Are you a mountaineer too?" she asked.

He laughed. "Me? No. I like to keep my feet firm on the ground. He gestured to the pack in Tristan's hand. "Is that his pack?"

"Yes," Tristan said.

David held out his hand. "Thank you for bringing it all this way."

Tristan didn't relinquish it. "May we ask you some questions about Malcolm?"

"Actually, I have to pick up my kid from soccer practice. She's taking the news hard."

"I'm sorry," Farah said. "Are you having a service?"

"My brother wouldn't want that. He was a quiet man. I'm sorry I don't have time to spend with you today. Perhaps another time."

"We're only in town for today," Tristan said.

David checked his watch just as the phone rang. "Excuse me."

Tristan stood and stretched. He looked around the room, pausing to study the photos on the fireplace. Farah walked over to a table by the entryway. He watched her in his peripheral. Even though it was only a few feet, any distance between them made him nervous.

*Stop it. You're acting like a fool.*

He turned back to the mantle. Most of the photos were of a girl at varying ages. The few with adults featured a stocky man with a toothy smile and a red-haired woman. He heard David moving around in the other room. He'd expected a token picture of Malcolm. Even Tristan, who had lived in a small shack in Nepal, had a photo of Drew. But even more disturbing, he did not see any photos of David. And the girl in the photo didn't look anything like him. She had blond hair and Nordic features like Malcolm. In the most recent photo, she was in her early twenties. David acted as if she were a child.

There was something missing. Some piece. He racked his brain, searching for it.

Malcolm had only mentioned one niece. She was in college. Why would she need a ride home from soccer practice? He reasoned his mind was searching for an explanation, so he didn't trust his conclusions fully. Still, it was possible.

He turned to Farah, about to open his mouth. She was already facing him across the room. "We need to go," she said.

"I know. Something's off."

They had both come to the same end.

He tightened his hold on Malcolm's pack and headed for the door. His heart beat in his chest, a warning drum. He practically pushed her out of the house, keeping her in front of him. They had reached the car when an angry David came barreling out of the house.

"Where the hell are you going?"

"We'll be back," Tristan said, having no idea what else to say.

"Stop right there."

Tristan fumbled for his keys, giving David just enough time to pull out a black metal object from his pocket.

Shit.

Farah got into the car. Thank God, he had left the doors unlocked. His normally steady hands shook as he held up the keys. Then he dropped them. "Fuck!"

He arched his back as sharp pain emanated from his shoulder. He bent to retrieve the keys and then practically dove into the car. Something loud and menacing whizzed by his ear. He reversed, his foot bearing down on the accelerator. The tires squealed, leaving behind the caustic scent of burnt rubber in their path.

Her breaths came loud and harsh. He took her hand and squeezed. "Are you okay?"

She didn't answer.

"Farah."

Her eyes widened as she took him in. "He shot you."

Tristan had suspected the sharp pain was a bullet. They had no time to pull over. He moved forward in his seat. "How bad does it look?"

"I don't think the bullet is in there, but I can't tell for sure. We need to wash out the wound."

"Not right now."

"Tristan…"

"I'll stop as soon as I feel it's safe." He had no clue when that would be.

Tristan sped through several blocks of residential homes until he finally came to a four-lane divided main street.

"What tipped you off?" he asked her.

"I was just thinking about Malcolm. I remembered the conversation that night I told the story of Koh-i-Noor. He said his brother was supposed to go with him to Kala Patthar. But this man said he didn't climb."

"Good memory. Yeah, he wasn't in any of the photos on the mantle either. Not to mention his daughter was older."

"I'm fairly certain Malcolm told me his niece was in college on the west coast. Could he have more than one niece or one brother?"

"I only heard him mention the one and just saw the one in the photos. Do you think that was their house?"

"Yes. The mail was all addressed to David Ball. The same name as Malcolm."

Except, that man, the one with the gun, wasn't David Ball.

Tristan checked the rearview mirror. He switched lanes.

"It was strange to me that he didn't seem very interested to hear about his brother."

He turned right onto another busy street. "Put your seatbelt on, Farah. And hang on. I need to make some quick turns up here."

"Why?" She slid on her seatbelt.

"Because he's following us."

The black SUV with tinted windows had been behind them since they'd come onto the major street. It had stayed a few cars back, but moved with them in each new direction. Tristan wasn't familiar with the area, but he wagered David, or whoever the fuck he was, had the same handicap. He wished the rental place had options for a manual transmission. He didn't feel enough control driving an automatic, nor was he used to it.

He inched his foot down the accelerator. Farah screamed as the car in front of them slowed down to stop for the yellow light ahead. Tristan veered right and passed four lanes of traffic as the light turned red.

The black SUV, having no choice, screeched to a stop.

Tristan took the ramp onto the expressway. Once he was sure they had lost the SUV, he pulled out his phone. He thought about calling Elliot, but he had no idea what to tell him. *Help, random people are shooting at us... again.* He'd banked on the idea that the distance would keep them safe. Whatever was going on in Pakistan followed them to Albany. Elliot would be here soon anyway. It seemed better to have the conversation in person.

He thought about his father too, but that would require a lot of explaining and listening to a chorus of well-intentioned lectures.

He squeezed Farah's hand. "We're okay now." He said, as much to confirm it for himself as her.

"We're not okay. What are we going to do? A man shot you."

"We need to find shelter. I know who to call."

Tristan almost lost hope at the fourth ring. Then a groggy voice answered, "Who the hell is this?"

"Hello, mate."

"Sinclair? What the bloody hell is wrong with you? Do you know what time it is here? Oh wait, you're here too."

"Actually, I'm not. I'm back in the States."

"Yeah? Then like I said, what the bloody hell are you doing calling me at this hour?"

Tristan held the phone away from his ear. "Long story. Look, I don't have time to explain, but I need a favor. Can I use your apartment for a day or two?"

A few more choice words were exchanged before they disconnected.

"Who was that?" she asked.

"A friend. He has an apartment in the city. We can hide out there for a bit."

"What city?"

"New York City."

# Chapter 32

Farah had searched through their luggage until she found a jacket for Tristan to wear over his shirt. After all, walking in with a large blood stain on your arm would draw suspicion. She tried to pretend that she belonged and this was all normal. But this was as far from normal as the moon was from the earth. When Tristan had said an apartment in the city, she'd expected a few rooms in a building, not a luxurious high rise in the city center with multiple floors, including one with just a swimming pool.

She'd found some antiseptic in the huge bathroom on the ground floor. As she suspected, the bullet had grazed him. Thank God. He winced as the cloth touched his shoulder. She almost laughed. She'd seen this man use the pads of his fingers to scale up the side of a rock and here he winced over a little sting.

"I think you might need stitches."

"Just slap a bandage on it. I'll be good to go."

"I don't think—"

He grabbed her wrist and kissed the underside. "Please Farah. We need to protect ourselves and figure out what's going on. If it incapacitated me, I would go, but this… This I can handle."

"Okay," she agreed with reluctance. "What about the police? Should we call them?"

"I thought of that. But we have no idea how to explain what's happening. We survived the Savage, and now random people are trying to kill us. Well… I don't think it's random."

"Maybe it has something to do with the body? Edelweiss's grandfather?"

"That's what I was thinking. You're the history buff. What do you think?"

She took the seat next to him. "It's plausible, but if the year is correct, the war was still going on."

"It's not as if Edelweiss is a trusted source. But it makes sense him and Malcolm were working together. They knew each other."

She chewed on her bottom lip. "I think he was telling the truth about the year. I understand he wasn't the most reliable person, but I don't think he'd fake the date. I remember the way he looked when he spoke about his grandfather. The man may have been part of a horrible cause, but Edelweiss loved him."

"Okay, let's say Grandpa E did climb the mountain at that time. Maybe he wasn't commissioned by Hitler. He could have been a deserter too. What better place to go than where no one can find you? He might as well have been on Mars."

"That's true, but why would anyone want to track down a deserter now? Especially, a dead one."

Her head needed a breather, a chance to catch up to all that had happened. She started at the wall of windows in front of her. They overlooked Manhattan, and casted long, luminous shadows across the marble floors. "Whose apartment is this?"

"Liam Montgomery. He's in India for business." Tristan laughed. "It has to be three in the morning there. I woke him up. Anyway, he said we could make ourselves at home. The security here is really good, and I doubt anyone will track us back here. Not many people know that we're friends."

"Liam Montgomery? He has the same name as the hotel mogul."

"That's because he is the hotel mogul."

She searched around the room again, struck silent by its luxury. "How do you know him?"

"Boarding school."

"You went to boarding school?"

"Sure did. Had the blue blazer with red elbow patches and a paisley tie and everything."

As tense as she was, her lips curved into a smile. She couldn't imagine strong, rugged, outdoorsman, Tristan Sinclair, wearing a...suit.

"I went to boarding school too. Mr. Jat sent me after my mother died." He was her father, yet she still could not bring herself to refer to him that way. After all, he'd never publicly acknowledged her as his daughter.

He pulled her into his lap. "We have a lot in common, milady, even if we do hail from different corners of this world."

"Did you enjoy boarding school?'

"It's a Sinclair family tradition. But not one I enjoyed. It was just an expectation like everything else in my life."

Tristan's phone rang. He ignored the call.

"Who is it?"

"Elliot. He's called twice. I really don't have much to say to him right now. I do think we need to tell him what we know. He can probably help, but right now, I just want to gather our thoughts."

Her stomach groaned.

"Hungry?" he asked.

"A little."

"A little? Sounds like your body would disagree."

He headed to the kitchen. He looked through the cabinets and fridge. He closed the last one. "Nada."

"I don't think we should go out right now."

"We don't have to." He picked up a phone. "There are perks to being rich." He paused before he dialed, an amused smile on his face. "Funny, I know you prefer step-in, lever-lock crampons, yet I have no idea if you like Chinese food."

She smiled. "I do."

He ordered them a feast fit for ten people, not two. She would have objected except her stomach whined again.

"General Tso makes better chicken than Colonel Sanders."

She flipped through her photos and laid out a picture of each man. "You know he was an actual general, right?"

"Are you serious?"

"Yes. During the Qing Dynasty."

"I bet you were that girl who had all the answers in class."

"Wish I had some answers right now."

"Me too." He studied the photos. Were they all pawns in someone else's plot?

"First, we think it has something to do with Malcolm and Edelweiss." She counted off with her fingers. "Second, we don't think we have the right history regarding Edelweiss's grandfather. And third, we've been shot at twice now, but everyone who could be involved is dead." She shivered again and flattened her hands against her lap. "And why? Because we saw something we shouldn't have? Like a dead Nazi?"

"Doesn't really make sense," Tristan agreed.

"It's like you said, the man at the hospital could have killed you but he didn't."

"The man today could have done it when we arrived in Albany or last night at the hotel. He didn't have to lure us to that house."

She swallowed. "Do you think he did something to the people who lived in that house? The ones in the photographs?"

Tristan was quiet for a moment. "We can place an anonymous phone call to the police. We'll just say we're a neighbor and saw a stranger lurking in there. There's nothing more we can do right now besides that."

He was right. She thought back to the short exchange at the house. The man claiming to be David Ball had a strange disposition. Really, the only remark he'd made was to ask about the pack. Malcolm's pack. The one he had in his lap when they visited him in the hospital. "Maybe it's not something we saw. Maybe it's something we have."

He shifted his gaze to the black canvas pack, clearly coming up with the same conclusion. The old, battered bag looked out of place on the opulent shiny floor. But she felt a small prickle of relief as if a huge awkward puzzle piece finally fell into place. Farah bent down and unzipped it. "The shooter could have grabbed it. It was in the room."

"Maybe he didn't know what he was looking for."

"The police checked it out before handing it over to us."

She nodded. "True, but here we are."

"Security at the airport looked through it too."

"Yes, but they didn't know what they were looking for. We don't either, but we have a clue."

"We looked through it ourselves, and it just has the souvenirs."

"The pack isn't obvious…and yet it is. Let's go through it one more time."

She carefully removed each of the objects, turning them over to examine them in the light. Inside there were a pair of gloves, goggles, ice screws, extra rope, and a few novels. Nothing stood out. There was no journal, no photos, no documents or clues to explain why they were being chased. Farah wondered for the hundredth time if her love of fiction books was causing her to create an intricate plotline where none existed.

Yet, they had almost been killed. Three times now. Once on the mountain by nature. And twice on the ground. Or was the mountain even an accident?

Tristan took the bag and flipped it over, shaking it. Tiny grains of dirt littered the shiny marble floor. He felt along the fabric for any hidden compartments. "There is nothing here."

Farah sighed. "I'll get a dustpan," she said, heading to the kitchen.

"The Purloined Letter."

"What?" she asked, turning around.

Tristan was holding the snow globe, staring at the pink crystals inside. "The damn purloined letter. Hidden in plain sight."

# Chapter 33

Her eyes widened before she shook her head. "They're just crystals," she said.

He begged to differ. There was something here. They just had to find it. "Maybe. But you said you don't remember them from before. That has to mean something."

"I only glanced at it for a minute before Malcolm grabbed it from me."

"That means something too. Whatever this thing is, he was very protective of it." Tristan rifled through drawers until he found a small hammer. He laid out a towel. "Close your eyes." He swung the hammer up.

"Wait," she said. "Maybe we don't need to crack it. If there is something inside, then he must have had an easy way to get it in there. Therefore, there has to be a simpler way to get it out." She took the object in her hand and studied it from every angle. "I've always been really good at puzzles." She felt around the rim of the metal base and across the glass top. She held it under the light in all directions.

"Farah, we don't have time for this," Tristan said after the third time she spun it around, his voice ripe with frustration.

"I feel a latch. I need something to pry it open."

Tristan ruffled through a few more drawers until he found a flat-head screwdriver. She pried the latch loose. Inside was a compartment with three screws. She held the globe while he removed each of the tiny little screws. When the last one fell, the globe spun apart from its base like a jar lid. He covered a large bowl with several towels. "Do it slowly," he said.

She released the water. She tried to control the spill, but the water sloshed a bit. Pink jewels fell onto the towel, splashing up with the water. He picked one up and held it against the light. It sparkled and glinted. It appeared much larger outside of the globe. They discovered another little compartment on the side with even more pink jewels. She took out a dry white porcelain bowl. They gathered the pink jewels into the bowl. *Plink, plink, plink* they went, one by one.

When they were done, there were sixty, perfectly polished pink gems. They had been carrying around a fucking fortune with them. Well...if they were real.

"I think they're diamonds," she said.

"Pink diamonds?"

"Diamonds have different colors. The Hope Diamond is blue. These...sparkle."

The doorbell rang, causing her to jerk. She threw a kitchen towel over the jewels. He would have laughed except the tension suffocated him too. He placed a hand on her shoulder. "It's our food." At least he thought it was, but probably best not to add that. Instead, he told her to stay hidden in the kitchen while he checked the door. On his way, he grabbed a small sharp knife from the kitchen. It was most likely the best weapon available to him at this point.

He exhaled when he saw a doorman with plastic bags in his hand. He retrieved the food and left a generous tip. He was so relieved he wanted to thank the delivery man for not trying to kill them. When he returned, she was staring at the diamonds.

He set down the bags. Grasping her waist, he whispered to her. "Farah, we have to eat. We're both starving. If we're going to make any sense out of this, we'll need nourishment."

"You're right."

Tristan set everything up. There was a fancy mahogany dining table in the other room and a glass table in the kitchen and probably a hundred other dining areas in this behemoth of an apartment, but neither of them thought of those areas. Instead, they sat cross-legged on the kitchen floor, surrounded by containers of delicious-smelling Chinese food, the plate of pink diamonds between them. Just a casual romantic dinner.

He pushed the plate toward her. "This is better than a pebble, wouldn't you say?"

"I prefer the pebble." She speared a piece of broccoli with her chopsticks and popped it into her mouth. "We should take them to the police. At least we know what they are after now."

Tristan dragged a hand through his hair. "It's not as simple as that."

"Why?"

"Because we don't know a goddamn thing about these diamonds, if they are diamonds. And if they are, they could be blood diamonds, and we broke a million laws by transporting them to this country."

"You think they're from Africa?"

"Maybe. We don't know what Malcolm was into."

Farah was quiet for a moment.

"What are you thinking?" Tristan asked her.

"What if these were on Edelweiss's grandfather's body? Maybe that was the reason he wanted to find the body in the first place. I remember Edelweiss taking the man's pack. Plus, he didn't even help with the burial. He seemed more interested in the actual pack. I don't think these are blood diamonds, but I bet they are stolen just the same."

"That's true, except at that elevation, people's minds don't work the same as they do down here. So we really can't trust our guts."

"But let's say I'm right."

"And you think Malcolm stole them from Edelweiss? He had the snow globe before we left, remember?"

"That's what makes it stand out. He was protective of it, and I don't remember the pink stones. He said he got it in one of the shops at Hunza. I've been to most of the souvenir shops in Hunza and never seen anything like this. He had ample opportunity to take the pouch from Edelweiss and place the real diamonds inside the snow globe. They both shared a tent. They could have been working together too."

"You're missing a very crucial angle."

"What's that?"

"Why would Grandpa E take the diamonds up the mountain in the first place? The changing topography would make the mountain one of the worse places to hide something. Where the hell would he even get the diamonds from?" Tristan picked up one of the gems. It was roughly the size of a pistachio. God, if this was a real diamond, it had to be worth quite a bit, and they had sixty of them.

"I don't know, except in that story Edelweiss suggested his grandfather was superstitious. Remember how he referred to K2 as Koh-i-Noor. The actual diamond, Koh-i-Noor, is said to have very bad luck for any man possessing it. That's why only the queen can wear it. A lot of diamonds in history have that type of curse associated with them."

Tristan dropped the diamond back onto the plate. "Well, guess that trend has held so far. These diamonds must be cursed too. At least for Edelweiss and Malcolm. Let's hope I fare better."

Her lower lip quivered. "It's not funny."

"I know. I'm sorry. I don't know what else to do." He took her hand. "Look. If Edelweiss wanted the diamonds, then why climb the mountain once the diamonds were in his hand? He could have just faked an injury and gone back to camp."

"I don't know, except Edelweiss and Malcolm both seemed like real climbers to me. Plus, the higher we got, the more exhausted we all were. Like you said, people don't think clearly at those elevations. If that's all true, then maybe Malcolm was looking for an opportunity to get rid of Edelweiss? Does it sound crazy?"

"Insane...but true too."

"It wasn't our ice screws."

"Maybe you want to believe that so badly you'll make up a terrific story."

"Fuck you, Tristan."

"I'm sorry." He cupped her face. "There is one thing that I remember clearly. I mentioned a few times that Edelweiss should not go on, but Malcolm would argue every time."

"Tristan, that night we descended, I thought my eyes were playing tricks on me, but Malcolm was below me. It was taking him a while to move. We were all exhausted, but he's a very fast climber. When I looked down, he was next to the rope, but he wasn't using it anymore. It's as if he knew the screws wouldn't hold. Plus, if you think about our climbing positions, he insisted he lead on the way down. I thought Ahmed and him might even fight about it, right there on the summit."

"So?"

"Why would he use the ropes on the way up, but not the way down?"

"You think he loosened the screws on his way down?"

"Maybe. He definitely had the opportunity. I think he somehow got tangled in the rope when the others fell."

What she said made complete sense, but some part of him didn't want to rationalize that Malcolm had killed four men in cold blood. His anger was threatening to spill out. Malcolm had almost killed Farah. They had come within an inch of losing their own lives to save that bastard.

This was beginning to sound like an Agatha Christie novel, but her theory had merit. Killing men at eight thousand meters would mean a clean getaway. After all, accidents like that happened all the time. No one would question it. There would be no one to examine the bodies or perform forensic testing. And most of all, there would be no witnesses... well, except for Farah and him. That's probably why Malcolm wanted them to head down in a certain order. They would be clipped to the ropes, and when the screws came loose, all of them would have tumbled into the abyss.

"The only reason I didn't descend in that order is because I wanted to spread Drew's ashes," Tristan said.

Her voice was as soft as a whisper. "The only reason I didn't is because I wanted to stand on top of the world with you for one moment longer."

They were both quiet, digesting the revelations. He pressed his lips against her head and held her close.

He remembered the prayer he said as they made their summit bid. *I love her, Drew. I love her so much. Keep her safe for me.*

Drew had come through.

*Thank you, little brother. Thank you for keeping us safe.*

# Chapter 34

Needing more answers, they searched the four-floor flat for a computer. As it turned out, Liam Montgomery had a plush corner office at the far end of the second floor. He had a subscription service to several libraries and journals as well. Farah, being the scholar she was, had experience with such sites. Tristan placed a second call to his friend to inquire on the password. At least it was a more reasonable hour this time.

They worked quietly, clacking away at various searches. Having written numerous papers at university, she had a more methodical approach than him. He looked up the backgrounds on each climber in their group and went through their social media profiles. They all checked out, their bios matching what they had stated on the trip. He should not have wasted his time. Ahmed would have checked out their backgrounds. He did search after search regarding any climbs of K2 during the 1940s. He could find no references.

"Any luck?" he asked her after an hour.

"Not much."

"I guess our imaginations are more than sufficient to fill in all the gaps. I mean, what more do we need besides Nazi mountain climbers and pink diamonds?"

"I did searches on the 1940 climb, but there is nothing written about it. I looked for anything on Fritz Ditel. I found a reference to him being an SS officer, but nothing else. We already knew that. But here is something. Pink diamonds exist. Did you know diamonds get their distinctive shade from the elements contained within their carbon structure? Sort of like genetics."

He scrolled through the article he was reading, searching for keywords. "How does that help us?"

She twirled a strand of hair. "Well, it can give us the possibility of a location where these gems may have been mined. Yellow diamonds have more nitrogen. Blue diamonds contain boron."

"And pink diamonds?"

She bit her lower lip. "That's the thing. From everything I've read, there are no impurities in pink diamonds. They are an anomaly that science can't account for yet, which is why they are so rare."

"Just our luck."

"But there are theories. One explanation is a seismic shift like an earthquake."

He picked up a diamond on the plate. "How much do you figure one of these would go for?

"If they are real, it would be impossible for us to tell. I'm seeing prices all over the map."

"You think they might be fake? We could be spinning all these theories, and these aren't even real. I'm not a geologist or a man who's got a lot of knowledge when it comes to diamonds."

"Me either. But then why are people chasing us? Why is there a hidden compartment in the snow globe?"

"Farah, it's possible we're envisioning things. Sort of like how the Specter of Brocken makes you look like a giant. Sometimes the illusion starts to make sense."

"I don't think we're wrong here."

"Maybe not, but is there a way we can tell for sure? Diamonds cut through glass, right?"

"Yes, but there are other minerals that cut glass too." She picked up one of the gems and breathed on it. He leaned over her shoulder. "They say if the fogginess clears up in less than three seconds, it's real."

"I barely even saw it fog." He tried again with the same result.

"There are other tests we can do," she said.

"Is there a way to know their worth or where they might come from?"

"We'd need a jeweler to tell us for sure. One of the articles I read is written by this man who lives here in New York. He's a geologist, diamond expert, and an historian. He works in the diamond district. Can go see him?"

"And bring our lot of stolen diamonds?"

"We can just bring one. People come to this man to verify the authenticity of their diamonds. We could tell him this is a family heirloom we need appraised. If they are that old, there wouldn't be any reports of theft, but it is a risk."

He wasn't sure if it was a great idea, but he had none of his own. "Let's do it."

# Chapter 35

Tristan took a long shower and shaved his beard. It had been a while since he'd seen his bare face. He trimmed his hair. He found one of Liam's suits that fit him well. If he was to play the part of a wealthy Manhattan businessman with his blushing bride on a quest to legitimize a precious family heirloom, he should dress the part. When he stared at the man in the mirror, he thought there was someone his father might be proud of in the reflection.

Either way, the reflection staring back was a stranger.

They'd called down to the front desk. He wasn't even sure what to ask for, but the doorman knew exactly what he needed. A half hour later, two women with painfully tall high heels swept into the room with a rolling cart full of dresses for Farah along with boxes of makeup and jewelry. Tristan almost keeled over in laughter at the jewelry.

He wished this wasn't a role they were playing. Right now, he wanted nothing more than to take his girl for a night on the town. He wanted to open the car door for her and pull back the chair at dinner. He wanted to snuggle up with her on the couch and watch crap television. He wanted weekend mountain adventures. And brunch. Yes, the man who lived for adventure wanted to do Sunday brunch…with her.

It wasn't that he'd changed. He still thirsted for the adventure, but he craved something more now. He craved normal.

He wondered if there was any way their two worlds could join. He called Liam last time for one last favor.

Tristan headed toward the other bathroom where she was changing and knocked on the door. "Are you ready?"

"Almost," she said.

"I'll pack up."

He'd found an empty velvet box to place the pink diamond they would take to the shop. He gathered the rest, counting them out again as much to confirm none were missing as making sure they were in fact real. He placed them inside a small tin used to house tea bags. He packed up their belongings and cleaned up any signs they'd been here. He wasn't sure if they would be returning to Liam's penthouse again. Danger seemed to lay in wait for them everywhere they went.

He turned when he heard the click of heels. Sexy black heels. His gaze traveled up her very long legs. He'd noticed Farah's beauty straight away, back in that tiny shop in Islamabad. She had a stark real beauty, the kind that made men want to be artists and poets. But now...in a body-hugging royal blue dress, he had no words. She was stunning. Her hair looked longer as it hung in loose, silky strands framing her face. She wore powder and color on her lips. But her eyes. Her eyes blew him away. When the two women had shown up, they had cooed about how gorgeous they were. There was black kohl around them. They looked like jewels themselves.

"What's wrong?" she asked. She looked down at her dress. "Am I overdressed?"

"Yes, you should take it off. Take it all off." He took her hand and kissed the back of her wrist. "You're beautiful, milady."

She laughed and linked her arms through his. "You clean up well, yourself."

What he'd give to spend an evening tangling the bed sheets with her until they were both messy again.

# Chapter 36

Farah felt in her purse for the small stone. Not the diamond they were bringing. They had placed that in a little box. She felt around for the small rock she had taken from the mountain. She knew he had a similar one in his pocket. She usually held fast to logic, but she needed to believe in the magic of the stones. That they somehow intertwined her and Tristan, and as long as they had them, they would be able to keep each other safe.

She'd spoken to Ezra Fischer on the phone. At first, he said he was booked until the end of the month. When she explained she was in possession of what she thought was a rare pink diamond, he suddenly had an opening in his busy schedule. She knew they had found the right man. He had a passion for his craft.

Tristan pulled up to a nondescript building. He looked at her, his green eyes bright and intense. "You really think this is going to work? We're just going to waltz in there with the diamond, and he's going to tell us what we need to know?"

The valet opened her door. "Can you give us a minute?" she asked.

The man nodded and walked away. She closed her door and turned to Tristan. "Maybe he'll tell us something useful that will fit the pieces together and confirm some things. I know the man loves what he does for a living, and when you love what you do, you want to impart your knowledge to anyone who will listen."

"I don't know, Farah."

"You're right. Hey, I'm nervous. Can we talk about something else for a minute?"

"We should get this over with."

"Just a few minutes, Tristan."

"What do you want to talk about?"

"Anything off the subject. What's your favorite place to go big rock climbing?"

He thought about it for a while. "It all depends. Red River Gorge in Kentucky is beautiful, but you can't beat Jackson, Wyoming. And also there's..." He quirked his brow when he caught her expression. He burst out in laughter. "I see what you did there."

She smiled and signaled for the valet. "Let's go in now."

The inside of the store boasted case after case full of brilliant jewels. The carpet was a dark gray, so soft and plush her feet sank into it. Overhead, several large chandeliers twinkled. They were both handed flutes of champagne when they entered. She was glad they had the foresight to dress up. She doubted they would have been allowed within ten feet of this place in their jeans and T-shirts.

"We have an appointment with Mr. Fischer," Farah explained to the woman who greeted them.

"Of course, you want to have your engagement diamond appraised."

Tristan choked next to her. She shot him a look. What did he expect? She had to give Mr. Fischer a reasonable story.

"Yes."

The salesgirl led them into a back room. She smiled widely at Tristan and managed to brush up against his arm several times. She wasn't the only one. It wasn't lost on Farah how the other women in the large shop scanned Tristan longer than pleasantries required. She dismissed the childish thoughts. She couldn't blame them after all. Tristan had a feral masculinity and a boyish charm wrapped up in one delicious package. His too-long burnished-gold hair was combed back tonight, but it still looked unruly, the kind of hair a woman's fingers were meant to roam through. He filled out Liam's suit beautifully. Her mouth went dry just staring at him.

Mr. Fischer was an older gentleman with a full black and gray beard. When he shook her hand, her whole body rattled.

"Ms. Nawas, please have a seat."

"Thank you for meeting with us on such short notice."

"To get a chance to analyze a pink diamond...well, that privilege is all mine." He reached his hand out toward Tristan. "This must be your groom?"

"Yes, I'm the groom. Tristan." Ezra leaned in as if waiting for something. "Sorry, Tristan Sinclair."

Farah chided herself for not realizing they needed to come up with fake names. Maybe she should have read more mysteries and fewer historical novels. If you wanted to know how a haberdashery worked, she was your girl. But she was definitely not cut out for this intrigue and espionage. Next to this, scaling a mountain seemed easier.

They each took one of the antique Spider Back chairs next to a long mahogany table. The table contained several lamps and long metal boxes with under-lit squares. Ezra Fischer rolled up his sleeves. A gold Rolex glinted on his wrist, even in the low light. "That is a lovely dress, Ms. Nawaz."

"Call me Farah, please. Thank you for the compliment. I imagine it's somewhere close to Tavernier blue?"

Ezra's brown eyes twinkled as he smiled. "Indeed, I do believe you've gotten the shade correct."

Tristan looked at each of them, the confusion evident on his face. "Could someone point me in the right direction before I get too lost in this conversation?"

Farah smiled. "Tavernier was the man who brought the Hope Diamond from India to France. They named the shade of blue after him."

"That's quite right."

"Our diamond is nowhere in the vicinity of the Hope. Yet, I do believe you may find some historical significance."

"I'm definitely intrigued." Mr. Fischer searched through a drawer and took out several instruments. He rolled up his shirtsleeves and clapped his hands. "May I see it, please?"

She slid the box over to him. Ezra lifted the diamond with a pair of tweezers. He placed it under the light and examined it with a microscope. He placed it back on the table. His mouth gaped for one brief second before he snapped it shut. "Excuse me for one second. I want to get another tool."

"What if he's calling the police?" she asked when they were alone.

"He isn't. That wasn't the look of a man who suspects wrongdoing."

"Then what?"

"He's intrigued."

"By the diamond?"

"Yes, and by you too. Can't blame him there." Tristan squeezed Farah's hand, his tilted smile bordering on accusatory.

"What?" she asked, feigning innocence.

"You're quite charming. Do you know that?"

"Just trying to be friendly."

"Well, when we're married, I'm laying down some rules."

She chuckled. "That's what you think."

Ezra returned. On the outside, Farah tried to act like a newly engaged woman, but on the inside her heart thumped wildly.

"Ms. Nawas, you told me on the phone this was a family heirloom of your fiancé's family." He turned toward Tristan. "Can you give me any more history?"

Tristan shifted in his chair and cleared his throat. "It's been passed down for generations. My family hailed from Germany."

"Your name is Sinclair?"

"Yes...the... The diamond hails from my mother's side."

Tristan Sinclair may have been many wonderful things, but she'd seen dolls give better performances. She prayed Ezra didn't grow suspicious. Luckily, he seemed transfixed by the diamond suspended between his tweezers. "What year did they purchase it?"

"It would have come into the family around 1940."

"I see."

"What can you tell us about it?" Tristan asked.

"It's definitely real and old. Too old to have any coding. The clarity is flawless. I'm assuming you know how rare pink diamonds are?"

"I've heard."

"It makes them quite valuable. May I ask why you've never had this appraised?"

"My mother was concerned about its...origins."

Farah stopped herself from exhaling. Tristan may not have been an actor, but he could improvise well.

"I see." Ezra set the diamond down. "They didn't have too many sales recorded in Germany at that time so it's difficult to pinpoint."

"Why not?" Tristan asked.

"Hitler confiscated any valuables for the war effort. In those days, the only other buyers of diamonds hailed from America. They had the means and weren't in the war yet. Of course, even those diamonds came through Europe."

"How so?" Farah asked.

"If you wanted a diamond cut and polished correctly, you sent it through a small city in Belgium called Antwerp. The Jews there had passed down the skillset from father to son. It's one of the reasons Hitler didn't invade Antwerp until close to the end of the war. He needed them to polish and preserve his diamonds."

Tristan adjusted his tie. "You believe this diamond was stolen by Hitler?"

"I do."

"Could this diamond be stolen from the Jews?" Farah asked.

"No, dear, if that was the case, you would not be leaving here with the diamond since they would legally belong to Israel. As I said, Antwerp was a clearing ground for gems. They came from all over the world there. Chances were, if you wanted to buy, sell, cut, or polish a diamond during that time, it came through Antwerp."

"But it's impossible to figure out where it originated from since the records don't exist," Farah said.

"On the contrary, young lady. I said there weren't records of sales. But the diamond cutters of Antwerp kept immaculate records of the diamonds that came into their possession. When the SS invaded, they also maintained records of all their confiscated goods. Miraculously, most of the Antwerp records survived the war." He tapped his finger against his lips and took off his glasses. He stood and ambled over to a long book shelf. "I've always been interested in the history of gemstones. They've been at the root of wars and love affairs since the beginning of time." He turned back to them. "I'm not referring to the plot of *Titanic* either."

He reached for a huge book with leather binding and yellowing pages. It landed on the mahogany table with a thump. Ezra turned the pages until he found what he was looking for. It was a picture of a letter written in German. "This is a Nazi manifest of items recovered during the invasion of Antwerp. They list the diamonds, the carats, and batches. None of it would be especially interesting except for one description. Seventy-three pink diamonds, about five carats each. Perhaps the largest cache of pink diamonds ever recorded."

Tristan leaned forward. "Sir, did you say seventy-three?"

"I did. They all came from one single stone. They called it the Rose Diamond, and like most uncovered diamonds from that era, it was mined in India. As a rough stone, the Rose Diamond's weight and size rivaled the Hope. They might have been cousins and came from the same mine."

"Who owned the Rose Diamond?"

"The British Raj. You have to remember India was under colonization at the time."

"What happened to all the diamonds?"

Ezra shrugged. "Scattered to the four corners of the world I'm sure." He held the small diamond in the tweezers again. For someone with large hands, he had great dexterity and grace. Farah doubted she could grasp the diamond like that without it bouncing out of her grip.

"But I believe you are holding a piece of the original Rose Diamond right here."

They were actually holding sixty pieces of it.

"It's possible it fell into other hands over the decades or was sold to payoff war debt. Throughout history, diamonds were often used as currency, since they were universally accepted, easy to move, and difficult to trace. The only reason these are traceable is due to their rare color. But the reality is we really don't know what happened to the other diamonds. This manifest is the last known historical document in connection with the Rose Diamonds. I can get more information if I send it to my lab. They can possibly verify the region it was mined from and make confirmation."

"That's all right," Farah said. "I think we have enough information on the history. Thank you."

Ezra slammed the book shut. "As you wish. Either way, let's get down to the brass tacks."

"Brass tacks?"

He held up the gem. "You came here to find out what this is worth, no?" He looked pointedly at Tristan.

"Yes."

"Well, rest assured, young man, it is befitting a bride as lovely as yours. I cannot put an actual price on it without lab work, but this diamond has to be worth at least two in my estimation."

"Two?" Tristan asked.

"I'd put it between two-point-one to two-point-five."

"Million?" Tristan asked, his voice three octaves higher than before.

"Of course, million."

# Chapter 37

By the time they'd left Ezra Fischer's store, her legs felt rubbery as if she'd hiked for six hours. He'd continued on about mounting the diamond in the perfect setting. He'd brought up different styles and suggested a rose gold band, but she'd stopped paying attention.

Tristan had made some excuse and led them from the shop.

"Did he really say two million?" she asked after he'd driven for a few miles.

"He said two-point-one to two-point-five to be exact. We're holding on to about a hundred-and-twenty million dollars' worth of diamonds."

"We need help here."

"I agree, but we can't just stroll into the police station and hand them a hundred-and-twenty mill in diamonds. And then tell them we accidently transported them into the country. How will we possibly be able to convince them we're not complicit?"

"What else are we supposed to do? We're innocent in this."

Her shaking knee stilled when he placed his palm over it. "Farah, if we do that, they might deport you. You're only here on a visitor's visa. I won't risk that." He was quiet for a while, his thumb running across her wrist.

"I can look after myself."

He banged his fist on the steering wheel. "Well, maybe I want to fucking look after you too."

She quieted then. His words may have caused an argument, but she could summon no anger toward him. There was hurt in his voice. The truth was, she wanted to look after him too. They drove in silence for a while.

"I'm sorry, Tristan. No one has ever cared for me the way you do. I'm not used to it. I'm not used to this heavy feeling inside my heart for you either. It scares me more than anything. I've never had so much to lose.

So much to gamble with. That's why I want to pull out of this. I just want us to be safe."

"That's all I want too."

"Where are we going?"

"Home to Richmond. It's about a ten-hour drive."

"Do you think that's a good idea? Whoever is after us knows where you live."

"We don't have a play here, Farah. Not from what I can see. We know we're holding on to a large fortune and really bad people are after us. I wish there was just a way for us to explain it all, but I doubt they'll let us live. I say we hide the diamonds somewhere along the way. You're right, we might be leading them, but like you said, we need help. What is today?"

"Tuesday."

"Elliot is coming back to the States tomorrow. We can meet him. At least he'll be able to advise us. He is a lawyer, and we need legal counsel."

"Okay," she said. "I agree it's the best choice we have. Maybe the only choice."

"Good." He put his arm around her and pulled her close. He pressed his lips against her temple. "Maybe this isn't the right time. There doesn't seem to be a right time with us, Dimples. There's just a wrong time and a worse time. I don't care what holds us back or what obligations wait for us, I just need you to know this. I love you, Farah Nawaz. I love you with everything I am. All my life all I've wanted to do was climb the highest peak and conquer the next challenge. But you... You make me feel like I don't need to climb anymore. That I can be still. That I can be happy just looking into your eyes."

She slid her hand into his. "I want to look after you too. I'm used to being on my own and not relying on anyone else. I thought it made me weaker to be tied to anyone. But the last thing I feel when I'm with you is weak. I love you, Tristan."

# Chapter 38

Elliot would not be home until the next day. They had both grown tired from the road. They had barely gotten any sleep since they had come off the mountain. Typically, Tristan would have slept roughly ten hours a day for a month straight after such an expedition.

They had managed to keep awake on adrenaline, fear, and coffee, but their bodies and heads ached for rest. He kept checking his rearview mirror and taking odd routes. Only when he was positive no one was following did he pull off the expressway. They passed residential neighborhoods and commercial buildings. They went farther until they came up to a wooded area. He flipped on his high beams as they drove down dusty, single lane roads until the traffic lights became sparse and streets didn't intersect for miles. He flipped on the radio. An old country tune played. The breeze blowing through the open window was sweet. He felt twelve years old again, climbing the old oak tree in his backyard. He was home.

He didn't trust staying at a hotel. True, they hadn't incurred any trouble since Albany, but she was right. Trouble didn't need to find them, not when they were driving toward it at seventy miles an hour.

She stretched and yawned as the sun dipped into the horizon. "Why are we stopping?"

"Figured we could rest here for the night. This looks to be a good place for a morning hike."

"You want to go hiking?" she asked.

"It always helps to clear my head. Plus, this looks fairly remote, wouldn't you say? A good place to bury some treasure? I think it's better not to carry the jewels with us. If anything happens and we get detained, we'll have a huge bargaining chip…sixty of them to be exact."

Realization flickered across her face. She nodded. "Yes, I see your point."

They got out and stretched their legs. Early autumn in North Carolina had always been Tristan's favorite time of year. The trees were ripe with foliage, the tips of the leaves starting to color in brilliant reds and golds. The air tasted crisp and fresh with the breeze carrying the faintest scent of pine and blackberries. It was in woods similar to these, on a day much like today, that he and Drew had decided they would be life-long adventurers.

As beautiful as the day was, it was the site of Farah in the middle of the woods that commanded his attention. This woman with her large violet eyes, plump lips, and mane of dark curls owned his heart. He wished they could stay trapped here forever in their own little fairy tale.

God, he was worried. What if he was making the wrong decision and she got hurt as a result?

She must have sensed it. She rubbed his shoulders. "Tomorrow will take care of itself, but tonight we need to take care of each other."

The same words he had whispered to her in a tent not so long ago. "Did a wise man tell you that?"

"A very wise and beautiful man."

He took her wrist and kissed the underside. "I could sure do with some normal tonight."

She smiled. "It sounds to me like you're asking for another cheap date."

Creatures rustled away as Tristan's laugh echoed through the remote landscape. "Very funny, smartass." He pulled her against his chest. "Come here." He claimed her mouth with his. She smelled like dessert and tasted even better.

She pulled away. "Where are you taking me?"

He took a few steps so he was in front of her and gestured to their surroundings. "A romantic fire-lit dinner al fresco style followed by an evening of star gazing." He bowed with a flourish.

Her smile inched up enough to see the dimples on her check. "I'd like that very much."

They found a few branches and lit a small fire. Tristan set up the tent while she changed out of the Tavernier blue dress into sweats and a T-shirt. Damn, she still looked lovely.

She arranged packs of trail mix, chocolate bars, chips, and two bottles of water purchased from their last gas station stop. It looked like a feast. He added a bottle of red wine and popped the cork. Okay, so it was more of a screw-off deal. But in his defense, the gas station didn't have many choices. They sat down on blankets, ready to enjoy their picnic.

"When did you get this?" she asked, holding up the wine.

"When you weren't looking. Now, I know what you're thinking. This isn't the best time to dull our senses, but it's not very strong and I really think it can take the edge off right now."

"That wasn't what I was thinking."

"Then what?"

Her mouth quirked, her expression turning naughty. "I was just wondering if you got any for yourself." She took a long swig and passed him the bottle.

"How is it?" He took a swig himself and passed it back.

"Better than that horrible liquor we had in Concordia. I don't know how you drank that."

"That was actually 'Hunza water' or 'Juniper gin' as some refer to it."

She grimaced. "I believe it's strong enough to remove stain from furniture."

"Probably." Not for the first time, he wondered how she could make him laugh at the most intense times. He took a long drink for himself. The wine fell somewhere between swell and swill. They munched on their treats and passed the bottle back and forth.

"Take off your shirt," she said.

"Say please."

She punched his arm. "I want to change your bandage."

"We can do it later."

"It would make me feel better if we did it now."

He removed his shirt. She grabbed the first-aid kit and inspected the wound.

"How's it looking, doc?"

"Better. It's healing."

She covered his wound with fresh antiseptic cream and replaced the bandage. She kissed his shoulder. He grabbed her arm before she moved away. "If this was a real date…"

"Go on."

"No…forget it."

"Bloody hell, Tristan. Hasn't anyone ever told you to never start a sentence you can't finish?"

"Nope. No one has ever given me that advice." He twirled a strand of her hair around his finger. "But here is what I do know. There are no winners in the game of what if. You told me that once."

"I don't care. I want to play anyway."

He stood and reached for her hand. He pulled her up. "I would love to dance with you."

"In this game, can we pretend I'm graceful?"

"You are graceful. Graceful and strong and so fucking sexy."

"All we need is a song then." When he opened his mouth, she put her hand over it. "So long as you're not singing it."

He kissed her nose. "Everyone's a citric."

Staring at her, Tristan wondered how he could have justified leaving her. There wasn't a doubt that he would have come back. He would have tried his best to move on with life, but what his head worked toward, his heart would have fought. It would have been a short matter of time before he came back to Hunza Valley in search of her. He opened the car and turned on the ignition. He flipped on the radio. Station after station spewed out static. The only thing he could tune in was a country station.

Willie Nelson singing about being on the road again wasn't exactly his idea of a sweep-a-girl-off-her-feet kind of dance, but Farah stepped into his arms nonetheless. He spun her around and dipped her. She craned her head back, laughing like a child. With her in his arms, the world felt like a better place.

"I was wrong," he said, spinning her around.

Her laughter echoed through the forest. "About what?"

"I thought I was the happiest when I'm on the mountain. I'm not." He pulled her close. "I'm the happiest when I'm with you."

She hugged him. "I'm happiest with you too."

The kiss started soft, a barely-there whisper. He touched her lips and covered a light trail down her slender neck. The thing he loved most about intimacy with Farah was that she wasn't afraid to ask for, maybe even demand, what she wanted. She wrapped her arms around him. Her soft hair brushed against his face. She parted her lips, inviting him in. He tangled his tongue against hers, his hands drifting lower. She straddled him.

He wasn't sure when it had started raining. He was too busy tasting her delicious mouth. The kiss devoured every other sense. She pulled back and leaned her forehead against his. They were both breathless. He brushed her wet hair away from her face and kissed along her jawline.

"So much for watching the stars, huh?"

She craned her head back, her laugh wild and carefree. As if she was teasing the rain. "I think you can still make me see stars."

"Are you throwing down a challenge, girl?"

"It's thrown."

He set her down and then turned off the car engine. She disappeared into the tent. He almost dove after her. They peeled off each other's wet clothes. Everything was rhythmic, done with a steely urgency…that was until Tristan got to Farah's bra, which stubbornly refused to come undone.

When he finally managed to do away with the garment, he wasted no time on the panties, pulling the cotton material until they ripped.

"Ouch," she said.

"Sorry, sweetheart."

"At this rate, I won't have any clothes left."

"I have to admit that would make things much easier for me."

He gazed at her naked body, so hungry for her and yet holding himself back. He tilted her chin. "Let me look at you, Farah Nawaz. Let me remember this perfect moment." Her body was a duality, strong and soft and curvy and hard. He wanted to explore every inch and leave his mark. He wanted to claim her in every moan and grunt and breathless murmur. He wanted to fuck her raw.

He pulled her into his lap. With his hands on her hips, he positioned her. She slowly sunk over him. She rolled her hips forward. Each move drove him crazy. He nipped at her ears and fondled her breasts. He swallowed her moans.

The high moon created long shadows against the tent walls. Her palms lay flat against his chest. She tightened around him, her cries becoming more urgent. He changed their pacing, wanting the moment to last.

"I'm close." She closed her eyes.

"Not yet." He flipped them over so she was on her back. He pressed his hand flat on the floor of the tent to get leverage. He thanked the Lord they both had amazing stamina.

Farah wrapped her long legs around his hips. He thrust slow and deep until she called out his name. Then he lost control and increased the tempo. The tent filled with their harsh breaths. There was a cadence…a rhythm in it. It might possibly be the only time someone could accuse Tristan Sinclair of rhythm. He dragged his fingers through her hair. She bit his lip. They both begged for release and held each other back. Then neither of them had the energy. They had to descend. She came, her body quaking, his name on her lips. He followed.

She rested her head on his chest, their bodies covered in a light sheen of sweat. The rain had stopped, except for the drips sliding down tree branches and off leaves. He listened to the earth's melody and the sounds of her soft breath. He relished the taste of red wine and Farah still fresh on his lips.

"Did you see stars?"

She gave him a soft, lazy smile. "An entire galaxy."

"Me too." He kissed her head.

Her voice turned serious. "I don't think I've ever been this scared," she said. She shivered from the cold. "At least on the mountain, I know how to be prepared. What to do. I have instinct. Here it feels like I have nothing."

He covered her with his body. "The most important thing is that we stay together. We're better together."

"How are you so calm, Tristan? You were that night when we almost froze to death on the mountain too. It's like the worse the situation, the more resilient you are."

"That's not true, sweetheart. It's just I have been through something more frightening. This right now? Holding you in my arms under the stars, even in these circumstances, is bliss."

"To me too." She snuggled closer to him. "What do you mean you've been through something more frightening?"

"During our climb."

"The night on the side of the mountain."

"I was scared, but I had you in my arms. I knew where you were and I had some control. It was the moment before though, the moment when I heard the rope snap and you didn't respond. The moment I called your name in the dark and prayed you could follow the sound of my voice. The whole time I felt helpless not being able to get to you. Then there were the gunshots at the hospital and not knowing where you were for that brief instance. The gunshots in that subdivision in Albany." The whole time he had felt a void of loss so deep and fierce he was sure it was a hole he'd never crawl out of.

"Farah Nawaz, I fell in love with you before then. It happened in our small intimate moments and talks. Even when we didn't talk, and all we did was hike for hours in silence. They say a Specter of Brocken is a once in a lifetime sight. Don't get me wrong, it was special. But you are my once in a lifetime."

# Chapter 39

They were silent as they walked off the trail, trying to locate a remote area to bury the diamonds. It was miraculous to think how these diamonds could have traveled from India to Belgium to Pakistan to right here in rural North Carolina. Men had fought and died for them.

He just hoped he wasn't one of them.

As usual, the fresh air and long walk helped to clear his head. They had been so busy running and working with no knowledge, there was no time to link all the connections they had made. Not that he could connect them. All he knew for sure was that he loved this woman who walked beside him. They had gone through hell and back and survived. Now, they were nearing an end. He wanted to plan a life with her, but first, they had to get through this.

The thoughts scattered in his head, knocking around like ricocheting squash balls. It felt like the closer they got to the truth, the farther away from it they were. He felt foolish. They had managed to travel with that snow globe without knowing what they were carrying. Then again, it went through customs and airport security, not to mention the police station in Hunza, without anyone realizing what it was.

*We met at Kala Patthar.*

*My grandfather died on the mountain. His expedition left him to rot.*

*The dead deserve respect.*

Edelweiss, Malcolm. Lino, Bjorn, Rana. All of them were dead. If the diamonds did come from Grandpa E, why the hell had he taken them up into the remote mountains?

The answer hit Tristan with sudden clarity.

"There's one part of a mountain that never changes its topography, Farah."

"What's that?" she asked.

"The summit. The summit of a mountain never changes."

"You're right."

"Maybe that's why Grandpa E was taking the diamonds there. Maybe he needed to hide them. And he chose the most remote place in the world to do it."

"That's possible I suppose. It sounds far-fetched though."

"Well, I don't think he was a sane man to begin with. He stole diamonds from Hitler, after all."

"True. I doubt we will ever know what he was doing on that mountain with the diamonds."

"Yeah, it doesn't matter anyway."

Not that any of it mattered. What mattered was that Malcolm killed the others and then someone killed him. Scratch that, the real question was that whoever had shot Malcolm was now after them. After the diamonds. That was the missing piece.

"Here," she said.

He stared at the ground and then back at her. It was a good spot, secluded and out of the way. He hit the shovel against the ground. The rains had made it soft. She checked the area against the GPS for the coordinates. They dropped the metal box containing the jewels inside. Tristan wasn't sure if he wanted to see them again or never see them again.

"Farah, I'm going to see Elliot alone."

"What?"

He placed a hand on each of her shoulders. "Listen to me. I'd rather you not be there. We have no idea if someone is waiting for us. I need you safe."

She shook her head. "I'm going with you."

"No, sweetheart, you're not. I won't take that risk. I'll make sure Elliot takes care of you if anything happens."

"Don't do this, Tristan. We're better together. You said so yourself."

"There's no part of me that's better by putting you in danger. We don't have time for arguments. This is not a choice to debate. We're partners, you and I, but in this, I have to go alone."

A single tear fell down her face. "I love you. I'll do this for you. But if anything happens to you, I'll kill you."

"I'll keep that in mind."

# Chapter 40

Farah had agreed, but she had waged a silent protest the whole way to the station. He kept scanning the area. It didn't appear anyone was following them, but then again, he wasn't an expert at these things. At least an avalanche gave you a few seconds notice so you could brace for impact. In this situation, they were sitting targets.

He bought another prepaid cell phone from a shop in the terminal. He purchased five tickets for the farthest routes they had—Miami, Los Angeles, New York, Chicago, and Denver. She stared at the tickets and back at him.

"I don't understand."

"I'll explain." He reached into his wallet and handed her a wad of bills. He'd asked Liam for a cash loan. The man had given him the personal combination to his safe. He handed her the money.

"Get on one of these buses. Don't tell me which one. Whichever one you choose, don't take it to the final destination. Get off somewhere in-between. Check into a hotel and wait for me."

She stared at the tickets and cash. "You've watched too many movies."

"I never said it was a great plan. It's just the only one I have."

"Where will you be?"

He'd either be in jail or dead or coming back for her. He prayed it was the third option. "I don't know yet." He handed her a business card. "This is Liam's personal number. If you run into trouble, you can call him. I want you off the grid for now."

"How will I find you?"

"I'll call that number."

"This isn't right. I'm a witness too. I can help."

If Farah came with him, there was a strong possibility they would send her back. He'd taken many risks in his life. Hell, he'd made a career out of risk-taking. But he refused to take a chance when it came to her safety. "Don't argue anymore. There isn't time. Just kiss me."

He tilted her chin. The kiss was deep and long. He wasn't one for public displays, but he had so much to tell her in that kiss.

*I'll be back for you.*

*We're almost at the end.*

*I'm going to start a life with you.*

*You. Are. My. Lady.*

I love you.

# Chapter 41

Tristan drove to the Georgian-brick Tudor Elliot kept in Richmond. Before he rang the doorbell, he shoved his hands in his jacket pocket, grateful for the tiny pebble that was there.

"You look like hell," Elliot said.

"I feel like hell."

"Come in."

The two men embraced.

"I've been trying to reach you for days," Elliot said. He looked outside toward Tristan's rental.

"Farah isn't here. I wanted to come alone."

"I need to know where she is. I've staked my reputation on her visa."

"I understand. I have a lot to tell you first."

Elliot led them to the living room. Half the furniture was still covered in sheets. "Well, let's get started then."

"I need your help again, Elliot. Farah and I are caught up in something that's too big for us. We need to sort it all out."

"Something more than the hospital shooting?"

"That's just the tip of the iceberg."

The two men sat at a table. Elliot had arrived shortly before Tristan. He'd set up the chessboard in the kitchen.

Elliot moved a piece. "I would offer you something to drink, but as you can see, it's all still a work in progress."

"You unpacked the chess set."

"Indeed. It helps me to focus to move around the pieces. Now, tell me everything. I need to know every single detail."

Tristan took a deep breath and began. The story was much longer than he anticipated. It started in Hunza when they first saw the snow globe and ended when he dropped Farah off at the train station. He recounted each detail and all the strange theories they had from mountain curses to Nazi diamonds to loosened ice screws. The whole time, even he questioned if it all really happened. When would the Savage Mountain leave them alone?

Elliot was quiet, fingers steepled, the whole time Tristan spoke. He absorbed all the information, occasionally asking a question or two.

"Who else knows all of this?"

"Just you."

"Not your friend, Liam?"

"He only knows I need to protect Farah."

"I see." Elliot stood and stretched. "Your theories are interesting, but it's all circumstantial. You don't have evidence to support it. You should have come to me as soon as you found the diamonds."

"I know."

"We need to go to the police on this. Whether you meant to or not, you illegally transported stolen diamonds across international waters. You've been a key witness in several murders and have withheld information. I'm going to make some calls starting with my friend, the Attorney General. I'll explain you're willing to cooperate."

"Will they deport Farah? I don't want her in any danger."

"I can negotiate to keep her here until the investigation is over. That's protocol." He took out his cell phone. "Oh, one more thing. Where are the diamonds now?"

Tristan remained silent.

"Tristan?"

"I don't know if it's a good idea to reveal that. It's the only evidence we have."

"I'll need to give them the location as a sign of good faith. We need the diamonds to corroborate your story."

Tristan looked at the chessboard. For a moment, he saw all the pieces. Not the ones on the chessboard, but the ones in his life. Then it went blank. He was a boy again in his grandfather's study, playing on an antique Staunton board. He could see two moves ahead, maybe three.

There had been only three rules for the expedition: go with a group, go home when it was over, and of course, don't die. Rules Elliot had created. He'd even made the contact with Rana.

The most obvious explanation was usually overlooked.

Fuck.

Tristan nodded. "We buried them in the woods off the I-85. I've memorized the longitude and latitude lines."

Elliot chuckled. "Buried treasure?"

"Something like that." He rambled off the long rows of numbers to Elliot, who jotted them down on a piece of paper.

Elliot patted Tristan on the back. "I'll be back."

There was no time. Tristan took out his phone and made a call. The man on the other end had always been prepared for even the worse news. Tristan prayed he would just do what he asked.

"Send the police to Elliot's house in Richmond now. I can't explain. Stay on the line." Tristan put the phone in his back pocket. He ran to the kitchen. He searched around the room and went through every drawer until he found a knife. A knife was not ideal. He'd have to be close. Much too close.

Elliot's footsteps padded down the hall. He stuffed the knife into his back pocket and turned around as he entered the room. "How did it go, Uncle?"

"What are you doing in here?"

"Got thirsty."

"The water isn't turned on yet."

"Yeah, I figured that out."

"Well, we can get a drink after this. We deserve it. I told him the gist of it. Of course, the story is much too long for me to get through all the details. He wants to meet us at his office."

"Now?"

"Of course now. We'll need to locate Farah. Both of you should make your statements together. No worries. I'll be right there to act as your counsel. I'll do everything in my power to get you immunity."

Tristan turned his head toward the window. He saw the black car with the dark tinted windows. If he got in that car, he'd be getting out a dead man.

"What's wrong?" Elliot asked.

"I'm not resigning, Elliot. You haven't checkmated me."

Elliot was silent for a moment, his brow furrowing. The smile that followed spelled doom all over it. It was a triumphant smile. "Haven't I though?" Elliot shook his head. "I was hoping this would be easier. I really don't want to do this in here."

The chessboard had helped him figure it out. This whole time he'd searched for that missing piece on the board. But the piece he sought was never on the board to begin with. It was the invisible hand moving all the other pieces.

A tall dark-haired man walked in and stood next to Elliot.

"How was the drive from Albany?" Tristan asked Malcolm's imposter brother.

"Rough."

"Did you kill his brother's family?"

It was Elliot who answered. "That's really not my style, Tristan. Only make moves that are necessary to the game. Didn't I teach you that?"

"Is that what this is? A game?"

"It's much more than that." Elliot took out the gun and pointed it at Tristan. "At least the furniture still has sheets over it. How did you figure it out?"

Elliot, the consummate player, needed to analyze the game. Thank God for that because Tristan needed time more than anything else. "Kala Patthar. It was staring me in the face. You were there at the same time as Edelweiss and Malcolm. Then I thought about how we carried that damn snow globe through all those checkpoints. Hell, the police station in Hunza practically thrust it upon us. That was all you. Your man, Shaw, made sure we got through customs without a hitch. Why didn't you just take it yourself?"

"And risk everything? I don't think so."

"So the three of you were partners this whole time. Was Rana in on it? Bjorn?"

"Just the three of us. That idiot, Edelweiss, loved to talk. One night when we sat around the campfire, he tells us this incredible story about his grandfather who stole at least a hundred mill in diamonds from Hitler. That's insane, right? I didn't buy it at first. But the research checked out. We figured, what could it hurt to see if the diamonds were still on the old man? So I staked Edelweiss and Malcolm on the expedition. If the diamonds were there, the plan was to split them three ways."

"The plan wasn't for Malcolm to kill Edelweiss?"

"Not originally, but let's face it. The man couldn't keep his mouth shut. Who can trust someone like that? Malcolm felt he had no choice. If the accident caused others to die, well, collateral damage can't be avoided in these cases. Just so you know, Tristan, you tagging along wasn't planned either. If you want to know the truth, I wanted you to go home, but you were just a thorn in my side that would not go away."

"You're saying it was all a coincidence?"

"Don't you know anything about strategy? When a piece presents a problem, you make it work for you. I didn't trust Malcolm and Edelweiss. But you... You I could trust. If anything went wrong up there, you'd report it back to me. Without even knowing it, you'd be my loyal pawn. It's kind of brilliant."

"Why did you do it?"

"If it's any consolation, it was never supposed to be you. Malcolm was going to transport the diamonds, but then he lost his damn leg and a little of his mind too. I couldn't wait months for him to recuperate. Truth is, I had very slim hope the diamonds were even real. I mean, Drew was really out of it when he gave us the coordinates for the body."

Blood rushed through his ears. "Drew?"

"The timing was perfect. Drew was headed up there anyway. So I just asked him to check the general vicinity where the man was last seen. Sure enough, there was a body there."

"What the fuck did you do to my brother?"

"I couldn't have him tell anyone else. Finding a dead Nazi on a mountain is liable to invite a shit storm of media coverage. I begged him to keep it to himself, but he wanted to go to the police. He wanted to tell you."

Tristan backed up, shaking his head. "He died of an aneurism. You didn't kill him."

"Do you think it's that difficult to pay off a doctor in a third world remote hospital?"

His head throbbed, and he could not breathe. A chill flooded his veins. He could barely focus on Elliot's voice.

"I thought about cutting you in, Tristan, but you wouldn't go for it, would you? Money never meant anything to you. So this way, you could help me indirectly. All you had to do was deliver the package to Albany. I took care of everything else. It was so simple and brilliant."

"I'm going to kill you, Elliot."

"Are you? Doesn't look that way from where I'm standing."

Tristan felt the shot before he heard it. The pain didn't register for a few seconds. He clutched his stomach, trying to stop the bleeding. Thick blood pooled against his hand and seeped out from his fingers.

Elliot stared at the gun in his hand as if he couldn't believe what happened. "It feels like I have the upper hand here." He was a terrible actor. He was struggling. His hand shook and his face was pale.

Tristan's legs could no longer hold his weight. He slumped to the ground. Elliot lifted the gun again. Tristan held out his hand. "Elliot, I wouldn't do that."

"I'm sorry, Tristan. I am. This does not bring me joy."

"I gave you the wrong coordinates. You'll be looking in the wrong spot for the diamonds."

Elliot's stance didn't change, but his smile faltered. "You're bluffing."

"Check it. That longitude line isn't even in this state."

Elliot stared at the paper and back at Tristan.

Tristan pressed his hand against this wound. "Best part of chess…even a pawn can win. You said that to me once."

Elliot considered the statement for a moment. "I also said you have no idea when you've already lost. You're bleeding out in my living room, and you're talking about winning."

Tristan was losing too much blood too fast. He had no idea how he'd survive. At least he had the knowledge Farah would be safe.

Elliot's accomplice went inside the bedroom. When he came out, Tristan's heart collapsed. She had her hands tied behind her back and a gag over her mouth. Her eyes were wide. "You should know by now, I always have a backup plan," Elliot said. "Did you think I wasn't following you? Granted, we lost track of you in the woods. Couldn't exactly have a car in there without you knowing. If you'd given me the right coordinates, this would have been over by now."

"You would have killed us no matter what."

"Yes, but it wouldn't have to hurt."

"She isn't part of this."

Elliot's laugh sent chills down Tristan's back. "She wasn't. She would have been free, at home, safe and sound. You were the one who said you wouldn't leave if she didn't come with you. Irony at its best. You're the one who put her in harm's way, my boy. Love really does blind you."

Tristan had to keep Elliot talking. That was the only way. "She doesn't know where they are."

"Stop lying."

"It's true. I swear. I buried them after I put her on that train. The less she knew, the less danger she was in."

He pulled Farah closer. A tear ran down her face. He ran the barrel of the pistol against her neck. But Elliot was not a killer. He was nervous. Tristan could see it in his stance, the uncertainty in his expression. The guilt in his eyes. He removed the gag on her mouth. "Where are they? Tell me now."

He looked at Farah, praying she understood the game. *We need time, sweetheart.*

"I don't know," she said.

Good girl.

Elliot shook his head. "You're lying. Don't make me do this. I didn't want any bloodshed. None. But it all got too big too fast. We could have all been rich. Just tell me what I need to know, and it can all be over."

"This isn't you, Elliot."

"Do you know what I've seen over there? The games we play with each other over land, over resources? Tristan, I figured out a long time ago we're all pieces for someone else to move."

The sirens came then. They were in the distance, but it would not take long from them to arrive.

The color drained from Elliot's face. "Take her to the car," Elliot said to the man beside him. "We have to leave."

They would keep her alive until they found the diamonds. Tristan was sure of that. But in his last revelation to his uncle, he'd planted a few seeds of doubt. What if Farah didn't know? Then everything had been for nothing. Elliot had laid down his hand too soon.

Elliot had gotten stuck in his own trap and was out of time. Tristan closed his eyes. He had no more strength. He had just one last card to play. He would wager his life against Elliot's greed.

He heard her voice come to him. "We're survivors. You can do this." He knew she hadn't said it aloud, but he heard it just the same. It gave him strength.

"I'll tell you, Elliot. Just let her go." His vision blurred, but he heard the sound of Elliot's footsteps coming toward him. He closed his hand around the wooden handle of the knife.

"Tristan," Elliot said, checking his pulse. "Tell me where they are, and I'll let her live. I promise. I never meant to harm Drew. This thing became bigger than me."

Tristan mumbled, making his voice low.

Elliot leaned in closer. "Speak up."

He summoned strength somewhere deep inside of him. He pulled out the knife. He jabbed the blade into Elliot's throat. Once. Twice. Three times. Then the world went dark.

# Chapter 42

"Where are you?" she asked. "Wherever you are, take me there. I need to be with you."

*Not here, milady. It's dark here. Too cold.*

"It's never too cold when I'm with you," she said. "Let me keep you warm."

*Too tired.*

"Tristan, please wake up."

*Only sleep.*

"I'm praying to every God I know, and I know all of them. Please Tristan, open your eyes."

She spoke to him like this for hours. He heard the words, fuzzy at first, until they started clearing. The sound of machines, beeping and clicking became clearer too. He felt the squeeze of her hand.

Then he opened his eyes. Even though his vision was blurry, he could see the tears on her cheeks. She'd been crying…a lot. There was a tube in his mouth. He tried to offer her a comforting smile, but it was impossible. The next time he woke up the tube was gone. "Farah." He barely recognized his own voice.

He wasn't sure if it was a dream. She looked so relieved. She smiled the dimple smile right before kissing his cheek. "I'm here."

He tried to sit up, but his whole body screamed in agony. "Farah."

"Lie back." She took a glass of water with a straw and held it for him. He choked at first.

"Slow sips, Tristan. I have much to tell you."

She explained that the wound had been deep. He'd gone into surgery, and they'd removed the bullet. It was touch and go for a while.

Farah had never left him. He felt her presence, although for a while he wasn't sure if it was on earth or somewhere in heaven.

"You're safe?" He dared not breathe, afraid she wasn't real.

"The police surrounded us before he pulled out of the driveway. It was brilliant, Tristan. Your father recorded the conversation. We're both safe now."

"I brought you into this," Tristan said. "You would not have been in danger."

"Don't ever say that again. You saved my life in every way."

"The diamonds?" he asked.

"The police have them. I provided the coordinates. The investigation is almost complete. Many of our theories were correct. They did geological testing. The diamonds were part of the famous Rose Diamond. They were stolen by a high-ranking Nazi official, who happened to be part of a secret expedition on K2. The police interviewed Edelweiss's descendants and learned that the story had been passed down in their family as part folklore and legend. Apparently, the man was very eccentric and paranoid. Edelweiss's grandfather planned to bury the diamonds on the summit and come back for them after the war. At that time, no one else had made the summit of K2, and there were only a few attempts. He figured no one ever would."

Yeah, you couldn't make this stuff up.

"Wonder why Edelweiss didn't just quit when he had the diamonds? He could have gone back down."

Farah shrugged. "I'm not sure, except he was a climber. It's hard to be so close to the sun and not take flight."

"Icarus's Wings," Tristan said.

"Something like that."

He tried to sit up again.

"You need to rest," she said. "I'll go find your father and tell him you're awake. He's been here with me the whole time, but just left to get coffee for us."

He wanted to see his father, but he needed a moment with her first. "I have something to say to you."

"It can wait."

"It cannot." They had come so close to losing each other way too many times for him to waste another second.

She took a seat. "As you wish. I'm listening."

"Come closer," he said. She leaned forward. "I'm not prepared, but I refuse to wait any longer. You need to know what's in my heart." He took a deep breath, which hurt.

"Stop."

"No." God, he felt so much emotion, but right now his brain wasn't forming the right words.

Her lip quivered. "Tristan, you need to rest."

"Stop interrupting me. I may not be able to bend at the knee. I don't have a ring. I don't even have words prepared. Those are things you deserve, but we've never been people who follow tradition. So I will just ask you, plain and humble and hopeful. Farah Nawaz, we belong together and—"

"No, Tristan."

"No?"

"Don't propose to me."

"Why the hell not?"

Instead of an answer, she handed him a letter. He regarded it with suspicion.

"What is this? Are you trying to kill me, woman?"

Her smile contradicted his fears. "It's for you. I wrote this the night we camped in the woods in Richmond. But I've been thinking these words for much longer. I wanted to give it to you that night, but you needed your focus."

"If this is a good-bye note, you can have it back. I won't say good-bye you anymore." He held it taught, ready to rip the note to shreds.

She clasped his hand. "Is that what you think this is? Oh Tristan, as brilliant as you are, you can be very wrong sometimes."

"Then what?"

"Don't you remember? Where I come from the woman chooses her mate."

He thought back to the day he was invited to the small hut for tea and Farah explained how a Kalash woman proposes. He grinned, relief flooding him like a soothing balm for all his aches. "She writes him a letter." He fumbled with the paper. His fingers were connected to several devices making it difficult. He let out a frustrated groan and tried to rip them off so he could use his hands.

Farah curled her fingers around his wrist and kissed his cheek. "Let me." She took the note from him. "Tristan, I've been so careful guarding and protecting my heart. I decided long ago freedom and independence were synonyms. But I never bargained for you. A man, who could spark something in me that I didn't know existed. A man, whose kindness and bravery rivaled the heroes in every book I'd devoured. I thought love was a virus. It had to be. What else could affect the head, the lungs, and the heart all at once? It left me confused and panicked and emotional. It left me full and happy and dizzy too. Love is a virus. But I discovered it's also the cure.

"I choose you, Tristan Sinclair. I want to walk beside you in this life and all the lives after this. We held hands on top of the world once. But I realize now that whenever I am with you, I'm already standing on top of the world. Kissing you is like kissing the sky. And loving... Well, loving you has been the greatest privilege of my life. I love you. Be mine. Be mine forever. Yours in every way, Farah." Her voice choked on the last sentence.

"I'm already yours, milady." He patted the area next to him. He had to hold her right now as much as he had to take his next breath. They barely fit on the narrow hospital bed, but Tristan had no intention of letting her go.

"Am I hurting you?" she asked.

"No. I need you close to me."

"I love you, Tristan. I never want to hold back again. I don't care where we live as long as we're together."

"I love you too, Farah. We'll live in Hunza Valley," he said. "You belong there. I belong next to you. I want our children to know where their mother comes from."

A single tear fell down her cheek. He kissed it away.

"Are you sure? It won't be easy, you know."

"You're wrong. It will be easy because we will be together. We're better together. I know the real heartache is being without you."

"My entire life was built around climbing that mountain. I used to think standing on top of it was my once in a lifetime moment. But I was wrong. Tristan Sinclair, you are my once in a lifetime."

He kissed her head. "And you're mine."

"We were wrong about something else too."

"What's that?" he asked.

"The Goddess of the Mountain wasn't jealous of us. She wasn't after us. She protected us. We could have died a thousand ways, but we didn't."

"You're right."

They slept, a deep dreamless satisfying sleep, their limbs tangled together. The position should not have been comfortable, but they could not imagine sleeping any other way.

# Epilogue

He stood on a clear day in spring underneath the oak tree in the backyard of his family home. He wasn't nervous. But he was worried. Grandma El was having an exceptionally good day so far, but she now looked displeased. Scratch that, she looked as if she might whoop his ass. He bent down on his knee before the woman. "What's wrong, Grandma?"

"I don't approve."

He stiffened. "Of Farah?"

She waved her hand. "No, silly. I adore Farah. She's got the right amount of backbone and sass to keep you in line. She is perfect for you."

"Good, I'm glad we agree. But what has you so upset, Grandma?"

"This wedding. It's so…non-traditional."

Tristan nodded. "We really needed something simple. We've had a lot of complicated. We need normal now."

"There is nothing normal about this, Tristan. There are hardly any guests. We're having it in the backyard under the oak tree like a summer barbeque."

"I couldn't think of anything more perfect." The music queued then. He took his place under the canopy of the tree.

She wore a simple white dress, a few sprigs of jasmine in her hair. She didn't need extra decoration. She was lovely on her own. His father gave her away. Only a handful of close family came. Farah insisted they spend the last six months in Richmond. It gave Tristan a chance to recuperate and spend time with his family. She'd won over his family, even his father. In fact, she'd helped him mend that relationship.

They had received a generous award for uncovering the diamonds. Enough to fund a school in Hunza and purchase supplies for the children. Farah would teach there. They would have a comfortable life. He could not be prouder of the woman he loved. The one who saved him every single day.

They decided to divide their time between their two homes. It didn't matter really because they had discovered home was not a place but a feeling. They were each other's homes.

His heart swelled with every step she took. When she got to him, he pulled her in for a deep kiss.

The pastor cleared his throat. "We're not at that part yet."

"I'm sorry," Tristan said. He could not help himself.

Their guests laughed. When the pastor told them to exchange rings, they both took out small pebbles and placed them in each other's palms.

Grandma El shook her head. "You couldn't buy the girl a decent ring? Do you need money?"

Tristan smiled at his bride. "Do you want a diamond? They are forever."

Farah shook her head and smiled at his grandmother. "I asked for this. It's the perfect symbol of all the perfect days we have to look forward to." She turned to Tristan. "Besides, I never want to see another diamond again."

He would have laughed, but his desire to kiss her overtook everything else. He looked to the pastor for permission. As soon as he spoke the words, Tristan took his bride in his arms and kissed her. He couldn't wait to get her alone and walk her over the threshold of their small cottage in Richmond. He'd even bought her a wedding gift.

A painting of the Karakorum range by their favorite artist.

Maiden Shina.

# Unwanted Girl

If you are looking for another heartwarming story with compelling characters and lots of emotion, pick up the highly acclaimed *Unwanted Girl* by MK Schiller.

## On sale now!

### *When a man loves a woman*

Recovering addict Nick Dorsey finds solace in his regimented life. That is until he meets Shyla Metha. Something about the shy Indian beauty who delivers take-out to his Greenwich Village loft inspires the reclusive writer. And when Shyla reveals her desire to write a book of her own, he agrees to help her. The tale of a young Indian girl growing up against a landscape of brutal choices isn't Nick's usual territory, but something about the story, and the beautiful storyteller, draws him in deep.

Shyla is drawn to Nick, but she never imagines falling for him. Like Nick, Shyla hails from a village, too…a rural village in India. They have nothing in common, yet he makes her feel alive for the first time in her life. She is not ready for their journey to end, but the plans she's made cannot be broken . . .not even by him. Can they find a way to rewrite the next chapter?

# Chapter 1

Nick Dorsey ran every morning, although he no longer ventured to guess whether he was chasing dreams or fleeing demons. As he exited the brick building on Bleecker to a grim, grayish sky, the promise of another sunless day revealed itself.

His feet pounded the pavement in a stride that ranged from sprint to run to jog, matching the same footpaths as TS Eliot, Faulkner, and Poe. He'd insisted on the Village because it was a literary mecca. Although, these days, it could be argued the high rents favored capitalists over the creatives.

He'd hunted for months with a petite blond realtor until she found a place in his price range. The realtor was intelligent and assertive—during negotiations and sex—two traits Nick valued. In the end, it got him a nice place in the West Village with a working elevator, architectural charm, and original hardwood floors. It got her a fat commission check and about the same number of orgasms. Too bad the only thing he turned on these days was his computer...and that relationship was near terminal.

He rounded Thompson Avenue, passing the bookstore where his latest novel occupied the window. He allowed the smallest flicker of pride before picking up speed. How far he'd come from the poor kid whose life was hand-me-down clothes and secondhand books.

He reached Washington Square Park ready to do a complete loop. Nick's runs used to consist of random thoughts about his characters and plot points. The beauty of being a writer was you could work anywhere anytime. One of the best scenes he'd ever written was during a tax audit. Now, his mind lacked the spark required to conjure creativity. He emerged from the park, slowing his pace until he reached the glass door of The Ole Time Floral shop with its annoying wreath of greenery and bells that signaled his arrival.

"A white rose, please," he said to the florist, who was already reaching into the barrel to retrieve the item.

"You know, dear, it's romantic how you buy her a rose every day, but I'm sure she'd be more impressed with a whole bouquet at once."

Nick frowned. "I don't want to impress her. I just want her to know I'm there."

The lady arched a bushy brow, waiting for further explanation, but Nick did not intend to satisfy her unsolicited curiosity. He shoved the money at her and clutched the thorny bud in his hand. She no longer asked if he wanted it wrapped with a sprig of greenery.

He ran an additional mile until he reached the tranquil snow-covered grounds behind an ornate metal gate on Sullivan Street. It looked like a park with its lush landscape of willow trees and benches, but the stone angels, marble pillars, and simple markers jutting from the ground gave away its identity.

He fell to his knees, the crunch of fresh snow against hard earth disturbing the serenity. Nick gulped in the cold desolate air, reading her gravestone for the thousandth time, even though every curl of the fancy lettering chiseled on the surface was already etched into his brain. He'd become a creature of habit, and the repetition of every act provided a strange comfort. He bowed his head, joined his hands together, and begged in silence for forgiveness that would never come.

An hour later, showered and freshly dressed, he walked through the heavy wooden doors of the old church on Grand, the location of his second daily errand. Nick originally chose the ten a.m. timeframe to avoid crowds. It was flawed logic, bordering on reckless naiveté since the term "avoid crowds" was a fool's ambition in this city. Although there weren't any stockbrokers or executives, plenty of actors, singers, and housewives packed the large room. They all chatted amicably while drinking percolated coffee, which Nick, a coffee connoisseur, admitted was the best he'd ever had.

He sat in the uncomfortable metal chair, waiting for the meeting to come to order. When the time came, Nick spoke clearly and honestly.

"I'm Nick Dorsey, and I am a meth addict. It's been eighteen months, two weeks, and three days since my last fix." He talked about his addiction until his three minutes of indulgent introspection were up and his Styrofoam cup runneth empty.

He arrived back at the Bleecker Street loft with all his errands accomplished, but no sense of accomplishment for it. Gaping at his keyboard, a fresh cup of caffeine in his hand and a stifling lack of imagination, he sat down.

Wanting to alleviate the harsh glare of the blank page, he clicked on the keyboard in quick snapping strokes. The rain fell in thick sheets as if the sky weighed in on Max's decision.

Shit.

Did he actually start the fucking book with a weather report? The greats— George Orwell, Charles Dickens, or Dr. Seuss were capable of such openings, but Nick Dorsey was not. He hit the backspace, erasing every individual character with a scorning strike. He wondered what other words could describe rain. He walked over to the large bookshelf that spanned an entire wall. As it turned out, Webster's had thirty-two words for precipitation from the descriptive drencher to the very simple wet stuff.

He slammed the book shut, tired of his pathetic attempts at procrastination.

He didn't mind the timid knock at nine p.m., though. That was a welcome break from the unrelenting flutter of the cursor.

Sandwich girl was here and right on time.

He opened the door, and there she stood as she had almost every night for the past year since he'd discovered the corner deli delivered. The tall, thin girl with raven hair offered a nervous smile. He often speculated on the length of her hair. She always wore it in a tightly coiled bun except for the few loose strands that framed her face.

When her smile widened just right, it would create the slightest dimple on her left cheek. As much as he enjoyed the appearance of the dimple, what struck him the most was her accent. He'd heard all kinds of Asian accents, but never one as lyrical as hers with each simple word drawn out softly, a seductive hum as it left her lips. Her loose trench coat, too mild for this weather, slipped off one shoulder as she inched her knapsack higher on the other.

"Hello," she said cheerfully, handing him the brown paper bag that contained his turkey and Swiss on whole wheat.

"Hiya, Sandwich Girl." It was their usual greeting. No names—the time for civilized introductions had passed long ago.

He fished a twenty from his wallet. She shoved her hand in her pocket searching for change.

"Keep it," he said.

"Thank you. That's very generous."

Why they went through the same motions, he didn't know, except she was polite and unassuming, and he found a certain comfort in the repetition. "Don't mention it."

Her head began shifting downward, but she paused and lifted her gaze to meet his. In the beginning, the shy girl would never look him in the face, throwing the bag at him and taking off before he yelled after her that he had yet to pay. Then she'd slowly shuffle back, her head down, holding out her trembling hand. Now, they held actual conversation between them, and although it lacked any depth, those few minutes became the most enjoyable part of his scheduled day.

"It's getting nicer outside. I think spring will arrive early this year," she said.

"Is that so?" Maybe she believed Nick never went out, and her weather reports were a necessary service to give him insight into the subtle climactic shifts of his own environment. Or maybe she was just making small talk.

"Yes, but it might rain." She dropped her voice as if conveying a secret. "I think it will rain actually."

"Will it be a soaker, a mist, or a monsoon?" he asked, happy to apply the seldom-used words to his vernacular. The thesaurus hadn't been a waste of time.

She clutched her jacket around her. "Definitely a drencher. I don't think we have to worry about monsoons on this side of the world."

"Your forecasts have never been accurate...not once."

She bit her lower lip, her expression thoughtful. "Really?"

"Nope. But in case you're right, do you have an umbrella?"

"I don't have far to go."

"Wait here." He set the bag on a console table and grabbed an umbrella from the hall closet. "Take this."

"Oh no, I couldn't."

"You can return it tomorrow." He held it out to her until she gripped her fingers around it.

"Thank you."

"Be safe."

She'd rewarded him with a brilliant, dimple-inducing smile the first time he'd said that, and it became his customary farewell to her in the days that followed. The smile never disappointed.

"Good-night."

"Night," he said, leaning against the doorjamb until the elevator arrived.

A minute later, he strolled to the window and watched her exit onto the street, headed north on Bleecker, her coat flapping around her. He reassured himself it was the comfort of routine along with the quality deli meat he craved. It had nothing to do with the delivery girl. Never mind he opted for Chinese or pizza on Wednesdays and Sundays—her days off. Sure, she was a pretty girl, but definitely not his type. He preferred the kind of women he wrote about…buxom blondes and rambunctious redheads with confident personas and hungry appetites.

This girl was shy, awkward…and for some reason, intriguing. He had no idea why he looked forward to their silly chats, except they made him a little happier. Any ounce of happiness was such a rare occurrence in Nick's life, he seized it gratefully.

Nick started the process of shutting down the computer. He'd eat, work out for a few hours, take a shower, read, and go to bed. The same as he did every night. He hesitated at the customary question of Do you want to save changes? There were no changes to save.

He cracked his knuckles and stretched his back. His fingers landed on the keys like a mocking friend, both beckoning and humiliating him in that order. Except now, the words coursed through his hands with great speed and little consideration as the page filled.

Sandwich girl, you are a mystery. A sweet, sad smile that never reaches your big brown eyes. Silky hair tucked and clipped away as if forgotten, save for the few rebellious strands struggling for freedom. Would you welcome my advance or retreat into the shadows? I can see your inexperience, an odd fit, wrapping around you like another coat. But there's something else there, too. A profound strength that exists as if you're a lone soldier, battling your way through a battered life.

Nick highlighted the section and hovered a finger above the delete key. Instead, he labeled the document Sandwich Girl and saved it to his hard drive. It wasn't his best work and nothing he could use in a novel, but it meant something to him. It represented the first paragraph he'd managed in almost two years.

\* \* \* \*

Shyla Metha watched his window from a darkened corner some distance away. On warmer days, she'd stand in this area for twenty minutes until sufficiently shamed by her lurking. Still, she was drawn to him.

It wasn't just his looks, although she couldn't deny the pull of his broad shoulders, sandy hair that fell somewhere between brown and blond, and dark ocean-colored eyes. The beard was interesting, too, creating an air of mystery around him. Funny, she'd never expected to be attracted to physical characteristics so different from her own, yet she'd developed a dimwitted crush on this boy…man.

He'd been aloof in the beginning, and she was timid, a combination that never mixed, but one day she'd added a comment about the weather, and he had grinned, the rigid stiffness of his posture easing for a few seconds. Although they came from different worlds, they had something in common. Nick Dorsey was lonely and sad...perhaps even broken.

She clutched the black umbrella in her hand. Her time was growing short. She'd be returning home when her student visa expired at the end of the semester. Now was the time for risks! Or rather tomorrow when he ordered another sandwich.

# Meet the Author

Not knowing a word of English, **MK Schiller** came to America at the age of four from India. Since then, all she's done is collect words. After receiving the best gift ever from her parents—her very own library card—she began reading everything she could get her greedy hands on. At sixteen, a friend asked her to make up a story featuring the popular bad boy at school. This wasn't fan fiction…it was friend fiction. From that day on, she's known she wanted to be a writer. With the goal of making her readers both laugh and cry, MK Schiller has penned more than a dozen books, each one filled with misfit characters overcoming obstacles and finding true love.

Printed in the United States
by Baker & Taylor Publisher Services